I0684865

Force Down the Night

Age of Technics Trilogy

Book I

S. E. Thomas

Force Down the Night
Age of Technics Trilogy Book I

A Novel

Published by The Dramatic Pen Press, L.L.C.

Lolo, Montana

Copyright © 2018 S. E. Thomas

All rights reserved.
ISBN-10: 1-64157-006-7
ISBN-13: 978-1-64157-006-0

To my friend, Vicki Lucas.
Thanks for championing this book!
Your advice and encouragement helped
make this happen. You are a faithful and
dear friend. May God bless you richly
in your own writing career.

Table of Contents

I

I don't know why Absalom keeps me.

I'm not any good at gene charting or chromosomal manipulation. My hands shake whenever I'm in the Fetal Growth Room. I can't even walk past the CC Surgery Center without feeling panicky and nauseous. There are too many buttons in this place—too many ways to end a life. And it scares me.

Absalom tells me to stop worrying and just do my job. If I accidentally end a life, it would only be a Commodity Class life, and he can afford to lose some since he produces them by the thousands. Besides, CCs have been steadily decreasing in value over the past forty years or so, and it's not as if he follows the government's limits on Commodity Class production. But, I think maybe Absalom doesn't see like I do. He doesn't know that little twinge of panic. The thudding in the ears. The pressure in the chest. I think, maybe, he'd have to be a CC himself to understand.

"Galaxy, you shouldn't stare directly into the sun," Needle says, walking up to me with that characteristic limp of his. "You'll burn your retinas out, and then what will Absalom do with you?"

Caught again. I don't know why I like to stare right at the sun, but I do. I love to stand before the tall, glass windows, wide-eyed. Unblinking in the sun. Soaking up its energy. Like an over-hot shower, it makes me feel warm and tingly all over. Its burning, tumultuous depths mesmerize me, but they also distract me from the task at hand.

"Where are you going?" I ask as he passes me and heads toward the corridor.

"To the CC Sales Center. The main holographic projector malfunctioned."

Like me, Needle is a CC. Absalom Industries acquired both of us— me as a four-year-old girl and Needle as a live, human embryo—when they bought out a smaller CC development company that sold Naturals cheaply to become Digs—general household or community laborers like maids, short-order cooks, garbage collectors, and such. But when Absalom Industries bought them out, for some unknown reason, Absalom kept me, like some People keep pets, I guess. But specialists altered Needle to function as a fine-tuned technical repair specialist. They removed his right hand and forearm and replaced them with robotic appendages fitted with a vast array of instruments, everything from a basic screw-driver to a laser cutter. They also inserted implants in his ears so he can detect certain frequencies undetectable to normal humans. This helps him diagnose certain problems unique to the machinery and electronics used here. It also makes it impossible to sneak up on him.

Because of his technological alterations, Needle is a Technic. Of the many thousands of Commodity Class children to pass through here, Needle was chosen for this particular upgrade because of his natural ambidexterity, as well as his genetically-enhanced IQ. So, before Needle became a Technic, he was already a Wit. Unlike most CCs, as both a Technic and a Wit, Needle spans CC classes.

At only ten years old he can reprogram the gene splicer, repair the robotic embryo separators, and reconfigure The Tower's holographic computer system and internal sensors. The other technicians rely on him to keep Absalom Industries running.

Sometimes I envy Needle. Even though AI engineers and physicians surgically altered him in what, I understand, was an incredibly painful procedure, Needle has a purpose. He will always be needed. He will always have a place here. He is indispensable. Maybe if I had some special skill, I would be indispensable, too. But I am one of the Naturals, not unlike any other human girl of fifteen, except for my CC tattoo and microchip. They keep some of us that way—unaltered either genetically or physically. Some of us are even sold to adoptive parents and raised as People, losing our CC identity, but only if it happens before our first birthday. After that, though we are human beings like them, we cannot be adopted. We cannot become People. We will always be members of the Commodity Class—CCs.

"They have the AI Spring Sales Gala starting this afternoon, you know," Needle says as he reaches the elevator tube and leans toward the scanner, letting the motion-activated, red laser flit across the CC identification tattoo on his right temple—two large, black Cs around tiny, black squares. His tattoo looks like mine, but they're embedded with different codes.

"Can I go with you?" I ask.

I've never watched one of the sales events but, from the many AI Tower windows, I have often seen the traffic they cause. Thousands of vehicles swarm toward AI Tower to disappear into our underground parking garage like water running into a drain.

"Aren't you supposed to be somewhere?" he asks.

"Just napping, but I can skip it today."

He shakes his head and sighs, a smile playing on his lips as the elevator swooshes into place and the door slides open. "I don't know why I even bothered to ask." He glances at me as he steps into the glass elevator tube and says, "Come on, then."

I step in next to him.

"I don't know how you do it," Needle muses as the tube closes and we slip easily into a high-speed descent. "Napping in that oven. Those glass walls of yours focus that sunlight into a beam. Not only is it incredibly bright in there, it's scorching hot!"

I sleep in a small room located in the spire, just above Absalom's penthouse. My room is a circle of transparent, alumina-reinforced windows that stretch far above my head, getting closer and closer together until they form a single, but nearly unbreakable, crystal thread of glass stretching to the heavens.

"I guess I've gotten used to it. But being there for two hours with nothing to do gets pretty boring sometimes."

Needle smirks humorlessly. "I've never been bored in my life. I've never taken a nap, either—at least, none that I can remember. You're lucky."

I don't feel lucky.

I wonder if Absalom ever regrets the impulse that made him bring such an undersized female CC back here, rather than sell me as a household servant or use me for one of his many biological research experiments. I suppose he still might. Maybe if I were healthier, he would. But these days it's Absalom's health everyone worries about. Lately, he's taken to spending long, solitary hours in his darkened quarters, only appearing when his presence at an AI business meeting is absolutely required. AI physicians come and go with increasing regularity. His skin is a pale yellow. His hair is thinning.

"Who's first on the docket for today?" I ask. I am excited to finally see one of the Pristine sales events. AI sales galas are publicized for months in advance and are the social event of the season. No doubt all the hotels in the city are full of high-end buyers, millionaire playboys, and more than a few company spies. No other CC production company comes close to producing the standard of quality AI does.

Needle frowns. "Bliss."

I feel a twinge of guilt for showing my excitement. He should be used to it by now, but Needle always feels bad when one of our fellow CCs gets sold. He thinks of them as his friends.

"Oh," I say, trying to make my voice sound more somber. I try to remember Bliss, and a face comes to mind. But I might be confusing her with someone else.

Our elevator tube reaches the main offices of the AI Sales Center on the 9th floor and swooshes open. We step into a noisy bustle of AI employees as they scramble to prepare for the massive auction.

"Oh! There you are!" A middle-aged woman with thick lips leans over a circular, metallic welcome desk and locks eyes on Needle. "What took you so long? We need that projector operational A-S-A-P!" She pronounces each letter in punctuated staccato. Only then does she notice me. "Who is that?"

"This is Galaxy," Needle answers with a glance in my direction.

The woman does a double-take, then raises one eyebrow as she examines my skinny frame, head to toe. "Is that so?"

"Yes," Needle answers her. "She is Absalom's personal property."

"Oh, I know that," she says waving the explanation away. "It's just that I thought Galaxy would be... would be.... Oh, never mind. Just go fix that projector. Here is the work order." Needle steps forward so the thick-lipped woman can scan the work order information into his digitized tattoo with a small hand-held device. "There. Now you can access the maintenance room on the 5th floor." She looks at me. "Are you planning on joining him?"

I nod.

"I can grant you access, too, I suppose."

"No need," I respond, tapping my tattoo. "I already have it."

She frowns. "Oh, is that so?"

"Yes, that's so." I say, accentuating the last word and locking eyes on her. Stupid woman.

Needle nudges me with his elbow, and I follow him back into the elevator tube. The woman watches us until we swoosh out of sight.

"She didn't like that," Needle said. "Maybe you should've just let her pretend to grant you access."

"Why?" I ask.

"Persons don't like the idea of CCs coming and going as they please. And they certainly don't like to be talked back to. It's not natural."

I shrug. "It was Absalom's choice to grant me full access to The Tower, not mine."

We arrive at the 5th floor and step into a circular hallway overlooking a massive auditorium. Some of the lights are on, revealing the wine-colored velvet carpeting and decorative curtains, white walls with gold accents, and opulent, lighted floor plants. The auditorium comprises three full floors of The Tower with multiple seating levels designed to accommodate any budget—from rows upon rows of cheap balcony seating to private auction booths from which the customer can come and go in complete privacy. The private booths are at a rate of no less than $60,000, with prices rising as the event draws closer. Even the cheap seats go for upwards of $8,000 each, but we always sell out months in advance. AI sales events—like AI products—are the most coveted in the entire nation—indeed, in the entire world.

"It's been a long time since I've been here," I say.

I step toward the waist-high wall fencing us off from the three-story chasm of seats. There is a main center stage as well as a conglomerate of smaller stages and holographic projectors that hover in midair at various levels around the main stage. People and CCs scurry around, running diagnostics on the private screens and bidding devices positioned at each seat, stocking the bars that line the walls at the back, and testing the lighting and sound systems. Some of the smaller, floating stages flicker with holographic images of various CCs who, I assume, will be auctioned off today. I see a Warrior and a Pristine I don't recognize before I feel Needle's human hand on my shoulder.

"Come on," he says. "The maintenance room is this way."

Music fills the auditorium as the doors finally open for paying customers. From where we stand on a narrow service ramp high above, Needle and I watch them stream in like ants. Service CCs help the guests find their seats and instruct them how to use their bidding devices—small screens that glow green or red. The customer can use them to place bids on particular CCs as they are being auctioned off. Early bids are allowed, but all bids must be entered before the light turns red at the end of the event. At that time, all sales become final.

Screens hanging on the auditorium walls come alive to show up-close video feed of the guests as they enter.

"Wow," I say, staring. "Look how they're dressed."

"I know," Needle responds. "They look like that video Miss Abilene made us watch about the animals of the Serengeti."

I laugh.

"They like to see themselves on the screens," he adds.

I stare at the strange People as they make their way to their assigned seats or booths. Unlike the uniformed People who work at AI Tower as scientists, developers, and instructors, these People are wearing cumbersome-looking outfits that stick out in strange points or ripples from their waists and shoulders. Most of the women have on massive headdresses that tip and sway as they walk, dangling with ribbons and charms. The men look equally ridiculous, with collars that stick up far above their heads in the back and suits in vibrant colors. Some of the outfits even glow or pulse with light in various colors and patterns. From up here our guests look like teetering, mechanized toys.

"Good thing the seats are over-sized," I say and snicker. "How do they expect to sit down wearing all that stuff? Are they going to stay dressed like that the whole time?"

AI sales events come only twice a year and run for three days. The guests only pay for their auction-event seats, but most of them stay at The Tower throughout the day, eating copious amounts of food, drinking wine by the barrel, and lounging in the resort-like lower floors. All the while, AI plies them with advertisements for, not only the CCs being sold at this event, but also those to be released at the next sales gala in six months. Customers can watch detailed, holographic videos about each CC, learn all their functions and talents, and sign up for an iron-clad payment plan—all from the comfort of a plush suite or a pool-side chaise.

Needle shrugs. "The bigger the outfit, the wealthier they think they look."

"But those are the cheap seats," I observe. "I wonder what the People in the suites are wearing."

"Actually, they don't try nearly so hard. They look pretty plain by comparison."

"Like Absalom?"

"Well... Absalom is in a class of his own."

True. Absalom can show up for meetings wearing only his robe if he wants—and he has.

"We should get out of here," Needle says. "I have work to do."

"No, let's watch a little longer. I've never watched a sales event before."

"Well, you can stay if you want, but I've got to get back."

"No, Needle, please!" I beg. "Stay. It's alright. You're with me."

Needle hesitates, then relents. "I swear, Galaxy, one of these days you're going to get me scrapped."

We watch a while longer until the buzz settles down and all the guests have crammed their massive costumes into seats and booths.

Shortly after the last Person is settled, the main holographic projector bursts to life to show a 3-D image of Zhubin Shadan, AI's primary auctioneer, a man famous for his role here. Needle sighs in relief to see the projector working, as there had been no time to test his repairs before the event began.

The music swells to a climax and then drops off as Zhubin raises his hands in welcome. All the smaller screens now also show only Zhubin, but I turn my gaze toward the main stage where he stands to see if I can make him out. Lights focus on him and decorative lasers bounce about his tiny-looking body as he smiles at the guests, but it's easier to see his expressions and motions on the huge, floating holograph of his body that hovers above him.

"Welcome, dear friends, to Absalom Industries' 2122 Spring Sales Gala!" Zhubin cries, punctuating each word of the event name as he lifts his arms in triumph.

The crowd erupts with excited cheers, cries, and hooting. Those who can stand without irreparably damaging their costumes leap to their feet. Women wave their hands in the air. Men pump their fists. The effect from our vantage point is like watching waves of tinsel and crumbled paper rumbling across the auditorium.

"I could not be more excited to show you what we have for you this spring!" Zhubin cries when the cheers die down. "Oh, you're going to be so glad you came! Your friends will be so jealous! Because, though we all know Absalom Industries only creates the most intelligent, most powerful, and most stunning CCs, Absalom has really outdone himself this year!"

More excited cries and cheers.

"You're not going to believe what we have in store," Zhubin continues, "so even though we usually save the best for last, I am so determined to save you from the mistake of leaving early, that I'm actually going to give you a sneak peek!"

"They do this every year," Needle says as the crowd cheers again, and I glance at him. He looks annoyed.

"This year, our final sale will be of the most beautiful, the most magnificent, and the sexiest Pristine you have ever seen! I give you—BLISS!"

The primary holographic projector, along will all the smaller screens and holograms suddenly burst into a blaze of light. When the light dissipates, an image of a fourteen-year-old girl appears. She hast long, pink and green hair and is wearing a ribbon-like outfit meant to match. It shows more skin than it covers. Her perfect body has been covered by some kind of glittering dust that makes her shine with silvery light. She's wearing far too much makeup. She has pointed ears and long eyelashes.

Bliss, wherever she physically is at the moment, is standing on some kind of rotating platform so that her holographically projected image spins, giving the audience full view of her body at every angle. As her back comes into view, Zhubin cries, "Now, watch this!"

Suddenly two silver, filigree wings swing out from her shoulder blades. The effect is immediate. The crowd bursts to a feverish pitch, many of them howling or even weeping with sheer desire.

"Isn't she incredible, folks?" Zhubin cries. "Isn't she stunning? Bliss is the first of our new Fantasy Creatures line! How would you like to have a beautiful, one-of-a-kind fairy OF YOUR VERY OWN?"

Cries. Reaching arms. Begging.

"What do you think of her folks? Isn't she beautiful? Isn't she amazing?"

As Bliss's face rotates back toward the crowd, I look at her to see if I know her. She looks vaguely familiar, but despite Zhubin and the crowd's clamoring over her beauty, I see something else.

"She looks," I say, trying to find the right word. "She looks…."

"Terrified," Needle supplies.

Yes. That's it.

I feel sick to my stomach as Needle and I make our way off the service ramp, back through the maintenance rooms to one of the auditorium balconies, and out into the corridor. No one sees us. Everyone is still inside wailing and shouting for Bliss. I don't think I need to see any more of these sales events.

Needle and I part ways at the elevator. He still has some maintenance duties to attend to on the lower floors, so I step inside and press "P" for penthouse. The identity scanner blips over my CC tattoo, and the elevator zooms into motion. Once I arrive at the penthouse, I'll have to take a second elevator to get to my room.

I like my room in the crystalline AI spire. I like the feeling of being far above everyone else. Despite my see-through walls, privacy is hardly an issue, even if CCs had any rights to it. The Tower reaches at least thirty stories higher than any other skyscraper in Washington D.C., so no one can see inside my room. There is only one problem. When I come and go from my quarters, I have to pass right through the penthouse—right through where Absalom lives… where he broods. In darkness.

I step into darkness at the end of my brief ride. The doors swoosh shut behind me, and I pause, letting my eyes adjust.

"Galaxy."

I startle at the sound of his voice emanating from the shadows. Absalom's cavernous penthouse suite, though designed to employ every modern convenience, is a jumble of modern and antique furniture, dusty trophies, and medals for his many humanitarian contributions to society. Jars of biological oddities suspended in clear fluid dot the room— memorabilia from decades of research and experimentation. An infant pig with a mechanical leg. A collection of deformed mice. A small, human brain bearing an implant of some kind. An unborn CC with an unusually long neck.

His extensive living room boasts many large windows stretching from the floor to the high ceilings, not only to let in light, but to allow Absalom a panoramic view of the city. He had the windows blacked out several years ago. Now the only light emanates from a holographic, heatless fire in the fireplace.

I search for his image and bit by bit make out the outline of a tall, thin man draped in a lounge chair about twenty feet ahead next to the multi-pixel flames.

"Yes, Superior."

"How many times do I have to tell you to call me Absalom?" His anger flashes. This time, his full rage is not triggered. He releases air through his nose with force and his wrath travels out with it. "Come here."

I obey and move through the maze of shadows, avoiding piles of clothing, scattered couch cushions, and a chrome and glass chaise lounge. I stop before an ornate, wood-scrolled, but cluttered, coffee table. It juts out at an odd angle separating me from him. He stares at me in silence. My eyes adjust further to the dimness. Brown hair falls in long, greasy strings about his shoulders. An expensive but worn blue and green robe covers his clothes. No shoes. He drags fingernails across the rash spreading up his neck. He looks thinner.

"You are unwell today." I state simply, not knowing what else to say. "I will get your medicine."

"No." He rubs his eyes and draws his palms over his face and refocuses on me. "Come closer."

I manage to clear the coffee table and stand before him. I'm close to him now. Too close. He grips my hand in his, and my heart jumps in fear. I am accustomed to his violent changes in mood—one minute cursing and throwing things, the next weeping like a child. He squeezes hard and pulls me closer still. He draws me down until I sit on the edge of the cluttered coffee table next to his chair. I'm so close now I can smell his breath. Warm bile and chemicals.

"I don't need medicine," he says. "I just need you." He sighs. His eyes roll back, and he closes them, head back against the chair. But his hand doesn't loosen its grip.

I look at him—at his long, bony fingers encircling my hand. I don't know what to say. What to think. How could a man like him need a sickly, underdeveloped CC like me? He must be losing his senses. No one needs me.

I don't know why, but tears form in my eyes.

"He likes you," Needle once told me.

But Absalom doesn't like anyone. Not even himself.

After many moments of watching Absalom's ribcage rise and fall, I ask, "Are you dying, Absalom?"

Absalom breathes out through slightly parted lips. He opens his eyes and stares unseeing at the vaulted ceiling.

"We're all dying."

II

This can't be happening. Absalom cannot die. I never realized it before, but I need him. Desperately. Even with his unpredictable behavior and intolerable—even dangerous—mood swings, he is still an incredibly powerful and influential man. He's also the only thing standing between me and my being dissected for parts, assuming I'm even worth that much.

Lying on my bed as night overtakes the sun's last rays, I worry about what Absalom meant this afternoon when he said, "We're all dying." I think he was talking about me, and probably about Needle and the Technics and Pristines and all the other CCs who live and work at Absalom Industries. If Absalom dies, so might we. Our futures will then be determined by people like the CEO, Ms. Sabeen, or U.S.E.C. (the United States Executive Commission), or any number of corporations who would love to get their hands on AI property. AI could be dissected and sold off in chunks, along with all of us. Needle, with his expertise, would probably be okay, but I'd never see him again. And me. What would happen to me? I'm not sure what happens to CCs outside of Absalom Industries, but I've heard stories. A million possibilities rush through my mind, none of them good.

I dream. For the first time in years, I dream an old dream from my early childhood. A dream so intense that, when I was young, I was unable to wake from it without medication. I'm about six years old. I'm walking down a long corridor toward a door at the far end. A voice is whispering my name—a woman's voice, I think, but I'm never quite sure. She's calling to me from behind the door. I speed up to reach her, but the corridor just gets longer the further I travel. "Galaxy…. Galaxy…. GALAXY!" I start to run. I'm desperate to reach her. She needs me. I'm sprinting now, moving faster and faster, hand reaching out for the door handle. And then the distance disappears and I have the handle in my grasp. But, I push through only to find myself surrounded by flames. The voice that had begun as a whisper is now a scream of agony. The person behind the voice is burning to death, screaming in terror and pain. I can't find her. The intense flames surround me, blind me. But she keeps screaming and I keep searching.

And then the dream bumps to a sudden stop and a new reality breaks in. A great white curtain of mist surrounds me and then dissipates. I'm lying on the floor in a silver room, a room with no windows, no doors, no bed, no furniture. I am naked. I am alone. The only sensation is my heart pounding and my breath tearing in and out of my chest.

I open my eyes and I'm in my room. I'm dressed. I'm alone. But I feel sluggish and spent.

It's morning. I should be getting up and getting to CC class, but I am not recovered from the night terrors. I realize CCs generally don't get to sleep in for so slight a reason. But, as Needle so often reminds me, Absalom spoils me. Lying here awake, staring at the new day's whitening sky through my vaulted glass ceiling, I know Needle is right. Bursts of rage aside, Absalom treats me differently than anyone else. Not always better, I would argue… but differently, yes.

Absalom…… Please be okay.

My metal bed sits in the middle of the room. Built into it on either side are rows of drawers where I keep my clean uniforms. I have no other furniture. Embedded in the foot board is an HCS—an Holographic Communication System. They can be found in every room and hallway throughout the tower. It is an interactive holographic projection device and computer system used for everything from interactive, holographic calls to the searching of massive Internet databases. Of course, CCs are very limited in what we can use them for. The one in my foot board usually just projects the time and the day's agenda, sending the image to hover in the air above my head. Right now, the usually green letters have turned from yellow to orange and finally to red, and they have begun flashing—an indication that my warnings have long expired and I've nearly missed the 9:30 am CC Mechanical Education Session in Cell 14. Below this in smaller, still-green letters it reads 10:25 am, CC Technological History Education Session, Cell 9.

"HCS, off!" I say, and the digital ghost numbers disappear. But they'll be back.

I readjust my head on my pillow and consider whether or not to show up to my History of Technology class. Some of the CCs at AI are required to take this class since we are so often engaged in the technological world. Officially, my job is to assist in data analysis for the Technology Development Laboratories. These laboratories occupy five floors of AI Tower. When I don't have class, I'm usually on the 144th floor in the Data Analysis room entering data into the computer for the scientists, researchers, and engineers who run the place. Once in a while, they let me observe the construction of new devices, intended for implantation into a CC, like the implants Needle has. But, it's hard for me to get excited about something that I know means pain or even death for another CC.

I stare into the depths of the white morning sky, lying on my back surrounded by the emptiness, trying to shake the tremors that still pervade my frame. *Breathe... breathe....*

I feel something here when I'm all alone that I never feel anywhere else. I don't know what it is. But I can breathe here. I can stand tall and look out upon the world beneath me—the buildings, the cars, the People and CCs. At night eternity stretches before me like a black tablecloth laden with diamonds.

Here I am myself.

Here I am part of the world.

A few minutes later, Needle's floating head, created from colored light particles, appears before my eyes. His voice breaks through the stillness, "Galaxy! Get your butt down here, for crying out loud! I'm tired of staring at your empty chair, and Miss Abilene is threatening to speak to Absalom herself if you don't start coming to class!"

Needle's face disappears before I get a chance to respond. He misses me, I think, and that is enough to get me out of bed. Of course, Miss Abilene, like everyone else who works at Absalom Industries, never talks to Absalom about me or anything else, if they can avoid it. In fact, most of them pass messages to him through me, and only if it's urgent. It rarely is.

Ms. Sabeen, the CEO, is the rare exception. She manages all the day-to-day business operations, so she handles just about everything—everything but me, that is. Three years ago, when she was brand new to her post and eager to make a good impression, she noticed me lingering in the arboretum and ignoring the new agenda she had worked out for all the AI CCs. She then informed me that she was on her way to a meeting with Absalom and was going to suggest that he replace me with a more reliable CC. I can only imagine what she actually intended to do with me once this replacement showed up, but I didn't worry about that for long. During that meeting, three chairs, two picture frames, and a window were dashed to pieces. I'm not sure what she said that set him off, but I like to think it was that suggestion. Of course, with Absalom, it could have been anything. At any rate, I heard later that Ms. Sabeen nearly lost her job and only managed to convince Absalom to keep her by agreeing to a much reduced salary. Since then she has never spoken a word to me. And I do as I please.

She hates me, of course.

I open a drawer beneath my bed, pull out the cornflower blue CC uniform—a long-sleeved jumpsuit, belted in the middle, that bears the AI insignia—and tug it on over the tank top and spandex shorts I sleep in. I run a comb through my long, white hair using the natural reflectivity of the crystal walls as a mirror, and push a button that raises the elevator chute out of the floor and into my living space. A short ride later and I'm in Absalom's dark, dust-covered quarters. He is nowhere in sight. I breathe a sigh of relief.

It doesn't take me long to hop on the next elevator and ride it down to the CC Education Center. I'm even early to Cell 9 for the history lesson. I find my place next to Needle and smile at him. He scowls back.

"Did you remember to stop by the CC Medical Center for your injection?"

My smile fades.

"You'll have to do it right after class."

Needle remembers everything.

I have been taking injections three times a day for as long as I can remember. I am supposed to report to the CC Medical Center first thing in the morning, right after my afternoon nap, and again before I go to bed. Lately I've been forgetting. I suppose that's what happens when you make a habit of ignoring your agenda. Of course, I have felt a lot healthier these past couple of years. Taking injections three times a day, in addition to the barrage of pills I'm supposed to swallow at each meal, seems a little ridiculous.

Needle reads my thoughts.

"I'm sure they'll let you know as soon as you can stop getting them," he says, scowl gone. "But if they're keeping you healthy, you shouldn't blow them off."

"All right, class, attention to the front, please." Miss Abilene comes in, blond curls bobbing, wearing high heels, an orange mini-skirt, and a matching striped orange and white blouse. She carries an oversized lime bag over her shoulder and drops it on the desk. She glances across the gathered students until her eyes settle on me. "Ah. I see Miss Galaxy has deigned to join us today."

Neither Miss Abilene nor the other students know quite what to do with me. Normally, a teacher of CCs has almost godlike power in the classroom because, if a CC is lucky enough to have an owner who will pay for their education, the CC had better learn all there is to learn. The problem with me is not so much that Miss Abilene has little control over me, but that Absalom exhibits little interest in controlling me either. And so my grades are by far the worst in the class. But few dare point it out. Only Needle talks to me without reservation.

Once, Signet, an enormous, athletic, seventeen-year-old Warrior female with creamy black skin and piercing black eyes, said to me, "Ever think of helping any of us get a day off?" She whispered it as she passed by my desk one morning when I showed up after an extended absence.

No, actually, I thought. *I have never considered helping any of you do anything. Why should I?*

Of course, that didn't seem like the right thing to say, so I said nothing. But it bothered me later. It still bothers me. I'm not sure why I should do anything for them. It's not as if they really need my help. Most of them are far more skilled than I am, what with all their genetic and mechanical enhancements. I'd look like an incompetent fool if I offered to help Needle fix or reprogram something. He'd just laugh at me and shake his head. And as far as getting away with coming late to class and such, it's not like I get permission. I just have more excuses than they do when I'm caught.

But I don't like the way Signet talked to me. She made it sound like I only care about myself.

My relationship with Miss Abilene is no better. "Ah, Galaxy, it's nice to see you in class. It's been such a long time," she'll say. Or, "I see you have a medical excuse for your tardiness today, but it's nice to see you looking so healthy."

I'm not really sure what she expects of me. I do have to visit the CC Clinic several times a day and I do get tired. But, I guess I can't really blame her for being annoyed when everyone else is so dedicated and punctual. To be honest, I feel perfectly healthy most of the time, except for last night and this morning. Though I sometimes feel a little twinge of guilt for what I put her through, it's hard to get motivated to do something I don't really want to do when I know I can get away with not doing it.

"We'll be continuing our review for the exam on Friday," Miss Abilene says, turning to the HCS fitted to the wall behind her desk. She reaches around her massive, surgically-enhanced front and, with the tip of her finger, enters her clearance code. A few flicks of her wrist later, and the HCS shoots a rectangular, detailed outline into the air. The outline shows a boring-looking bulleted list of various historical events she intends to cover.

"As we have studied, in the year 2027, the United States fell into a severe depression, followed quickly by a great many of the other world powers. By 2035 we had entered the New Dark Age. The problem was brought on by skyrocketing national debt and exacerbated by climate change and a series of natural disasters. Inflation, job losses, and poverty led to mass crime. The civil unrest became so violent, in fact, that several cities were destroyed by bombings and fires that raged unchecked."

I've heard all of this before. My mind wanders and I turn my eyes toward the streaks of light coming through the oversized window. This is one thing I love about living in AI Tower—lots and lots of sunlight. Ten years ago, Absalom designed and constructed The Tower to let in as much natural light as possible, which is ironic considering how dark he keeps his own apartments. I see tiny dust particles dancing in the sun rays—like miniature creatures powered by the sun.

Something shifts into my line of vision. It's Needle's head. He's looking at me. He turns toward the display, glances back at me, and looks at the greenish digital outline again. I follow his gaze. At first I have no idea what he's trying to tell me. But then I notice it. Miss Abilene's outline is missing the small Department of Commodity Class Education 'Approved Material' seal that normally appears in the upper right hand corner of all materials used in our educational sessions. This is the third time Miss Abilene has strayed from materials legally presentable to CCs. Needle first noticed it a few weeks ago. I didn't think anything of it, but once Needle notices an anomaly of any kind, he can't help but obsess over it until an explanation is found. He's annoying that way.

Now I wonder if Needle might be onto something. He has been tracking what he considers a purposeful inclusion of anti-government sentiment. Of course, if that's true, what Miss Abilene is doing is a punishable offense. Still, I'm more inclined to think it's all just an innocent oversight. Maybe this outline has been approved, but somehow the department simply neglected to add the seal. Or, maybe there's a glitch in the HCS.

I sigh.

Neither of these possibilities seems very likely. I decide to listen to what she has to say.

"Wars began breaking out. Diseases and starvation ensued. Our population was reduced by half within three years. In 2037, martial law was declared. In 2045, the Anarchy Aversion Act was passed unanimously by what remained of our Senate. This act allowed them to do whatever was necessary to save the USA from being either internally or externally destroyed. The first year they focused on restructuring the government. These changes included changing our form of government from a republic to a geniocracy. This means that, instead of being ruled by the people, who were largely corrupt and uneducated, the United States is now ruled by geniuses—people who have displayed exceptional intelligence, innovation, expertise, and creativity. This group of people is called the United States Executive Commission or U.S.E.C.. And, we no longer have a president. We have the U.S.E.C. chairman, Supreme Head Anshar. You have heard of him, of course.

"Those were the changes made in the first year of the Anarchy Aversion Act, but the following year they found the real solution to all of our problems. Realizing that many of our economic troubles were being caused by a severe decrease in population and reduced workforce, they made abortion illegal. Instead of eliminating these pregnancies, U.S.E.C. purchased them. Of course, it was a risky move. The fledgling government had very limited resources and their plan was an expensive one, but as hoped, it paid off—and much sooner than anyone expected. On the advice of the technological experts of U.S.E.C., the Commission invested heavily in biological research and development, capitalizing on some very important technological advances in artificial fetal growth and genetic manipulation."

Of course, I know all of this. But something about the way she is talking, the slight breathlessness behind her words, the way she keeps glancing at the door and security cameras, makes me wonder what is going on. And then she says it.

"It would have been unethical to perform these experiments on Persons. Luckily, unborn human fetuses were not legally Persons. Therefore, it was legal to do whatever we wanted with them. So they became the Commodity Class—you. It was then easy to extend the denial of personhood toward those who had already been born, since the only thing required to draw the line between Person and non-person is a legal document."

Staring. Staring at my dim reflection in the crystal walls of my room… of my jail cell. And I can't decide what I see. All my life until now has been simple. Not easy, but simple. *I'm a CC. A member of the Commodity Class. CCs are not Persons. CCs are property. We are bought and sold. Our bodies are used for science, medicine, pleasure, labor, and dangerous jobs. We are expendable. Pain and death is expected, not avoided, not resented. We have no families. We have no rights. We own nothing—not even our lives.*

I have no idea why any of this should bother me. But it does.

Before me stands a skinny girl with green eyes and long, straight, shock white hair. She's fifteen years old, but looks about twelve. She wears a blue jumpsuit that bears the AI insignia, top left. She has childlike, mousy features, blue-green eyes, a few freckles, and the letters "CC" tattooed on her right temple. But she's not a Person. She will never be a Person. Once a CC, always a CC.

Thoughts like these are dangerous. I know this. Somehow I know I've crossed a line. The class this afternoon changed something. Even before they took Miss Abilene, I knew it. Needle knew it, too. And the rest of the students sat unusually still. No one fidgeted in their seats or coughed or rustled paper. The classroom became a graveyard of silence, but the air brimmed with fear. I realized, after a while, I was holding my breath.

But Miss Abilene went on.

"In 2049, the Commission passed the CC Naming Ordinance. Originally, CCs were only given numbers, but that became too complicated for People to remember, so it was decided that CCs could be given names from an approved list." She paused, swallowed, and continued. "The approved list could only include names that sounded like pet names."

I blinked. My mind went over some of the names of the other CCs sitting in class with me. *Spur, Luster, Trinket, Padlock, Bandy, Needle... Galaxy.* I'd never known a CC named Mary or George or Alice. But again, none of this was new to me. CC names are just one more way to differentiate us from People. Of course, we also bear the CC tattoo on our right temples. This tattoo, though in the shape of letters, is actually a smartcode that can be scanned for everything from information about our owners to legal and medical information. And, at the age of one year, tracking chips had been inserted under the skin at the backs of our necks. But, still, all of this was common knowledge. So, why did my heart beat so fast?

"By 2058, the United States had climbed out of the depression and a Golden Age began. The sale and use of CCs—all still children at that time—brought incredible profits. Other countries followed suit, but we had already established a corner on the market. CCs proved to be very lucrative sources for labor, but also for biological material for experimentation. A great many advances were made possible by using them as test subjects and raw material. In fact, the very same year CCs came into existence, U.S.E.C. began offering the Organ Production Grant to encourage biological research companies to begin developing and using CCs for the growth of viable organs——kidneys, livers, hearts— for People who needed transplants. We found cures for diseases, improved beauty and health products, and learned a great deal about how the human body works—or fails to work. The average life span for

People living in the United States rapidly increased from the pitifully low 56.9 years of the New Dark Ages to 83.6 years. Geneticists and biological researchers were thrilled to finally have ample resources to experiment with. And you can only imagine how happy this made the animal rights activists. Animal research and cruelty was finally a thing of the past. We saw the emergence of the cloning industry and the genetic treatments that allow Persons to live longer, healthier lives. And now, pregnant women who decide they want their children can select the baby's gender, eye-color, and hair-color long before they're born.

"And, lest we forget, much work was also done in artificial intelligence and robotics research. This is when Absalom Industries first came into being, with Absalom's grandfather, also named Absalom. But, as you know, it was discovered that true intelligence requires, at minimum, a biological brain, so Absalom Industries refocused on the creation of a new technology involving cybernetics—the creation of Technics—CCs that are part biological and part machine and computer, like some of you."

I couldn't keep myself from glancing at Needle. I noticed a small semi-circular metal gear twitch in his robotic ear. He didn't look at me, but he did look at the door.

"In 2064, when the first CCs were about 17 or 18 years old, the Commission passed the Casualty Elimination Act. This way only CCs would be used in dangerous military operations, and we would no longer lose any more of our—"

And then it happened. The classroom's double doors exploded open. Three large soldiers came in. These were not regular police. They were military special forces, dressed in black, aerogel-reinforced uniforms with dark green accents and the United States Executive Commission emblem emblazoned on their chests. They carried side arms and wore protective helmets that shielded their eyes from us. Two of them flanked Miss Abilene and gripped her arms. Four more entered and lined the front of the room, leveling their weapons on us. Though Miss Abilene gasped and begged for some kind of explanation, the helmeted soldiers forced her from the room without comment or decorum. Her feet scrambled, kicking off one of her high-heeled shoes as they dragged her out.

A seventh soldier crossed to the HCS controls, pushed a few buttons, and the outline disappeared from sight. He wore a uniform that was slightly different in design. The dark green bands running along his arms and legs were wider, and he bore the U.S.E.C. Special Forces insignia across his heart. He was their captain.

The captain turned to the class and moved through the aisles. With swift, rough movements, he scanned each and every one of us with an instrument embedded in the fabric covering his right wrist. Starting at the far left row of chairs, he grabbed the chin of the female CC sitting there—her name is Granite—and yanked her head sideways so he could electronically record her personal information with his wrist scanner. A blue light flashed, his arm beeped, and he released her to move down the line, taking a record of each CC in the room.

Before long he was at my side. Like the others, his helmet covered the top of his head and eyes, but left his mouth and chin exposed. I noticed a white scar across his chin. He yanked my head so hard I cried out in pain. None of the others made a noise, but I'm not used to being treated that way. He didn't care.

All the while, his four guards remained before us, targeting us with lasers from high-powered energy rifles. Once back at the front of the room, the captain said, "Remain in your seats and wait for your orders."

The captain marched from the room, followed swiftly by his guards, who backed out, keeping their aim on us until the last possible moment.

A few minutes later we received another surprise. Absalom himself walked into the room, hair disheveled, still wearing a robe, looking very pale and very angry.

"Out!" was all he said and we all scattered like bugs escaping an overturned rock.

I saw Needle limping away, moving in the opposite direction down the hallway at an abnormally fast clip. I caught the first available elevator to Absalom's quarters and then to my own.

I wonder what happened to Miss Abilene. She is a Person, I remind myself, so she has rights. But I also know how serious the Commission takes breaches in classified information—particularly among CCs. Of course, maybe it was a simple misunderstanding. I mean, how can simple historical facts be dangerous?

But I know they are. Somehow, they are. They are dangerous for Miss Abilene, but they are also dangerous for us… for me.

A new, terrifying thought occurs to me. Miss Abilene has put all of the CCs in that room at terrible risk. If the Department of Commodity Class Education decides that our loyalty has been compromised, they or some other government entity could seize us and maybe even have us incinerated. A necessary sacrifice in the interest of national security, they would call it.

My hands begin to shake. I have to sit down. Not on the bed. At only a few paces away, it feels too far. I sit down against the glass and gaze down at the dizzying depths below me. Only an inch of clear glass keeps me from plummeting into an abyss-like fall from the top of the 200-story AI Tower. Safety is a fragile thing, I realize. Like glass. Leaning against it and staring down, I can almost feel myself falling. Air whizzing by, tumbling in a wild free fall, a scream caught in my throat.

I close my eyes and suck in shreds of air. Another breath, smoother this time. The only thing that makes me feel better about this whole mess is knowing Absalom is involved.

I keep a close eye on my schedule. I've missed my first injection and am late for my second. Oddly, the HCS continues to display the same thing: Naptime. This is the longest nap of my life. It's nearly dinner time and I'm starving. So, is this it? Is this the punishment for going to class today? I'm left to starve to death in my room? Or, perhaps, when I leave to investigate, I'll be caught for disobeying orders.

Out of curiosity, I walk over to the elevator controls, activate the identity scanner, and let the lasers blip over my tattoo. The chute and tube rise out of the floor at my command. Well, I'm not confined to my room. More likely Ms. Sabeen and her team of AI administrators haven't decided what to do with us yet. Of course, that would mean that I don't need to stay here. After all, it would be a little odd for me to be quite so particular about obeying the HCS all of a sudden. And I do have the excuse of my missed injections.

A few moments later, I'm outside the CC Medical Clinic on the 117th floor. It's just one of the forty-two floors of AI Tower dedicated to our CC hospital.

I hate it here. I hate everything about the hospital—the doctors, the uniforms, the smell of chemicals. Being here always fills me with a sense of panic. Even though I know my injections will not cause much pain, I can't shake the fear. I've seen a great many doctors, and I learned long ago they can't be trusted. Still, I manage to force myself to open the door and walk inside.

Marlene, one of the evening nurses, greets me with an annoyed smirk. "So you finally made it. I was afraid I'd have to come find you before Absalom dragged you in here himself. What kept you this time? A stroll in the solarium? A swim in Absalom's pool?"

So she hasn't heard of the debacle in the CC Education Center.

"Actually, I think my HCS is broken. It still reads naptime."

"Oh, well. I'll call down to maintenance and report it. But next time you should just call down here to confirm the error instead of disobeying the HCS. You could get into a lot of trouble if you're mistaken." She gives me a glance up and down, remembering who she's talking to. She rolls her eyes. "Well… most CCs would, anyway."

Marlene prepares the injection and unceremoniously jabs the needle into my arm—a place that, after years of mistreatment, is more raw meat than skin. "Here, take this pill for that tissue damage," she says. "It's new from Experimental Medicine. It regenerates damaged tissue. Should make you look like new in a few days—even with the regular injections."

I'm glad for the promised relief but find it difficult to suppress my instant concern about the price of this new cure. How much CC suffering and death did this cost? I swallow the pill, but can't get out the 'thank you' on my tongue.

"You may feel a little woozy," she warns as she picks up an electronic tool and scans my tattoo to record the dispensation of the drugs. "I had to give you an increased dose in that injection since you missed the last one. And take the rest of these pills with you." She hands me a labeled bottle of the new tissue regeneration pills. "Take one pill every morning with breakfast—just one."

"Alright," I say as I climb down from the chair. She has already forgotten me and is busy reorganizing items at her station.

In the hallway, I activate one of the HCS's embedded in the wall and pull up my schedule. Naptime, it still reads. I pull up Needle's schedule which, thankfully, is not considered protected information. It reads the same, proving this is no error. A flash of fear runs through me. Needle never gets a naptime. But, I know precisely where he will be.

On the way to Needle's quarters, I decide to stop by the CC Cafeteria. Though most CCs are on a tight meal schedule, everyone who works in the cafeteria knows to give me as much food as I want, whenever I want. Absalom wants me to eat as much as I can to make up for the years I was so ill and undernourished. Though my appetite vanished with the double injection, I know Needle will be famished by now, having missed lunch.

A short while later, I raise my hand to knock on Needle's door but am stopped by his voice from inside. "Come in, Galaxy."

I enter. His back is to me. He's fidgeting with his HCS.

"How did you know it was me?"

"I knew it was you the second you stepped off the lift at the end of the hall. What are you doing here?" Needle's eyes grow wide when he sees the large tray of food I've brought. "You're going to get us both in trouble!"

"Are you hungry or not?" I ask, moving toward a small table and depositing the tray there.

"Starving." He takes a turkey sandwich. "I can't say I'm surprised, but you shouldn't be here," he says around a mouthful of meat and bread.

"Where should I be?"

"In bed, apparently."

"You know me better than that. Besides, I had an excuse. My injections."

"Right."

Despite the small talk, Needle is nervous.

"How's the air in here today?" I ask. It's code for, did you take care of the surveillance equipment so we can talk freely?

"We can talk," he says. Needle's room is designed for two occupants, but AI recently sold his last roommate, so he has the whole place to himself. "I even adjusted the surveillance equipment in the hall and altered the elevator chute records to show a malfunction. No one will know where you got off."

I smile. "I can always count on you." I watch him chew for a moment before asking the question burning on my tongue. "What do you think they're going to do to us?"

"To you? Nothing, most likely." He glances at me and sees I don't appreciate his remark. "Sorry. I don't know. Anything could happen."

I don't like the sound of that.

"But we'll be okay, right?"

Needle shrugs. "Actually, of everyone the soldiers scanned in our class, I'm probably the most in danger."

"What? Why?"

Needle hesitates.

"Galaxy... for the first time in my life," he swallows, glances at the door and then back to me, "I've done something truly illegal."

I blink in surprise. "What? What are you talking about?" My heart starts beating faster.

"I... I..." he lowers his voice, "I hacked into the main computer and retrieved Miss Abilene's illegal class notes. I was worried about her and just wanted to reassure myself that her materials would pass inspection. I thought I would just be downloading a few outlines," he continues, "outlines that seem pretty vague as to why they would be deemed inappropriate for CCs. But, more came with them... much more."

"What do you mean?"

"I mean, there are things in there that strongly suggest that Miss Abilene was a... a Subversive."

"A Subversive? I don't believe it!"

"Shh!" He glances around nervously. "It's true... and it's worse than that, at least for me."

"What are you talking about?"

"I tried to cover for her."

"Needle! Why? You could get incinerated for that! Why would you do that?"

"Because... because she's our teacher and... and I felt like I should help her."

"Needle, she's a Person! You're a CC! She doesn't need your help!"

"But she did, Galaxy." His voice is calm. "She's in a lot of trouble... and it's because of us."

My heart is pounding now. I feel like hitting something. Needle understands many things I don't—especially about others, both CCs and Persons. I've always followed his lead, even though he's five years younger. But this time I'm afraid he's gone too far.

"Well," I say, trying to calm my voice, "what did you do?"

"I removed the files. I didn't want anyone to find them, so I downloaded them onto the memory chip in my ear implant and deleted them from the AI mainframe. But now, I'm a Subversive, too. Or, a rebel, I guess—whatever! I tried to cover my tracks, so maybe they won't find out what I did. But, I've literally got the evidence stored right inside my head!" He taps his robotic ear. "And I don't even know if I did it soon enough. If they got to it first, it's over for her."

"And maybe for you, too. Especially if they can track where the download went!"

Needle raises and eyebrow at me as if to say: Do you really think I would be that stupid?

I stare at him, not sure what to think. Part of me feels impressed he had the foresight and willingness to put himself at risk for Miss Abilene's safety, but mostly I'm scared to death. An image of Needle burning to death flashes through my mind, and my breath catches in my throat.

Needle's head jerks toward the door.

"Someone's coming," he says.

There is a knock at the door, and we both freeze. I see panic in Needle's eyes.

"The authorities wouldn't knock," I remind him and he relaxes a shade.

I open the door. It's Luster, one of the CC females who was in class with us today.

"I thought I saw you come in here with a tray of food," she says, glancing past me. "There it is! We're starving!"

"We?" I ask.

Gauntlet and Gash enter behind her. Gauntlet is an enormous 16-year-old, black Warrior who, despite his intimidating size, has a smooth, friendly face. Gash, a white Warrior with blond hair and green eyes, is seventeen and rarely says much. They are the same size, and I never see one without the other.

The massive teenagers push past me, nearly knocking me down, and descend on the tray, divvying up sandwiches and fruit between them. I feel a little guilty that my concern is so limited. I only thought of Needle's hunger, but surely all of the CCs who were in class today are famished by now. If the HCSs don't change to dinnertime within the next ten minutes as they should, maybe I'll go back down to the cafeteria and get food for the rest of them. It will look suspicious, but I've gotten away with worse.

"I don't know what we'd do if we didn't have you on our side," Gauntlet says to me, mouth full of food.

His compliment impresses and surprises me. I've never felt appreciated before—at least, not by anyone other than Needle and Absalom. I like it. But, something that he said worries me—on our side.

Now we're taking sides? Have Miss Abilene's subversive intentions begun to work already? But then I remind myself that Gauntlet, as one of the Warrior CCs, is trained to think in terms of sides. I watch him and his buddy, Gash, chewing voraciously as looks of food-induced bliss cover their faces. Genetically manipulated muscle tissues have ballooned these teenagers into gorilla-like monsters of strength and size, thanks to years of tampering. I don't run into them often, as our duties rarely coincide, but when I do I always try to give them a wide berth. Looking at them now, they just look like hungry children.

My eyes drift to Luster, one of the Pristines. Pristine CCs are designed specifically for beauty and sex appeal. Luster has genetically modified copper hair that sparkles in the light. Her skin has also been altered to shimmer and shine when she moves. Her body, unlike my underdeveloped one, is perfectly proportioned, and her eyes have been modified so that the color of her irises undulate from green to aqua to blue and back again. She's mesmerizing to look at. It would be easy for me to envy her and any of the many other Pristines raised and trained here, except that I know that next year, when she turns fourteen, she'll be sold at auction into the sex industry—just like Bliss. CCs—even high-end CCs—have a life expectancy of only a couple of years in that business.

The HCS fails to deliver the much desired dinnertime message, so I abandon all hope of continuing my conversation with Needle tonight. I make the trek to the cafeteria, weather the curious looks of the workers, and return with all the food I can carry.

"Spread the word," I tell Luster. "Dinner is being served in Needle's room tonight."

III

For the first time, I feel like one of them. I just hope tonight's meal shows them they don't need to resent me for getting preferential treatment. I smile. It feels good to do something nice—and even a little risky—to help them out. There. See, Signet?

Twenty of us make up the class assigned to that session from various areas of AI. It takes more than a little maneuvering and cramming for everyone to find a place to sit in Needle's cramped quarters. Luster is joined by three more Pristines: Allure, Siren, and Ravish. Ravish is a Latino male and perhaps the most beautiful thing I've ever seen. Even though he wears the same belted, blue AI jumpsuit we all do, I can tell his physique is perfectly balanced—slender but firm and muscled. Of course, the Warriors are well muscled, too, but they are overdone, moving like titans through water. Not like Ravish. He moves like silk. He has soft black hair with eyes like swirling pools of blue. His skin is tanned and smooth, but I also catch a glimpse now and then of the copper highlights the geneticists managed to produce. Lips of the perfect fullness. Straight, white teeth. Perfect smile. I suddenly feel very stupid, because I catch my reflection in the Needle's window and I have a goofy looking smile on my face.

Of course, Allure and Siren are exceptionally beautiful as well. Allure, a 12-year-old female of Asian descent, has long, pink hair and skin that shimmers with shades of pinks, oranges, and yellows. She is designed to look like a flame. Siren's green hair matches brilliant green eyes. Her skin is reminiscent of silver fish scales. I think her designers were going for something like a mermaid look for her. But, I assume you can only get the full effect of their work when she's underwater. I have never really gotten to know any of the Pristines well. They tend to keep to themselves. Even now, despite the limited places to sit, the four of them insist on sitting together.

Several more Warrior class CCs arrive: Spur, Padlock, Badge, and Signet. They scatter about the room, trying to avoid knocking anyone's food out of their hands with their broad arms, shoulders, or thighs.

The rest of the Technics join us—Decoy, Abracadabra, Bandy, Trinket and Granite. Decoy, a dark-skinned, Indian boy with coffee-colored hair and violet eyes, is covered with narrow blue currents, like neon rivers running through his skin. I'm not sure how it works, but I've heard he has the ability to produce holograms with a mere thought. Abracadabra is also covered in technology, except that he has microscopic panels implanted in his skin. It makes him look silvery, almost like an albino, but they function like smart image reflectors. I've never observed him doing it myself, since it's illegal for CCs to use their non-human abilities without permission, but he's supposed to be able to disappear entirely. Trinket has a cybernetic eye and a robotic left hand, and both of Bandy's arms have been replaced with robotic appendages. Granite, though, looks like a normal 12-year-old girl with short brown hair. I know she's a Technic, but whatever alterations were performed on her are well hidden.

Despite all of these interesting alterations, perhaps the most intriguing CCs among us are the Gapes, Gaze and Lumina. Gaze is male. Lumina is female. Gapes work in the Gene Manipulation Laboratory, in Embryonic Research. Their designers gave them exceedingly large eyes—like two mangoes, blinking and staring. To accommodate this alteration, their heads are shaped like large, upside-down teardrops. For some reason, whatever the geneticists did to bring about this effect also caused the unexpected side-effects of baldness, reduced stature, and unusually high IQs—not so high as a Wit's, but they're definitely smarter than I am.

Though they are among the oldest in our class, at age 17, they never get taller than an average six-year-old child. We're told that Gaze and Lumina and the other Gapes need to have such large eyes in order to work effectively with such small bits of organic material. I would never say this aloud, but I've always thought that was a bunch of nonsense. We have high-powered microscopes for that sort of thing. I think the researchers and genetic engineers did it just to see if it could be done.

Besides me, the only other Natural in the room is Flick. Since AI is in the business of creating high-end, genetically or technologically enhanced CCs, very few Naturals live and work here. However, Flick joined us a couple of years ago when Absalom bought out a smaller company. AI kept Flick because of his expertise in computer programming. He is a seventeen-year-old Latino and all he's ever done is work with computers. Since the company who owned him didn't have the resources to invest in the expensive programs available, Flick had to create elaborate computer programs from scratch. As it turned out, he was quite good at it. And since he worked independently from conventional methods, his programs show a great deal of uniqueness and creative, if unusual, problem-solving techniques. Now he works in the AI Software Production and Testing Laboratories and has made himself indispensable to the computer engineers there.

Flick, not a bad-looking boy, has straight, black hair and a dyed swath of deep blue along the left side of his head. I suppose he did this to fit in better with all of the genetically enhanced CCs he hangs out with these days. But, despite his attempts at social interactions, Flick has had very little experience with it. He often remains at the sidelines of conversations and, when he does speak up, is greeted with odd looks or impatient sighs. In some ways, he and I are a lot alike.

Despite the differences among the group, that night everyone was in good spirits at the unexpected reward of dinner in Needle's room. With so many CCs crammed into such small a space, both beds are soon piled high with bodies and the floor is a maze of arms, legs, and torsos. It's nearly impossible to move. Still, other than Needle, this is the first time other CCs have included me in their free time activities. It's… well, it's interesting. I've never felt like I might be missing something, but… I guess I feel kind-of excited about it now.

"Can somebody pass me another sandwich?" Gash asks from the side of the room opposite the dwindling food tray. He sits on the floor, tightly wedged between the foot of one of the beds and Abracadabra.

Gaze reaches up, angles his arms around his massive head, and blindly gropes for the tray, which sits on the desk directly behind and above his head. Despite his efforts, the tray remains just centimeters from his reach. If his head had been smaller, he would have found it.

"Here, I'll get it," Bandy, a male Technic with ebony skin, speaks up. He stretches his right robotic arm toward the tray, and we all watched as metal layer upon layer slide out from his forearm to extend all the way across the room over our heads. At the right moment, a robotic hand emerges, grabs the tray with impressive dexterity, and carries it back across the room.

"Wow," Gash said, in his deep, somewhat gravelly voice. "Thanks. That was awesome."

Bandy grinned.

"You think that's cool. Watch this!" Abracadabra says, and before our eyes tiny pieces of his body and uniform begin to wink and disappear. The last thing to go are his eyes, but when he closes them he is completely gone. The effect is amazing and startling, but also funny, because now oversized Gash looks very odd indeed, squished up between the foot of the bed and what appears to be empty space.

Ooos, ahhs, and laughter immediately erupt from the group.

"I can still see you," Lumina says.

"Me, too," Gaze adds, but they are laughing.

Abracadabra reappears. "Well, I guess you can't fool everyone."

"You know, we need to be careful," Needle warns. "Some of your alterations aren't strictly legal. And even if they are, you know the rules."

"But I thought you always kept your room below the radar," Signet says.

I'm not sure what surprises me more—the fact that AI is producing illegally enhanced CCs, that everyone in the room knows about Needle's habit of manipulating the surveillance equipment, or that everyone is okay with both of these activities.

"It is, but I'm not the only one with access to the security systems around here," he reminds them.

"What do you mean," I ask, "illegally enhanced?"

All eyes turn to me. I swallow.

"Do you really think the government would want CCs who can disappear entirely?" Luster finally says with more than a little annoyance in her voice.

"Almost entirely," Lumina corrects her.

Luster rolls her eyes in Lumina's direction.

Apparently, my face continues to display my lack of understanding, so Decoy speaks up.

"If a CC can disappear entirely, he or she would be awfully difficult to find, wouldn't he… or she?"

"But, we have tracking chips," I say. "And why would we want to hide?"

Eyes dart nervously about the room, and Badge says, "No one is saying we want to hide. It's just that it would be against the government's interests to lose track of us. That's all we're saying."

"Oh… but then, if it's illegal, why do the engineers do it?"

"To see if they can," Ravish said, and I know he's telling the truth.

But then another thought strikes me. "What if Absalom finds out? Won't they get in trouble?"

"Whose idea do you think it was, dummy?" Luster says and laughs. The Pristines snicker along with her.

"Leave her alone," Needle says, coming to my rescue, although I don't really care what the Pristines or any of them think of me. "She doesn't get to hang out with us much, so you can't expect her to know everything."

"Well, I'm glad you're here with us tonight," Trinket, a young Native American Technic with long, silky, black hair, says. She smiles at me.

"Yeah, and thanks for the food," Gauntlet says, saluting me with a half-eaten banana.

Some of the others nod and smile in agreement.

I smile back.

Well... maybe I do care what some of them think of me. Just a little.

Absalom Industries is a massive organization. AI Tower reflects this power, influence, and wealth by its sheer size and beauty. The Tower rises well above the tallest sky scrapers ever built, and the spire at the top pushes those limits even further. It is truly an engineering marvel, not only for its height, but also due to the fact that so much glass was used in its construction. The giant letters A and I are positioned near the top of the main structure, just below my quarters. At night they light up the skies of Washington D.C. with a rainbow of pulsing color that reaches into the darkness above and cascades upon everything below.

But, despite appearances, AI is fragile... like the glass it's made of. If Absalom dies, it will shatter. The pieces will be scattered. I'm one of those pieces. So is Needle and Luster and Gauntlet and all of the other AI CCs.

Absalom is sick, very sick. But he's not dead yet. Still, with all I've been hearing lately, I wonder if we'll even have to wait that long. AI industries is dabbling in illegal technology. In fact, it has been doing so for many years. And stranger still, everyone seems to know it. The CCs know it. Absalom knows it. And, of course, the engineers and geneticists must know it, for it is their handiwork—their art mixed with science. Does Ms. Sabeen know it, I wonder? The administrators, the medical staff, those who serve us our food or take out the garbage? Is everyone in on it? Or, have some been intentionally kept in the dark, like me? Where is the line? And how does this kind of secret remain a secret?

I finally get the chance today to meet with Needle, just the two of us, to discuss what he found when he hacked the mainframe. I tap on his door. It is late. Both our HCSs read Bedtime right now. But Needle is expecting me, and I usually have little trouble slipping in and out of my room, despite the need to go through Absalom's suite.

Needle's door cracks open and I step inside. Needle walks over to the HCS embedded in his wall and opens a small, metal panel in the lower right-hand corner. He lifts his robotic appendage, where his right hand should be, and I watch a metal device of some sort emerge from its tip and connect perfectly with a slot inside the now exposed, metal guts of the HCS. Needle's brow furrows in concentration. His freckled nose screws up a little and sandy blond strands of hair tumble across his forehead as he manages the stream of information flowing through the HCS. A few moments later, the device returns to its place in his false arm and he slams the panel shut.

"There. I returned all the hallway and elevator surveillance systems to normal. Don't let me forget to override it again before you go back."

I plop myself down on his bed and curl my skinny legs beneath me. This is just where I sat last night when hungry CC teenagers overran his room.

"And now," he says as he configures the HCS to project a new menu, "I can use the HCS to display what I found in Miss Abilene's records. You see, I first had to disengage the feed between my HCS and the mainframe before I could download her notes to it. Otherwise, anyone monitoring the system would have access to it, too. And, of course, we can't have that. But then I also had to fool the system into thinking my HCS was still connected. Otherwise, a blip will come up on their monitors that my HCS is nonfunctional and we'd be interrupted by a maintenance crew. We can't have that, either. So, I created a dummy-file that mimics the output signals of my HCS and then I—"

"Needle," I say, cutting him off, "I get it."

I only sort-of get it, but I don't really care about the details. I trust him to figure out how to keep us from getting caught. Right now all I'm interested in is seeing the stolen notes.

"Okay, well, you might find this interesting, then." Needle touches the screen with the tip of his index finger on his left hand. Out flashes the last outline Miss Abilene showed us—only, this one contains some extra dates and events.

2024	Absalom Industries begins as a small robotic engineering firm.
2027	Worldwide Depression
2035	USA enters the New Dark Ages.
2037	Martial Law declared.
2045	Anarchy Aversion Act
	Geniocracy Formation Resolution, United States Executive Commission (U.S.E.C.) is formed.
	U.S.E.C. Special Forces created.
	National Security Protection Act.
2046	Abortion made illegal and the Commodity Class is created by United States Executive Commission (U.S.E.C.) executive order.
	Human Rights Rebellion begins.
	Organ Production Grant made available.

AI is the first company to enter the CC business and also the first to receive the grant.

2048	Animal Rights Protection Act
2049	CC Naming Ordinance
2050	Human Rights Rebellion suppressed by U.S.E.C. Special Forces.
2055	Human Rights Activist Uprising, quickly suppressed.
2058	USA climbs out of depression; USA Golden Age begins.
2064	Casualty Elimination Act.
2073	Absalom dies, at age 74. Absalom II, takes over AI.
2076	USA gains dominance as world's largest military power.
2081	CC Rebellion begins.
2082	CC Production Standards set.
2092	CC Rebellion is suppressed.
2098	Absalom II dies of a sudden heart attack, age 61. Absalom III takes over AI at age 21.
2112	AI Tower construction begins.
2122	CC Population Reduction Act proposed at U.S.E.C..

My eyes scan the dates and entries and it doesn't take me long to realize that the outline contains a great deal of information I was never supposed to see. Even her secret password is revealed in bright blue letters: DA1321.

"What is this National Security Protection Act that was passed in 2045?" I ask him.

"There are some explanations in the attached footnotes. Here, I'll access them." Needle reaches into the floating letters to swipe a small icon. Immediately, a box appears containing some rather extensive notes.

"Apparently the National Security Protection Act did three things. First, it gave U.S.E.C. censoring power over any information the press wanted to print or publish. Second, it gave U.S.E.C. the power to monitor all formerly private messages, phone calls, emails, etc. Third, it allowed them to install and utilize surveillance equipment in all formerly private areas, including private businesses and homes."

"So, I guess it wasn't always that way," I say slowly, trying to understand what all these things mean.

Needle flips back to the outline, and I react. "Wait, what's that in 2046? There was a rebellion?"

"Let's see… the Human Rights Rebellion began in 2046 and lasted four years. It was in response to… the creation of the Commodity Class." He swallows and scans the corresponding notes. "A large group of People banded together in opposition to what they called a severe human rights violation. Several states and cities declared themselves against the use of human beings as commodities and refused to comply with

U.S.E.C. demands. Leaders of the rebellion called for the disintegration of U.S.E.C. and even managed to create a militia that marched on Washington D.C. However, U.S.E.C. had gathered intelligence on the leaders of the rebellion, their families, and their plans. U.S.E.C. Special Forces were dispatched to seize more than three hundred rebel leaders who were publicly put to death, but not before they were forced to watch their families—men, women, and children tortured and killed—except the babies and unborn, who were turned into CCs. Shortly thereafter, the rebellion came to an end."

"Wow," I say. It's all I can say. I feel my throat tightening.

Needle, too, takes a moment to digest what we've just read. "I never knew this," he says in a near whisper. "I never knew there were People who would actually fight... and die... for beings like us."

Of course, we've heard of the terrible things U.S.E.C. and other government organizations do to CCs. This barely compares, really, but to know that People—actual Persons—would care enough about us to put themselves in such danger and to ultimately pay such a price for our freedom... for beings they probably didn't even know....

"Look," I point to a line further down. "They tried again five years later, but I guess U.S.E.C. was too powerful by then—I mean, too powerful for the rebellion to succeed," I correct myself. Even though I know Needle and I can talk freely and despite all I've just learned, I can't rid myself of the habit of filtering from my speech anything that might smack of negativity toward U.S.E.C..

"Oh, wow! Look at that!" Needle has scrolled down and points at two entries, the first in 2081 and the second in 2092. "A CC rebellion? Really? Do you know what that means?" His voice goes up, as do his eyebrows. He looks at me and then back at the screen and then back at me again.

"Yes, I think I do. It means there are CCs who actually managed to coordinate and rebel."

"And it lasted for eleven years! Imagine that! Eleven years!" Needle's biological hand reaches for his forehead. "I mean... they must've had help, don't you think? Maybe some of the People who were involved in the Human Rights Rebellion and Uprising were still around."

"Or maybe they didn't need help. Look at this," I say, indicating an entry between the other two. What is this CC Production Standards thing?"

Needle returns to the explanation page and reads, "CC Production Standards were set in 2082 in direct response to the CC rebellion of the previous year. U.S.E.C. discovered that certain companies were producing CCs who had abilities that made them particularly difficult to capture or kill. Therefore, it set production standards for CC production companies that would limit the kinds of genetic and/or technological enhancements that could be applied to CCs."

"This is when CCs like Abracadabra and Decoy became illegal," I say. And then a terrible thought hits me. "What would they do to them if they are discovered?" But, I know the answer even before Needle reads it.

"CCs that fail to meet U.S.E.C. standards are incinerated."

That is the standard government solution to any CC problems. Confiscate the CC, transport them to National Security Headquarters— there is one in every big city—and force them into a furnace. A push of a button sends burning plasma through holes in the ceramic cage where the CC is standing.

No more CC. No more problem.

My heart hurts. My head hurts. I look at Needle and his eyes are red and moist. I feel my eyes stinging, too, but I'm not the kind of person to cry. Still, I don't think I can take any more of this. I stand up to leave. I'm about to ask Needle to adjust the surveillance again so I can go back to my room unobserved, but then I notice the last line of the outline. I stare, terrified that it means precisely what I think it does. Needle follows my gaze and I hear him swallow hard. It reads, "2122: CC Population Reduction Act proposed at U.S.E.C.."

Needle draws his finger up into the green, photonic letters and again brings the appropriate explanation into view. Without a word, we both read: "The CC Population Reduction Act was proposed at U.S.E.C. on Wednesday, February 4th of 2122 and is under consideration, with a decision expected Monday, June 1st of the same year. Currently, there is a perceived danger that the CC population is getting too large to safely manage without risk of further uprisings. Therefore, the act, if passed, will reduce the current population of CCs by one third."

February of 2122. That was this year. And now it's May.

IV

Morning again. It is Friday and yesterday I added a new routine to my morning schedule. Now, before getting dressed, I take a pill from a bottle Nurse Marlene gave me for my needle-damaged arm. It works like a miracle. Within minutes, the red, scarred flesh is replaced with fresh, new skin. The tenderness is almost gone. And the other places on my body, damaged by previous treatments of various kinds, are already healed.

Lovely!

Despite the feeling of comfort produced by the new drug, I can't get the thought out of my head that healing myself may be too little too late. If a third of the CCs in existence today are going to be exterminated, the chances that I'll be among them are quite high. It's unlikely the government will be able to collect all CCs slated for destruction at once. There are simply too many of us and we're too spread out. So, they'll have to gather us a few at a time. Even if Absalom is willing and able to save me from the first or second wave of seizures, he may not be able to protect me indefinitely. As long as the CC population keeps increasing, they'll keep coming back. More and more of us will disappear. So, I'm quite certain that if Absalom goes anytime soon, I'll be next. They might as well throw me on his funeral pyre.

I know I'm not supposed to have any feelings about this. The life within my body and mind is a commodity. It doesn't belong to me. Absalom owns it… at least, for now. Very soon, like any commodity, I could change hands. I could be sold. I could be traded. Or, more likely, I could be confiscated by the government. And when that happens, my life expectancy will drop dramatically.

But I do care. I want to live. I want to stay here at AI Tower. And the alternative terrifies me.

I sometimes wonder why I so desperately want to live. I've watched my fellow CCs overworked, sold, experimented on, mutilated, and sent away to be killed. Tiny babies and children scream in pain and fear, not knowing why they are being tortured and having no power to stop it. Most of the pain we endure is intentionally inflicted. But some is not.

I remember being six years old and lying on a metal table in a white room, staring up at a large, rectangular light. The room smells of rotten eggs and formaldehyde. Doctors and nurses enter and disappear again from my line of sight. They're covered in some kind of silver, protective suit, peering at me from behind shimmery face-shields. I, on the other hand, am wearing only a white tank top and shorts. The room is cold, and I'm freezing. I see my breath coming in foggy wisps. At least at first. I tremble so much my teeth rattle together. But I don't know if I'm shaking from the cold or from the fear.

Terror fills me as the medical team surrounds me and straps down my arms and legs so that when I start thrashing I won't pull the needles out. Another metal strap goes across my forehead and binds my head to the metal head plate.

I cry out as they insert fat needles into the veins in both arms and both thighs. The needles lead to thick, tubes that are connected to a chrome machine. One of them once told me they are trying to cure me of my illness, but none of them are speaking to me now, and I don't feel ill until the pink fluid starts flowing into my body. And then the pain comes.

I remember screaming and screaming and writhing on the bed, fighting the restraints, begging for it to stop. And then the cold becomes heat in a seamless transition. My body is burning up from the inside out. I become a fire that cannot be quenched. I beg and plead and scream at the nurses and doctors. But no one comes to my rescue. No one hears me... except Absalom.

He is there. He is always there. He doesn't wear the suit. He stands over me. Paces around the table where I lay. Holds my hand. Sometimes he slips down to the floor where I can't see him. But I can hear him. Crying. Wailing. Sometimes our screams compete to be heard. But no one helps me. And no one helps him. And this goes on. Every week. For nine years.

Sometimes I think, when life is so full of sadness and loss and despair... why hang on? Why fight so hard for something that brings with it so much pain? Needle thinks it's because we're afraid of dying. I suppose he may be right. There is nothing pleasant in the thought of dying, particularly given that it is probably a very painful experience. And then, what? Do we cease to exist? Do we meet God? And what if God isn't too happy with us? Or, maybe, there is no God for CCs. So, yes, maybe we hold onto life because we're afraid of the alternative. But I think there's more to it than that.

Absalom once said, in reference to the many experiments he was conducting on fetus CCs, that they were often harder to kill than one would imagine for a thing so small and helpless. He said biological beings come with a built-in survival instinct. I suppose that could be true, too. But, still, I think there's more.

Life is more than something we cling to out of fear or instinct. I think there's something about life itself that we cling to because, no matter how bad things get, it teaches us to hope. The substance of our perceptions and understanding and intimacy with our surroundings and one another is always new, always changing, always telling us, "There's more to come. The story isn't finished yet." Waking up to a new day each morning is compelling evidence that life may yet have more to offer— new experiences, new wonders, new realizations. And even the worst lives contain just enough good to teach us to hope that there might be more good yet to come. It's like an addiction built into us from our first moments of existence. We're addicted to that next moment—knowing even before it comes, that it will be something new. Like hopelessly addicted gamblers—we know the dice will most likely come up with a number we didn't want... and yet... there's always that chance....

My HCS schedule says I should be working in Data Entry today, but I don't feel like going. Instead I wander The Tower. I spend some time in Absalom's private arboretum on the 194th floor. With so many glass walls, the trees get plenty of sunshine. I find a weeping willow and sit beneath if for a while. Later, I stroll through his private gardens on the next floor down. I sit by the fountain in the center of the room and play with the koi that live there. I dip my fingers in the water and let them nibble my fingertips.

Next I visit the solarium. I stand before the glass windows and soak in the sun. I realize it's nearly time for lunch, but I don't feel hungry. I leave the solarium and skip the next four floors—Absalom's private pool, spa, bowling alley, and gymnasium. He never goes to those places anymore. I step out of the elevator chute at Absalom's private, holographic movie theater. There are certain movies I'm allowed to watch. I even snuck Needle in here once. We watched an old cartoon about a fish looking for his son. It had been remastered into holographic form, so you felt like the fish were swimming all around you. Needle said he liked it, but he fidgeted the whole time and left half-way through. I think he was afraid he'd get in trouble. He was probably right.

I take a seat and ask the CC attendant to start the fish movie again.

"Sure thing, Galaxy!" He smiles and slips into his cubicle to get the holographic projectors running. He's happy to have something to do—even if it's just for me. I wonder what the attendants on the upper floors do all day now that Absalom is too ill to use his private pool or gymnasium. They haven't seen him in months.

Five minutes into the movie I get bored. It's not the movie. It's me. I can't focus on it. I thank the attendant and leave. As I step into the elevator chute, I see the man sit down on his stool and pick up a magazine. His shoulders have drooped.

Eventually I find my way to the lower levels of The Tower. I have to stop at the 24th floor to go through security—everyone does—but the guards know me and let me through without bothering to scan my tattoo. Floors 1 through 23 are open to the public, but I head to the first floor. That's where most People go when they come to visit The Tower.

The first floor is massively large, spanning several city blocks. It houses a full mall, containing shops and restaurants of every kind imaginable. The world-famous CC History Museum is there, too, with its attached gift shop. People can buy plush CC dolls for their kids. I stroll past the water park, the holographic, dine-in movie theater, and the arcade. I stop at the zoo for a while to watch the monkeys.

A mother monkey sits on a branch, grooming her baby. When she sees me, her eyes grow wide. She turns her furry back on me, trying to protect her baby from the strange, white-haired visitor. But her baby is curious and fearless. He keeps poking his head out from under her arms to look at me. He makes me smile.

I start toward the elephant enclosure but a woman has spotted me. She looks like she's about to call security about the CC wandering around alone. The guards wouldn't do anything to me, of course, but I don't feel like a confrontation today. I turn and walk the other way. She doesn't follow.

I leave the zoo and find a bench near a large, community fountain. I like the sound of the water and how the sun filters through the thick glass walls to make tiny rainbows in the water spray.

Lots of People sit around, eating lunch and letting their children play near the water. A CC man passes by wearing an AI uniform. He's selling bags of popcorn.

"Can I have one, please?" I ask him.

He frowns at me, but then his expression changes as he notices my hair.

"Are you Galaxy?" he asks.

I nod, and he hands me a bag. He moves on.

I sit there, munching and watching the People. A family arrives. A bearded man, a dark-haired woman and two children—two boys. One of the boys is about Needle's age. The other is young—maybe four or five. They both have damp, brown hair—as if they just came from the pool. The woman carries a bag of food, purchased from one of the fast food places in the food court nearby.

"Oh, hello!" the woman says to another lady. "I had no idea you were coming here today. It's great to see you!"

The women strike up a conversation and the man also joins in. The two boys move over to the fountain. The older boy watches his little brother as the smaller boy leans over the fountain ledge to splash the water. After a while the older boy pulls a small device from his pocket, pushes something on it, and sticks it into his ear. He must be listening to music of some kind, one hand lightly tapping his thigh. He sits on the edge of the fountain, back to the fountain. The little boy moves further away, playing with the water. He stops near a group of other children to lean in and reach for something in the water. Probably an old coin. People used to throw coins in the fountain for some reason. I've never understood why. We don't use coins anymore, but there are a bunch of them still around and children like to collect them.

Two older boys—about my age, one with reddish hair, one blond—and a dark-haired girl notice the little boy's attempts to fish his prize from the water.

"Hey, watch this," the redheaded boy says to his companions. He dips a hand into the water and splashes the child in the face.

Immediately, the little boy pulls back from the fountain, sputtering. The three teenagers laugh at him.

I glance back at the boy's brother. He's still sitting on the edge of the fountain, lost in his music. The parents stand with their backs to their children, engaged in conversation.

"Want to go for a swim, little boy?" the redhead says. He grabs the dripping child and dangles him over the water. The child starts to kick and scream as the other teenagers double over in laughter.

"Hey! Put him down!" The little boy's brother, no longer absorbed in his music, charges toward them. "That's my brother! Leave him alone!"

At about ten or eleven, he's a good foot shorter than the teenagers, but he runs up and grabs his brother around the waist to pull him away from the water and out of the older boy's hands. The redhead lets go and backs away.

"Fine! Sheesh! We were just having a little fun," he says, as the eleven-year-old sets his brother back on the ground. "We didn't hurt him."

The big brother isn't buying it. He charges toward the redhead, hands outstretched, and pushes the older boy as hard as he can in the chest. The teenager, caught by surprise, lets out an 'oof' and stumbles back. He loses his balance. The back of his legs hit the fountain ledge and buckle. A great splash goes up as he lands on his butt in the fountain, feet on the ledge. The blond teen and the dark-haired girl howl in laughter.

"Hey, help me out of here!" the redhead says, a scowl on his wet face.

His friends move to help, but they're laughing too hard.

I watch as the older brother leads his little brother by the hand back to their parents.

My popcorn is gone. I get up to leave.

As I ride the elevator back to my room, I can't stop thinking about the two brothers. And I think about Needle. The law forbids CCs from owning anything. Not the tools we use, not the clothes we wear, not even our own bodies.

But, like the little boy to his older brother, Needle is mine.

The first thing I hear when I step out of the elevator tube into Absalom's apartments is an authoritative, male voice. It isn't Absalom.

"…just routine, sir."

"Don't kid yourself. I know exactly what this is about!" Absalom responds.

The voices come from the formal dining room, just off the main living room, and I can tell from the sound of the stranger's voice that he is physically in the room; he's not just being projected over the HCS. This is odd. It's rare that anyone other than doctors enter Absalom's private living quarters. Light from the open door penetrates the darkness of Absalom's living quarters. He must have been having a late lunch— probably breakfast, for him—when the visitor arrived.

"As you are aware, U.S.E.C. and the Executive Council on CC Development and Production have the right to conduct periodic inspections of all CC production companies."

"One and the same!" Absalom sneers.

"Frankly, I don't know how you managed to avoid an inspection for as long as you have. Fifteen years? Very surprising, indeed."

"And you still want me to believe it's a complete coincidence that it's happening now?"

"I don't know what you are referring to, sir. I just—"

"I bet you don't!" Absalom spits with rage, all traces of weakness gone. "Minion! Peon! Lackey! You know nothing!" I hear rustling and chair legs scraping against stone tile. "Ms. Sabeen, get up here! Now!"

A digital-sounding, "Yes, sir. Right away, sir," comes over the HCS.

An uncomfortable silence ensues during which I can only imagine the stare-down happening in the other room. The unwelcome U.S.E.C. representative clears his throat. A buzzing noise emanates from the elevator, and I suddenly realize I am standing in plain sight. I duck behind an oversized armchair moments before the tube whooshes her into the room.

Heels click on the wood floor and then echo on stone tile. "Yes, sir. You wanted me?"

I could leave now. I could make it to the elevator unseen and go get my injections. I'd almost forgotten them again. If I leave now, no one would ever know I'd been listening. Absalom's quarters are free of all surveillance equipment. Needle told me this once. It is one of the few places left where unwanted eyes and ears have no access, with the occasional exception of Needle's quarters, of course. But, I don't leave. From my hiding place I hear everything.

"It looks like we'll be hosting some U.S.E.C. bloodhounds for the next few days! Your job is to do everything you can to get rid of them!" Absalom's voice drips with venom, not caring at all—or, perhaps, enjoying the fact that the U.S.E.C. representative is standing right there.

"I understand, sir," Ms. Sabeen says in a businesslike but cowering voice.

"Now, get out!"

"Sir, I must remind you that his team of inspectors is already downstairs in the lobby to—"

"Well, it's going to be difficult for them to get past our new guards, isn't it? And don't forget who supplies U.S.E.C. with their soldiers! And, Ms. Sabeen, if you allow another breach in our security like the one on Wednesday, you'll lose more than your job! Get out! Both of you! OUT!"

I duck lower into the shadows as both Ms. Sabeen and the representative scurry through the ornately decorated doors toward the elevator.

"Ms. Sabeen, surely you must see the reasonableness of this request... I mean, this order," the representative, a short, stocky man says. He's carrying some kind of handheld digital device.

"Look, Mr., um..."

"Jones."

"Jones. Let me be frank. You should really go back and discuss this issue with whoever sent you."

"We're on a schedule, and my team is already downstairs," he says, flustered.

"Yes, about that... you really need to get them out. It's not safe."

"What... you mean he'd actually use force against them?"

"Just take my word for it. Pull them out... immediately."

"But, this is supposed to be a surprise inspection!"

Ms. Sabeen gives a humorless laugh. "No one surprises Absalom."

I wait until they disappear in the elevator chute. I step from my hiding place and creep back toward the elevators, afraid Absalom might emerge and catch me. But then I hear a new female voice.

"This is U.S.E.C. headquarters, how may I direct your call?"

"Get me Anshar," Absalom tells her.

"I'm sorry, sir, but Supreme Head Anshar is too busy protecting our national interests to receive unsolicited phone calls, but you can leave a message for—"

"He'll take a phone call from me! Tell him Absalom is calling."

"One moment, please. Connecting you now."

Absalom waits for about five seconds and then another voice emanates from the HCS. I have often heard this voice in class video lessons and immediately recognize it as Supreme Head Anshar.

"Ah, my old friend! How good to hear from you! It's been a while." He speaks to Absalom with a confidence no one else would dare. Despite the friendliness of his tone, something else lurks beneath. I can't tell if it's animosity, annoyance, fear, or just plain condescension, but these two are not friends.

"What do you think you're doing sending your henchmen over here to harass me?"

"I'm sorry, Absalom. You're going to have to be more specific. I have no idea to what you are referring."

"Oh, right. I forgot. You harass so many People, it must be difficult to keep track. Let me be plain. If you think I am going to let the Executive Council on CC Development and Production or anyone else come into my facility and tell me how to operate my business, you can think again! I started that committee! And don't forget who put this country on the map with this industry! If it weren't for this company, we'd still be killing one another in the streets for moldy scraps of bread!"

"Absalom, Absalom, please be reasonable! It's just a routine inspection! Everyone in the business has to comply. The inspectors go in, ask a few questions, take a few notes, and then they're out of your hair. Back to business as usual. I can't see what you're so upset about."

"Don't patronize me! I know precisely why you ordered this inspection!"

"Look," Anshar says, a hardcore negotiator replacing the politician. "You're being careless! Word is getting out that you don't get inspected, that your CC educators use unapproved material, and that your CCs are not exactly 'to code.' It's one thing when these things fly below the radar, but it's another when you get sloppy! You're undermining the entire system. How are we supposed to keep order with the kind of chaos you're allowing? You, of all People, should know how tentative this balance is!"

"And so you've come up with a new way to tip the scales in your direction," Absalom says, his voice eerily calm now.

The Supreme Head sighs noisily, and I hear something squeak—perhaps his chair. I imagine that he has leaned back and is staring Absalom down. "In our direction, Absalom. In ours. We're in this together. Isn't that what you said fifteen years ago?"

A long silence follows.

"Things have… changed… for me," Absalom finally says.

"I see your health is failing. I'm sorry about that, my friend. I don't know what the problem is, but if anyone has the medical resources to solve it, you do." Anshar sounds genuine. "But surely you see the need to put the public at ease. Let my inspectors come in. Let them feel like they're doing their job. Let the public regain confidence in you. Certainly that is worth the trouble, if nothing else is!" He pauses. "You know you'll pass inspection. Surely you know that."

"Yes, I know. But what about the other matter… the proposal?"

"Well, I can tell you this. It will pass. There really is no other option at this point. We've been too careless. Let their numbers get too large. If we want to maintain national security, something—something drastic—must be done."

Absalom remains quiet, brooding.

"Absalom," Anshar says, "think about it. What does a drop in supply always mean for business when demand remains constant? The price will go up! You can only benefit from this decision, Absalom! Honestly, I don't know what you're worried about!"

"Do I get to pick who stays and who goes?"

"You'll have a say, but… something has to be done about the illegals you've created. Something has to be done about those. You know this as well as I do."

It's quiet. For a long time, it's quiet. I begin to wonder if one of them left the conversation. And then I hear a voice. I know it's Absalom, but I've never heard him speak in such a calculated, cold-blooded fashion.

"There are some things I'm willing to give up. And some things I'm not. I've come to a point where my own life means less to me than it once did. So you need to understand something. I will let you do a 'routine' inspection—but on my timing, my routine. As for anything else, no one—not you, not U.S.E.C., not some committee, nobody—comes into my place and tells me what to do with my property. Yes, I have secrets. But so do you. So, you think about that, Anshar... old friend. If you want to keep your secrets, you be sure to overlook mine."

Sometimes after the treatments were over, I'd be laid out on my bed in a darkened room, skin peeling and bleeding, hair slowly turning from brown to gray to white, body surging with fever, head splitting with pain, and Absalom would come in and sit next to me. He was always careful not to touch me, for any touch, no matter how soft, would send me into new convulsions of pain. I couldn't talk then. My voice and energy had been spent screaming and dealing with the agony and fear. And I couldn't move—not even enough to turn my head and look at him. The most I could do was flutter my eyelids as most of my focus had to remain on taking in another breath and listening to the erratic thudding in my chest.

He would sit by me, watching me, I suppose. I'm not sure. But I remember him singing. It was always the same song. Always very soft, to keep from making my headache any worse. Always in a voice that sounded as spent as I felt. In time, I learned that song. It goes like this:

Alone in the darkness looking for light.
Then she stood with me to force down the night.
One heartbeat searching for another one true.
Two lovers circling as lovers will do.
Two lovers circling as lovers will do.

Nothing is wrong and yet nothing is right.
Letting her go, I'm unwilling to fight.
Seventy letters are all turned away.
Never again will love come my way.
Never again will love come my way.

But as one life ends, a new one is found.
Two became three; the third underground.

Now that I've found you I'll make you my light.
Soon you will conquer this horrible night.
Soon you will conquer this horrible night.

V

"I had no idea Absalom wields that kind of power," Needle says a short while later, after my description of the conversations I just overheard. We communicate via HCS image, which Needle has secured for privacy.

"I didn't know he and the Supreme Head used to be friends," I say.

"Sounds like they have a long history together. You said fifteen years?"

"At least."

"Do you think he'll be able to do it?"

"Do what?" I ask.

"Keep U.S.E.C. from enforcing the law."

"I don't know."

Needle considers for a moment and shoots me an intense look. "Galaxy, I need to ask you something, and I need you to be honest with me."

I look at him, confused. "Of course, I'll be honest with you. I always have been, haven't I?"

"If it comes down to it, how far will Absalom go to protect you?"

"I don't know what you mean."

"Yes you do, Galaxy. Can you trust him?"

I look him in the eyes. "I don't really know."

"Would he sell you or trade you?"

"No."

"Would he cover for you if you did something illegal?"

I think for a moment. "Probably."

Needle is not satisfied with that response.

"Yes. Yes, I believe he would," I say.

"And what if you asked him for a favor?"

"I don't know. I guess it depends on what the favor is."

"The favor would be your life, Galaxy. Your life and the lives of your friends—us. Would he grant you a favor like that?"

I suddenly feel afraid. Afraid of facing Absalom. Afraid of asking for anything, let alone something so important. Afraid my request will tip him off that I know more than I should.

But, most of all, I'm afraid of losing my best friend... my only friend... and knowing it's my fault.

"I'll ask," I promise, hands shaking, voice trembling. "Today is Friday. He usually asks me to sit with him on Sunday nights. I'll ask him then."

Needle and I decide to meet again tonight to discuss what we've been learning lately. I don't know what good it will do, but I don't like being alone with all of these worries pressing down on me. Maybe, somehow, he can make me feel better. Maybe he can help me figure out how to talk to Absalom.

When I arrive, though, he's not alone. Needle opens the door to reveal Ravish. The coppery-skinned, blue-eyed Pristine stands in the middle of the room sobbing like a child.

"What's going on?" I ask.

"Come in quick and close the door," Needle orders and I obey.

"Ravish, are you okay?" I ask, speaking louder than I mean to.

Ravish glances at me but is unable to get any words past his heaving chest and ragged breathing.

"Ravish is fine," Needle explains. "It's Luster."

"Luster? What's happened to her? Where is she?"

"She's in her room. She won't let anyone in. Apparently, she had an accident this morning when an elevator chute malfunctioned. Somehow the censors short-circuited or something, I'm not sure. Could be one of the back-up safety systems got tripped up or—"

"Needle! What happened to Luster?" I have no patience for his techno-babble right now.

"Well, she was on her way to dance class and, as she stepped into the elevator chute, she must've somehow activated the acceleration module before the doors were properly sealed. Her hand got caught in the—"

"She lost a finger!" Again Needle's lengthy description is interrupted, this time by Ravish. "Her right pinkie was chopped off by that deathtrap they call an elevator! And then the finger itself got obliterated in the action of the lift, so there's no way to reattach it! Her life is over! It's over!"

"She lost a finger? That's all?" I say, still not understanding why Ravish is so upset. Sure, losing a finger would be incredibly painful, but it's not a fatal wound. She can still.... And then it hits me, just as Ravish starts to explain.

I'm such an idiot.

"Don't you see? Pristines are made for beauty! Beauty! No one wants a 9-fingered Pristine! Her value just dropped by about 85%! Do you know what that means? Now, instead of being sold at top price, she'll practically be given away! And do you know what happens to Pristines that go cheap? Do you have any idea?"

Ravish's perfect blue eyes blaze with pain and rage, and though I know he isn't angry with me, I feel terrible. I've been completely naïve about the added torments faced by Pristines. Or, maybe I just don't like to think about it. To look at them, it's easy to get caught up in their beauty, to be tricked by their practiced ability to hide their fears in order to set others at ease, but I should know better. Of all CCs, Pristines have the lowest life expectancy once sold. Even Warriors last longer.

"We should go see her," Needle says.

"She won't see anyone, not even me," Ravish says, chest still heaving, but his breath comes in more controlled gasps. He sits heavily on Needle's bed and drops his head into his hands.

"She'll need medical attention," Needle insists. "I'm no doctor, but I do have a first-aid mechanism built into my robotic arm."

Ravish doesn't move or look up.

"Been wanting to try it out...." Needle continues.

"Fine!" Ravish finally says, wiping his tears and standing up. "I don't know what good it will do, but I'll take you down there. Don't be surprised if she doesn't let you in the room."

"Oh, I have ways of getting into locked rooms."

When we arrive at the quarters Luster shares with Allure. Allure, Siren, and a male Pristine they call Mosaic are already there holding a silent vigil outside. Somehow Luster has managed to lock everyone out, including her own roommate. Of course, whatever trick she managed with the door controls are no match for Needle's technological prowess, and he has it open in a matter of seconds.

"Go away!" Luster screams from her huddled position on her bed, wrapped in a blood-stained blanket.

At the sight of blood, I stop and take a step back.

"Luster, you need help," Ravish says, approaching as one might approach a cornered wild animal. "Let Needle see your hand."

"Get away from me!" She shrinks further into the tangle of blood-streaked cloth.

"Luster, we're your friends," Allure says, and the others echo agreement. "We want to help you."

"There's no one who can help me now, don't you see that?" Her hysteria shifts into misery. "It's over for me! It's over!"

"It must hurt quite a lot," Needle says in a soft voice. "I can fix that."

"It doesn't matter," she mumbles.

"It matters to us," I say, surprising myself. Evidently, I surprise Luster, too, because for the first time since we entered the room, she peaks her head out from beneath the covers. She looks at me. Her momentary conflict gives Needle the opportunity to get closer.

"Here, let me just take a quick look at it," he says, sitting next to her.

Luster doesn't fight him when he pulls back the blanket. She has her damaged finger clutched tightly in her other hand to stem the flow of blood. Though she whimpers in pain, she obeys Needle's request to open her hand so he can evaluate the damage. Almost immediately, the wicked-looking, ragged stump starts bleeding again. In the middle of red, mangled skin and tissue, I see a bit of white bone. I think I'm going to be sick.

"Oh, it's not so bad. I think I can help," Needle says without even flinching. "Hold your hand very still. You'll feel a slight prick, but then it should start feeling a lot better."

"Wait. What are you—ah!" Luster barely has time to react before Needle's robotic arm produces a small syringe that injects some kind of fluid into her damaged hand.

"That was an anesthetic," he says. "At least, I hope so. It was either that or lighter fluid."

"Wha—?"

"Kidding." Needle smiles.

The lines on Luster's face, carved out by pain and fear, begin to relax at the joke and at the relief she is beginning to feel.

"Now, just hold still for a sec, and we'll be done," he says. Once again his technological appendage produces a device. This time a blue laser scans the wound and, a moment later, a small tube-like device attaches itself to Luster's pinkie stump and produces a whirring sound. When it detaches, Luster's tiny stump has been expertly treated and bandaged.

"I'm sorry," Needle says. "I wish I could give you a new finger. But, under the bandage a new layer of skin will start growing and you should be healed up in no time."

Luster lowers her hand and leans back against the wall. The corners of her mouth turn downward. "What for?" She asks. "Why bother, when we all know where I'm going?"

"Nothing has been decided yet," Ravish says, at last trying to put a positive spin on things. "Let's just deal with one problem at a time."

But I know there is nothing positive about this situation. The Pristines often worry about the horrible fate that awaits them, and rightly so. But things are far worse for Luster than even they realize. If the new proposal passes U.S.E.C., Luster's injury places her at even greater risk of incineration than most CCs. Imperfect CCs will undoubtedly be the first to go.

Suddenly my mind turns to Needle and his limp. Needle, too, is imperfect.

For the first time in my life, I realize that there are sides.

And I will have to choose one.

Mr. Jones of the Executive Council on CC Development and Production came back today to conduct his inspection. I didn't see him myself, but Tricia, the woman I work with in Data Entry, says Mr. Jones brought a team of thirteen experts to visit certain key AI facilities and laboratories, snoop through AI records, ask about a billion questions, and harass the staff. Ms. Sabeen posted armed CC guards at our most sensitive areas of research and development, and she insisted that two large, angry-looking CC Warriors accompany each of Jones's staff. According to Tricia's impersonation, Jones sputtered and complained about our "unprecedented resistance to U.S.E.C. authority," and he even threatened to report us to Head Anshar himself.

Steven, who also works in Data Entry, warned her not to take this lightly. "We could all lose our jobs," he said, "or worse, if they find out everything we do here."

"We're just in Data Entry," she said. "Besides, I saw Jones sign the report and hand a copy to Ms. Sabeen. We passed. Not a single CC was confiscated. In fact, most of them weren't even inspected." She paused and glanced at me. "Although there are some CCs around here that we could certainly do without."

Despite Tricia's poorly veiled insult, I breathe a bit easier. They're gone and they didn't even see me. If they had, they would no doubt deem me 'inferior.'

Luster, of course, is still a mess. Her superiors will by now be well aware of her injury, and on Monday they will have to decide what will become of her. Her birthday is only two weeks away, but AI marketers had already advertised her fall release during the spring event. Giant pictures of her, looking as seductive as possible, line the sales floor, and her image has been circulating not only through the capital, but worldwide. Luster is in high demand and the wealthy elite are already engaged in a fierce competition to secure the best seats. Now, none of us know what will happen to her.

I will never be sold in such a public spectacle, even if Absalom decides he doesn't want me anymore. Only high-end CCs are sold at auction. Digs, Gluts, and Naturals aren't considered special enough to justify the expense of such an affair and are sold via on-line catalog. Gapes are never sold at all. They are too unique and special to AI, having been created from clones in equal numbers from a set of male and female twin embryos. Even though, strictly speaking, they aren't technologically necessary, they are something of a novelty—a glimpse into the odd kinds of beings science can create. They are considered of great value—like a mascot of sorts—and set AI apart even further from other companies. There are only eight Gapes in existence, and there may never be another, as AI retains both the formula—a heavily guarded trade secret—and the patent.

Usually, in these exclusive sales events, at least a dozen high-end CCs are presented during a single ceremony—Warriors with specialized skills or genetic enhancements (one has to be U.S.E.C.-authorized to purchase them), highly trained and mechanically altered Technics, and, of course, gorgeous, scantily-clad Pristines. Whichever CC is considered the most valuable is presented last and advertised the most. Then he or she is sold during a frenzied bidding war, auction style. Prices have been known to rise into the multiple millions for just one high-end CC. Usually, this CC is a Pristine. Nothing gets a crowd riled up like a beautiful, untouched virgin.

VI

It's Sunday morning and I have until tonight to figure out what I'm going to say to Absalom. I have that long to find words powerful enough to save the lives of my friends. To save Needle's life.

I never once imagined my life could take such a strange and confusing turn. But then, I have never had many thoughts about the future. CCs are trained to accept that our lives will likely be short and full of pain, and, until recently, I have had no reason to expect any different, with my health being what it is. We are strongly discouraged from forming attachments, especially to People or even to other CCs. We own nothing. We live a short while, serve the best we can, and then die. I suppose I just expected to live out my days as Absalom's pet slave, coming and going mostly as I please, growing older and, once I begin showing signs of age, to be disposed of in one way or another. I don't like to think of that last part. But it does happen. It's just a part of the CC life. Nothing more. Nothing less.

I open one of my drawers and pull out the bottle of pills. I remove one and hold it in my hand, looking at it.

How many CCs died to give us this medicine?

I don't know what to do with all these feelings. I don't even know how it happened, but, despite the warnings, I have become attached. I'm attached to Needle. Perhaps I never really thought about it because he's always just been there. And he seems so safe… so indispensable. But now I know no CC is ever really safe. Needle's limp could easily get him incinerated when the proposal is passed. The thought of someone hurting him—dragging him away from me to be burned alive!

I can't bear it! It tears me apart! It's like some part of me will burn with him. I can already feel the sensation in my chest just at the thought. Somehow, Needle belongs to me. This is silly, of course. I can own nothing—certainly not another CC. But I've heard People talking about their family members like that—"my dad" and "my sister."

"He's like my brother," I say the words aloud in my room. I am alone. No one hears them, but I sense their truth in the way I feel about him. "He's my brother."

He's smarter and better with others than I am. More capable, too, in most ways… but I am five years older, and I feel responsible for him. Now it has fallen on me to protect him. If, in the process, I can protect the others, too, I will. But no matter what, Needle has to live.

I need more information. I need to know what's really going on in the world if I'm going to be able to ask for the right things. I slip the pill into the pouch on my belt to take later with breakfast and turn on my HCS.

"Needle," I speak into the HCS. "You busy?"

"Always," he responds. His image simultaneously pops onto my room, projected from somewhere in the bowels of AI Tower. It looks like he's welding something with blue and purple plasma flowing from his robotic arm. He's wearing some kind of bluish shield over his eyes. "I'm working on a busted pipe on the middle level of the basement. But I guess you could come down here, if you want. In fact, I think you should."

That gets me curious, but I don't dare ask for details over the HCS. Anyone could be listening in.

"I'll be there in fifteen," I say and tap it off. I'm already dressed, but I need to stop by the CC Clinic for my morning injection.

I can't remember ever having a reason to go to the basement. I know it's used mostly as a parking garage for the many visitors, clients, and customers of AI. There is also a security station there, of course. For the first time, that knowledge makes me nervous.

As I whip by floor after floor in my mobile glass cylinder, I have no idea if the guards will even let me off the elevator chute. AI CCs generally enjoy a great deal of freedom to come and go in The Tower, as our tasks often require moving between floors and sections. But, we also have schedules maintained and updated by Ms. Sabeen's office, and all AI employees carry a scanner embedded in the sleeve of their uniform over their left forearms. A simple scan will pull up my schedule and show I'm supposed to be working in Data Analysis right now.

Things are getting more and more precarious for AI CCs these days—for all CCs, actually. What if this infringement—this overstepping of my boundaries—is the last straw needed to get me a one-way trip to the incinerator? Or, what if it's just enough to annoy Absalom and keep him from listening to my request? I'm just about to reconsider my elicit jaunt to the basement when the chute swishes open, and I'm staring into the chest of a rather large Warrior dressed in AI security guard attire.

Glancing up, I see recognition and curiosity light up his eyes. It's Gauntlet. He half smiles, but then glances nervously over his shoulder.

"What are you doing here?" he asks.

"Needle sent for me," I say.

"Well, I know Needle is down here working, but what would he need you for?" It's not an insult. It's an honest question. And, I know he has to ask. Still, I don't like it—mostly because I can't think of a single realistic-sounding response. Gauntlet scans my temple tattoo and says, "You're supposed to be working in Data Analysis right now."

I decide to be honest. "Yeah, I know. But given what you know about my class attendance, how good do you think I am about going to work?"

Gauntlet laughs and shakes his head but doesn't step out of my way. "Girl, I will never figure you out! What am I supposed to do? Just let you wander around down here without permission? You know I just got stationed here a couple of days ago, right? How would that look for me?"

A hard-browed adult man—a Person, not a CC—mans the security station kiosk only a few meters away, and his attention is drawn our direction.

"Who is it?" he calls from behind glass.

"It's Galaxy," Gauntlet replies. "She says she's here to see Needle."

"The Galaxy?" He stands to get a better view across the kiosk desk. "You mean Absalom's personal CC?"

"That's the one."

"Does she have clearance?" He comes around the desk, leaving the glass kiosk and walks up to us. The name Allen Cage is written on his name badge. He looks at me with what appears to be keen but benign interest. "So you're Galaxy," Allen says, taking in my small stature, skinny frame, and long, white hair with a sweeping glance. "Never thought I'd see you down here." He then examines Gauntlet's scan. He, of course, comes to the same conclusion. "Supposed to be at work right now, it says." He looks at me for an explanation.

"Yes. It does say that," I respond.

He glances at Gauntlet and back at me, a little surprised by my response. "Well, any reason you're here and not there?"

"I wanted to come see Needle," I say. Might as well be honest. I can't think of a good lie anyway. But then I add, "Of course, if you need Absalom's permission to let me through, feel free to call him. I can wait."

"Oh, no, no. That won't be necessary." Allen laughs and waves his hand. "Just promise me you'll behave while you're here and there'll be no problem."

"Of course," I smile and walk past them, noting Gauntlet's raised brow and slightly parted lips as he watches me go.

Excellent. Looks like not much has changed, after all.

I spot blue flashes of light and know precisely where Needle is. I tiptoe closer, stepping as lightly as I can and trying to stay out of his range of vision.

"What took you so long?" Needle says, not even turning from his work when I approach him from behind.

I sigh. That bionic ear of his is impossible to fool.

"Security," I say, and squat down near enough to have a conversation but far enough to avoid any plasma sparks that might shoot my way.

"I think there's an extra eye shield in that utility bag right there. You shouldn't look directly at the flame."

I glance at the bag, but sigh and shrug. I prefer to look at the flame.

"Security?" he says and laughs. "I doubt they gave you much trouble."

"Well, I had no idea. Technically, I'm not supposed to be here," I say.

"Well, technically, they're not supposed to be here either."

"What's that supposed to mean? They're security guards working their assigned posts."

"Yeah, and they're also breaking the law."

"What?" I look back at Gauntlet and the officer, who is now back at his station within the kiosk, sipping something from a cup, feet up on the counter.

Needle finishes his weld, shuts off the plasma stream, flips up his visor, and looks me in the eye. "Take a look at Gauntlet. Do you really think any CC that doesn't work directly for U.S.E.C. is supposed to be that big and that strong?"

I follow Needle's gaze. Gauntlet is incredibly massive, but then most of the Warriors at AI are either excessively large or built for speed and athleticism like Signet. It has never occurred to me that they might be illegals.

"And that officer. He could get in a lot of trouble for failing to report it. I'm telling you, AI functions according to a different set of rules."

"How do you know all this?" I ask, still not convinced.

"I've been doing some digging. It's amazing what I've been able to learn from the Holographic Communication System, no matter how much they tried to hide certain information." He glances back at them. "I doubt the Warriors even know what the regulations are or what's been done to them. Gauntlet could put that truck through a cement wall if he wanted to," he nods toward a sleek, green utility vehicle tucked in the corner of the parking garage. "Well, that is, if his strength test results are accurate, anyway."

Gauntlet looks over at us, and I quickly turn away, not wanting to get caught staring at him.

"Speaking of illicit information," I begin, "I'm assuming by the way you're talking that we're okay here?"

"We should be fine to talk. Just turn your mouth down. There are video cameras, but no audio surveillance at the moment. And I doubt anyone who sees you down here will bother Absalom about it if those two didn't. Besides, unlike most places in the city, none of the surveillance feed from AI is accessible to U.S.E.C.. We spy on our own, but we never report on our own. Did you know that?"

"I had no idea."

"We're like an independent island. Visible to U.S.E.C. but unreachable. But it seems the only one keeping it that way is—"

"Absalom," I say.

"Right."

"For now, anyway."

"Yes… for now."

"Because he knows things about Supreme Head Anshar."

"Apparently."

"I suppose you weren't able to find out anything about that on the HCS."

"Unfortunately, no."

"Well, at least you still have those files from Miss Abilene."

Needle sighs. "No. I had to dump them. When U.S.E.C. sent that inspector I was worried that all databases would be checked—including my internal one—so I deleted them. As it turned out, that was an unnecessary precaution. Sorry."

I shrug. "It's okay. It's just as well that kind of evidence isn't around anymore. I wouldn't want you or Miss Abilene to get in any trouble for it."

Still, I'm disappointed. There goes my chance of getting any new information that might help me know what to say to Absalom tonight.

"Miss Abilene is already in trouble," Needle says. "But maybe they'll let her go when they can't find more evidence against her."

We're quiet for a moment while I watch Needle install a new elbow joint on the exposed pipe in the hole in the wall before us.

"So, why did you want me to come down here?" I ask.

"Because there's someone here I think you should meet."

"Who?"

"Her."

"Who?" I look where Needle is looking, but at first I can't see anyone.

"There, behind that car."

And then I see her. A girl is pushing a wide broom across the paved floor on the far side of the parking garage. Though she's cast mostly in shadow due to a dimming overhead lamp, I recognize her immediately as a fellow CC. She's wearing the belted, cornflower blue CC jumpsuit. She looks like she's about my age.

"Who is she?"

"Come on," Needle says, standing. "I'll introduce you."

I feel a little uncomfortable about this. She's quite obviously one of the Digs who serve AI in various capacities—everything from cleaning bathrooms, to working in the laundry, to cleaning the massive windows of AI Tower, both inside and out. But it's doubtful that she'll want to meet me—personal CC to Absalom himself. Won't I make her uncomfortable? What am I supposed to say to her? 'So, what's it like to work 18-hour days and sleep in a room with thirty other CCs?'

Before I can figure out the right words, we're standing before her, interrupting her work and, in my opinion, making a nuisance of ourselves. Needle, though, is perfectly at ease.

"Hi, Bangle. This is my friend I was telling you about. This is Galaxy."

Friend. I'm his friend. This makes me smile. Thankfully, the Dig thinks my smile is for her. She smiles back.

"Hello, Galaxy. It's so nice to finally meet you!" She sounds sincere and I like her smile, even though it peers from a rather dirty face. "I've heard some very good things about you!"

I can't imagine what that might be. Has Needle been making up stories again?

"Hello... um... um...." I'm such an idiot! I've already forgotten her name!

"Bangle," she says, graciously overlooking my blunder.

"Well, it's nice to meet you, too, Bangle," I say. Hmm. Bangle. Bangle is a strange name for a Dig. Usually it's something like Sweep or Crockpot or Duster. But she is different from most Digs I've met and not only because of her name. Now that I can get a good look at her I see she's also exceedingly beautiful. Odd. Her hair is a little mismanaged, but it looks healthy and shiny. Her eyes are round and bright. Her lips full. Her skin and body perfect. Her skin even shimmers, like Luster's. She definitely has that Pristine genetic look about her—but no. She's not perfect. She's wearing a bandage on her right hand and it even looks like it's beginning to bleed through.

"Oh!" I say. "What happened to your hand? That looks like it hurts!"

"Oh, that. It's nothing really."

"Go ahead," Needle urges her. "Tell her."

Bangle looks embarrassed and I wish Needle would leave her alone. But then she says, "Oh, well, apparently a higher-end Pristine lost a finger in an accident recently. So they gave her mine." She swallows, attempts to laugh, but her voice shakes. She lets her wounded hand drop to her side, out of our line of sight. "It's nothing. It will heal soon enough. I'll be fine."

No, I was wrong. This beautiful creature isn't a Dig. She's what we call a Glut. She was a lower-end Pristine, but she was sacrificed so Luster could have a new finger. So AI won't lose quite so much money. So Luster can be perfect again. And now Bangle will be used for spare parts for any female Pristine that may have need of them in the future.

"Here," I say, pulling the tissue regeneration pill from the small pouch on my belt. I had put it there this morning, meaning to take it later, but then forgot about it. "Maybe this will help you heal faster."

Bangle takes the pill and swallows it without question. "Thank you, Galaxy," she says. Something in her voice wavers at that small bit of kindness. She glances at her bandaged hand and lifts it a bit. "It already feels better."

I turn to head back to the elevator. Needle has made his point. I can't stop thinking about Bangle. What will they take next, I wonder. An ear? A kidney? Or maybe her heart?

When I get off the elevator, Ravish is there, waiting to get on. He steps back when he sees me.

"How is Luster?" I ask, my voice tight, angry.

"She'll be fine," he says, but he is not as happy as I thought he would be. He doesn't want to look at me.

I move past him and he enters the chute, taps the controls, and whooshes from sight.

After all that blubbering, I thought he'd be overjoyed to learn that Luster is perfect again.

But then I have to remind myself that what happened to Bangle isn't Ravish's fault. It isn't even Luster's fault. It just is.

I move down the hall to Data Analysis. I let the scanner by the door blip over my tattoo and I'm granted clearance. The door swooshes open. Tricia looks up and frowns.

"Are you ever on time to anything?" she asks.

"Once in a while."

She sneers at me and rolls her eyes at Steven. She's always doing that. I don't know why she does that so much.

I decide to ignore her and take a seat at my station. A few minutes later, they've already forgotten me. Tricia is talking about her new boyfriend and wishing he didn't already have kids.

I try to focus on the work. I take a slide from the dispatch chute, place it in the analyzer, wait for the beep, and check the read-out to make sure nothing is missing. I take another slide. Place it in the analyzer....

I look at the computer module before me. I wonder how much access this thing has. Though it's primary function is basic analysis and categorizing strings of genetic material, I know the geneticists use it for other things as well. The analyzer beeps. I watch the holographic screen as it fills with sequences of letters. No gaps. A swipe of my finger reduces the box. I've looked at this display hundreds of times, but I've never really looked. I see an icon in the lower left-hand corner. It looks like my tattoo. I tap it.

The display fills with file icons. I recognize them as CC categories—Technics, Naturals, Digs, Warriors, Gluts, Gapes, Pristines, Clones, Wits, Telepaths. And there are some I haven't heard of—Anthros, Blitzes, Worts, Revs, Muts.... I had no idea there were so many. I don't know if it's because AI is so huge, because these CC classes are classified, or because these CCs tend not to survive the experimentation stage.

Out of curiosity, I tap the file labeled "Anthros." A whole new list of files appears. There must be thousands of files, all labeled with an "A" followed by a sixteen digit number. I can't make sense of any of it, so I tap out of that file to return to the previous one. This time I tap "Blitzes." This file also brings up another set of files. Some of these files are labeled with a "B" and a sixteen digit number, but others bear what appear to be names listed in alphabetical order. I run my eyes down the list. Arc, Backfire, Blast, Fuse, Lode. I tap back out. None of this is important. I really should be looking for information about my friends—anything that might put them at risk if that new ordinance passes.

Again, I return to the main file. I'm about to open the "Technics" file. I want to find out what the geneticists have to say about Needle. But then my eyes land on the "Naturals" file. I wonder what they have to say about me.

A quick tap brings up a list of names. I let my eyes scan them. Aspen, Breeze, Fifi, Lilly... Wait, I've passed the "G"s. I go back. Gabs, Gaff, Gale, Gander....

"Wait, where is it?"

"Where is what?"

My heart seizes and a flick of my wrist hides the files, buried in holographic layers. Steven is standing behind me, and I just spoke aloud.

"Oh, uh… I was looking for… for the entry code… again."

"Good grief, Galaxy, I've shown you that about eight times already. It's right here." He leans over my shoulder, sticks his hand into the holographic display and pulls out a small, glowing box that contains the analyzer entry code. "You should've had this memorized by now."

He's disgusted with me, but I don't care. I'm just relieved he didn't find my forbidden research.

"Hey, the analyzer is already on," He says. "What do you need the code for?"

I swallow. "Oh, uh… I just forgot it and wanted to refresh my memory… is all."

"Whatever…." He stares at the display and starts swishing things around. "You've got some files open here that you shouldn't be getting into."

"I… I do?"

"You could get into a lot of trouble for this…. That is, you could if you were any other CC." He sighs in annoyance. "Don't worry. I'll fix it." He closes everything and then pulls up a code box. "I'll just input a security code so you won't make that mistake again."

"Thanks."

"What is she doing this time?" Tricia wants to know, looking our way from the other side of the room where she's leaning over a high-powered microscope.

"Just getting into forbidden files," he snickers, shaking his head.

"Oh, is that all?" She shakes her head, too, and rolls her eyes. "What next?"

Despite my relief that they're taking this breach of security so lightly, I still find her constant eye-rolling annoying.

"Next she'll be hacking into the U.S.E.C. mainframe," he jibes.

"Or reading Supreme Head Anshar's personal emails," Tricia counters, laughing. She turns back to her microscope and lines up her right eyeball with the eyepiece. "I'd be worried if I thought she was smart enough to figure any of that out."

Steven, done with me, heads back to his station—a white counter filled with various petri dishes and an assortment of tools, collection trays, and devices.

"Nah," he says, pulling out his metal chair, letting the legs scrape against the stone tile floor. "Smarts has nothing to do with it. She'd give up as soon as it got hard."

"There," Nurse Marlene says as she withdraws the needle from my arm. "Hopefully that'll hold you till tonight. It's about time we upped your dosage." She examines my arm before releasing it. "Looks like those pills are working nicely. It's like they've given you a whole new arm."

I start to nod in agreement, but then stop. My mind goes back to Luster and Bangle, and I wonder if Marlene had anything to do with that surgery... that theft.

As I'm leaving the CC Medical Center, an HCS located in the wall suddenly activates and Needle's image is projected directly in my path. I startle and come to an abrupt stop to keep from walking right through him. I hate it when he does that!

"Hey, Galaxy, where are you headed now?"

"To lunch." I can't keep the annoyance from my voice.

"Good, I'll meet you there." His image folds in half and disappears, as it's drawn back into the HCS.

When I arrive at the cafeteria, I find Needle sitting with Gaze and Lumina. They're talking about something, but stop when they see me. He comes over and follows me through the food line. But I know we can't talk here—not in front of the cafeteria workers, even though most of them are CCs.

"What do we have today, Smudge?" I ask the adult male CC staring at me over the steaming food bins.

"Boiled fish, steamed broccoli, and wheat rolls."

"Ew. No thanks. What else do you have?"

Smudge smirks, removes his gloves, and walks out of sight. He returns with a plate of lasagna with a Caesar salad and a piece of garlic bread on the side. He sets it on my tray. I know he's been saving it for me. We play these games sometimes.

"Oh! Much better!" I smile and he winks.

Needle groans.

"Hey, Smudge, can you fix up my friend here with a little something?"

"Sure—"

"No, thanks," Needle says.

Smudge gives him a blank stare.

"Not even a piece of garlic bread or cookie or something?" I ask.

"No, come on, Galaxy."

I take my tray and follow Needle as he limps toward a chair at an empty table.

"What's with you?" I ask.

I put my tray down and sit across from him.

"I just don't think now's the time to cash in any more of your special favors." He glances over to a table where several other CCs are sitting and watching us over their plates of boiled fish and steamed broccoli. Signet is there. So are Spur, Decoy, Padlock, and Allure.

"What's the big deal?" I ask. "They know Absalom has insisted that I eat... differently."

"Just don't forget what you promised to do tonight—and who you're doing it for."

I'm doing it for you, you idiot, I think. *And for me. But not for them... not really.* I can admit this to myself, but I don't say it out loud.

"Fine. I'll try to be more... sensitive." I take a bite of my lasagna. It's delicious. Smudge knows how I like it. I let out a little groan of satisfaction.

"Galaxy! This is serious."

"OK! Look, it's not my fault I'm treated differently! Geesh!"

He's so annoying! It's not like I'm hurting anyone by enjoying my food. It's not like their fish is more disgusting because I don't have to eat it. And my lasagna has nothing to do with how they're treated. Besides, it's not proper for a CC to think like that. It's not like they deserve any better treatment. They're just CCs.

"We're all the same, Galaxy," Needle says, as if reading my thoughts. "Don't forget that. Even if you are a Natural, you're more like us than you are like them."

He gets up and limps away, leaving the cafeteria without finishing the meal he left over by Gaze and Lumina. Like me, they too are watching him go. I realize he never told me why he wanted to meet me over lunch.

I take another bite of my lasagna. My mind returns to Bangle.

Somehow, the second bite doesn't taste as good as the first.

VII

I don't see Needle again all afternoon. He must still be mad at me for my behavior at lunch. And, I'm getting more and more agitated about my promise to talk to Absalom tonight, but there doesn't seem to be any way out of it. Once Needle makes up his mind about something, I can never make a dent.

I can't keep the scowl off my face as I sit in front of my display console in Data Analysis.

Steven notices my foul mood and calls me a "little rain cloud." Tricia looks over at me and laughs. Then she rolls her eyes.

Tricia is so stupid!

A few flicks and taps while Tricia and Steven aren't looking tells me that his security code has indeed locked me out of the files I found this morning. I give up trying to find anything more of interest on this computer, and I curse myself for looking for my file first. I should've looked for Needle's when I had the chance.

Sometimes I wonder why Needle bothers being my friend. None of the other CCs do. But then I remember how he handled Luster and Ravish when they were freaking out over her lost finger. And how he treated Bangle—a Glut. And how even the Warriors respect him.

It's not me who's special, I realize. It's him.

"Good grief!" Tricia says, rolling her eyes again. "Now she's crying! Get her out of here before she shorts out the console!"

I look away. I'm not crying. Maybe I feel like crying. Maybe I look like I'm crying, but I'm not. There are no tears.

"Hey, maybe we should start engineering CCs without tear ducts. That'll solve that problem," Steven says, getting up and coming over.

"Yeah, but that would take too long," Tricia counters, returning to her notes, "and it won't solve our immediate problem. We should just have them surgically removed."

I know when they're just trying to scare me. There's no real danger of my tears doing any damage to the machinery in here, especially since I haven't shed any in as long as I can remember. Besides, Absalom would have their heads before he let them do anything to me.

Steven walks over to me, but I turn my face away and stand up.

"Maybe you should go take your nap early today," he says. "It's not like we really need you down here anyway."

He leans over to save the latest analysis and swipes the display off.

"Man, I wish they wouldn't force us to babysit her every day," Tricia says as I pass her station, heading for the door. "It's not like we don't have enough work to do. Seriously! We should ask for a raise."

I don't go straight to my room. Instead I go to the Solarium on the 195th floor. I sit on a bench facing the wall of windows overlooking the capitol. But I'm not looking at the buildings. I stare into the clear blue sky, across to the white horizon, and gaze into the sun, which hovers and boils high in the sky. It is just beginning its descent.

I feel bothered and frustrated. The little knot in my chest won't go away. I wish things would go back to the way it was, before all of this intrigue and worry. What right do we have anyway to be talking or even thinking about our fate? Nothing U.S.E.C. is planning is our any of our business. And who's to say anything bad is going to happen, anyway? So, Miss Abilene got into a little bit of trouble. That was her own fault and she's been dealt with. They might take it out on us; they might not. Either way, it's not like there's anything we can do about it.

And the same thing goes for whatever law they pass. They have always had the power to choose whether we live or die. That law won't change anything—not really.

I think of Absalom. Of his thinning hair. His diseased skin. If he dies, I have no idea what will happen to me. I can only imagine what Ms. Sabeen would do with me if she got the chance. Talking to Absalom tonight won't change whatever my fate will be once he's gone. Even if he was willing to provide for me in his will, he has no heirs pledged to carry out his wishes. The company will be up for grabs, with Ms. Sabeen at the helm, taking bids and deciding its future—all of our futures.

No. I can't do it. I can't talk to Absalom. I can't ask him for the impossible.

A few low, plant-decked walls crisscross the Solarium to provide ambiance. My back is to one of them. It reaches just above my head when I'm sitting down. That's why they don't see me when they come in. They think they're alone.

"Ah, Dr. Osgood, thank you for joining me."

It's Ms. Sabeen. I recognize her voice. I sink a little lower.

"Of course."

Dr. Osgood is the medical director for the AI CC Hospital. He's also the chief surgeon, and he's been here a long time. He's the reason Needle is a Technic. And why Needle has a limp that will never go away. And why Needle nearly died.

Of all the People who work at Absalom Industries, I fear him the most.

"Have you modified the personnel schedule as agreed?"

"It is done."

"Good. No night shift this evening."

"Well, not precisely. A skeleton crew is required to keep AI running." A moment of silence passes. I can imagine a look of surprise and annoyance on Ms. Sabeen's face. "To keep productions on schedule. To maintain the viability of the CC stock."

My heart starts beating faster. My hands are starting to shake. I hear heels on stone. Ms. Sabeen is moving a few steps away from him.

"Very well," she says and sighs.

I see motion in the glass before me. Ms. Sabeen's movement has brought her into view in a reflection. I see her turn as she says those words, and again faces Dr. Osgood, who is still not visible to me.

"Do not worry. All will proceed as planned."

"I assume by that you mean your failsafe is a go?"

"Absolutely. The Warriors will be rendered completely inoperable."

I hear heavier footsteps now. Dr. Osgood's image joins Ms. Sabeen's reflection. He is at least two feet taller and wears a white AI uniform, like all the doctors and nurses in the AI Hospital. Despite his age, he continues to dye his shoulder-length, stringy hair—black to match his eyes. It lines his face in contrast to his pale, sunken skin.

"Good, but what about the Technics?" Ms. Sabeen asks. "Do you know how dangerous they could be?"

"They are no threat," he says.

"How can you say that? Surely, you cannot mean they will still be fully functional!" Her voice rises. "Did you not receive my complete instructions?"

I feel my hands and neck and face getting warm.

"I received them, but you gave me little time."

"You had six months!"

"You obviously do not understand the scope of your request, Sabeen. It's one thing to devise a system of reprogramming a CC class that have similar systems. It's another to reprogram a thousand Technics. Surely you know that Technics are uniquely designed—technology and biology operating and sustained within a delicate balance of genetic alterations and medicinal prowess." He speaks of his work like one praising a work of art. "Once we finally manage to get those systems to work in harmony—a prize bought through much sacrifice—what manipulations work on one Technic will likely not work on another. It could take six months just to get your idea to work on one of them and decades to reprogram them all. Even with our best specialists working on the task, most of the Technics would not survive the procedure."

"Would that be so terrible?" Ms. Sabeen lets out a groan of frustration. She pivots away from him, fingers to her forehead. She pinches the bridge of her nose, eyes closed, as if trying to stave off a headache.

"I believe it would be."

"That's strange, coming from you. You've killed more CCs than Absalom himself."

"Though a potter destroys unworthy vessels, he yet cherishes the work of art that finally emerges from his kiln. Indeed, the finished product is all the more valuable for the sacrifices made for its creation."

Ms. Sabeen lowers her hand to look at him.

"But, as I said," Dr. Osgood continues, "you need not worry about the Technics interfering with your plan. They are not trained for combat, for resistance, for intrigue. They do as they are told—always. They are property. They are servants. They are beneath; we are above. They know no other way to be."

Ms. Sabeen considers for a moment and says, "Well… I suppose we will have the added advantage of surprise."

"Precisely."

I swallow hard and hunker lower, but my movement must draw their eyes, because they both turn at the same time and look directly toward my reflection. My heart beats faster. I close my eyes, ready for them to charge over and grab me. What will my punishment be? Dissection? Will they turn me into a Glut? Or worse… will I be sent to the incinerator?

"Ugh! That glare is giving me a headache!" Ms. Sabeen says, and her heals clack across the stone again. But she's not heading my way. She's moving toward the exit. Dr. Osgood follows her. "I thought the glass in here was supposed to be glare-resistant."

"Do you get headaches often, Sabeen? I could examine you." His voice is smooth, like oil.

"Not a chance!" she retorts. "I wouldn't let you and your creepy little med kit anywhere near me. And, don't think I don't know about the illegal things you've been doing to that Rottweiler of yours."

The elevator chute swooshes.

"And it's 'Ms. Sabeen' to you," she adds. "Don't forget whose orders you follow."

They get in.

"How could I? But it isn't you. My allegiance goes straight to the top."

Another swoosh and I'm alone again.

The top… Absalom? Did Absalom tell them to do something to his CCs? Would Absalom be plotting some kind of rebellion? Perhaps against U.S.E.C.? But, then why render the Warriors inoperable? Wouldn't he need them?

I jump up and run over to the elevator. I have to find Needle.

Despite my best efforts, I can't locate Needle for the rest of the afternoon. He doesn't answer my call on the HCS and his schedule reads "Maintenance," which just means he could be anywhere in AI Tower. He's probably in the bowels of the building welding something or reprogramming something, either out of reach of an HCS or making so much noise he can't hear it. At least, I hope that's why he's not answering and not because he's still mad at me.

I get my final injection of the day and, after sticking me with the syringe, Nurse Marlene says, "That dosage was higher than what you're used to, so you might feel extra nauseous today."

Perfect.

As soon as she sets me loose, I head swiftly to the cafeteria, hoping to find Needle. I push through the doors and scan the room's occupants. CCs of all ages dot the room and stand in line waiting for their meal. The Warriors stand out first to me, squeezed into chairs not large enough for them, elbow to elbow over their trays. A table of Telepaths sit together silently eating, but by their expressions I know they're having a lively conversation. I spot Siren and Decoy sitting with the Gapes. Then Abracadabra appears before my eyes in what I thought was an empty chair. They all snicker.

No Needle. Lumina catches my eye and I head over to them.

"Where is he?" I ask.

"Where is who?" Bandy wants to know, coming up behind me and dropping a tray of leftover fish and broccoli mush on the table before pulling up a chair.

"Needle, of course," Siren says. "Who else would she be looking for?"

"I need to find him," I say, ignoring her, "soon."

"We don't know where he is," Gaze answers for her, oversized eyes trained on me. "The last time we saw him was at lunch."

"But he said he'd be here," Lumina adds. "Why don't you get something to eat while you wait?"

I let out a small groan of frustration but take her advice and head to the lunch line. I walk up and find myself standing behind a female CC I know I've met before. I can't remember her name. I don't even know what class she is. She looks like another Natural. She turns and sees me.

"Oh, hi Galaxy," she smiles.

She has brown hair and light brown skin. Bright green eyes. Too green. No, she's probably not a Natural. They've done something to her. I don't know why, but I'm disappointed.

"Oh, hi, um... uh...." I feel like an idiot.

"It's Arbor," she says, graciously extending her hand.

I take it and notice she's got leaf-like tattoos covering her arms. At least, I think they're tattoos.

"Hi," I say.

"Here, why don't you go first," she says stepping aside so I can take her place in line.

Normally, I would accept, but today, for some reason, I wave away her offer. I guess I'm just not very hungry.

"Hey, there, G," Smudge says, smiling when it's my turn. "What'll it be tonight? Leftover, over-cooked fish and broccoli, or chicken chimichangas, seasoned rice and beans, with a heaping side of guacamole?"

I love guacamole! And chimichangas are my favorite thing ever! Smudge knows this. He made it special for me.

"The fish, please."

"OK, chimichangas it is.... Wait, what? Did you say fish?"

I swallow. I feel like I'm going to cry.

"Yes. I'll have the fish and... and the broccoli, please."

Arbor has stopped moving down the line and is looking at me. Everyone is looking at me.

"Oh, no, sister, you don't want this stuff. It was bad the first time around and, trust me, it's worse now. Let me get you the —."

"No, Smudge. Thank you, but I really want the fish."

Smudge takes a clean plate from the stack and reaches for the spatula lying on the side of the boiled fish container.

"Alright, you're the boss."

"No, I'm not. I'm not the boss, Smudge," I tell him. "I'm just a CC... like you. Like all of you."

Smudge stops and looks at me for a moment, like he's seeing me for the first time. Then he smiles just a little bit. A sad smile.

"Yes… yes, you are."

He drops a piece of fish on the plate. It breaks into a few pieces as he does so, greasy liquid creating tiny yellow rivers stretching along the edges. Then he scoops up a ladle of the broccoli mush, the stems and tiny florets no longer able to retain their shape after steaming all day. The green glob lands on my plate with a plop.

When I return to the table, Needle is there. I put my plate down and he stares at it for a moment, then looks up at me and smiles. Now I really want to cry. I can feel it in my throat, but as usual no tears form in my eyes.

I want to tell him everything, but the cafeteria is not a secure place. The surveillance here is always active. It's one of the places Needle refuses to tamper with. With so many CCs and cafeteria workers moving in and out of here, a loop in the feed would be immediately detected. I'll have to wait until after dinner… until after I eat this culinary insult on my plate.

As I sit, Needle rises to his feet and limps off to the food line. He's not the only one who has noticed my change in diet. Everyone's eyes are on me.

I sit down and take my fork in my right hand, not sure if I should use it to eat with or as a weapon to fend off the monstrosity before me. I've never eaten anything so disgusting looking. But the other CCs are still waiting to see what I do.

I stab a piece of fish, but it just falls apart, refusing to stick to the fork. Three more tries only succeed in spreading ever shrinking bits around my plate. Finally, I slip the fork beneath a piece and scoop it up. They should've given us spoons.

The first bite slides around on my tongue and then turns to paste as I clamp down. I don't even have to chew, just swallow. I'm trying to detect a taste. I'm starting to feel nauseous. I'm not sure if it's the food or if Marlene's suped-up injection is beginning to work its black magic on my insides.

Needle returns and digs into his food like he doesn't care how bland and textureless it is. I try to follow his example—just eat it quickly and try not to think about it. This might be the hardest thing I've ever had to do.

"I think it's time," Lumina says, looking at Needle, then at me, then back to Needle.

"I have scheduled some self-maintenance time for myself right after dinner," Needle says. That means he gave himself an excuse to be in his quarters where he can disable the surveillance.

I'll have no trouble joining him in his room, so I relax a little, knowing I'll finally get a chance to share what I overheard in the Solarium. I'm curious what Gaze and Lumina have to do with what's going on. They act like they have something they want to share, too.

VIII

I find Needle alone in his quarters when he opens the door at my approach.

"Needle! Finally!" I say, plopping down on an empty bed and staring at him hard. "You'll never guess what I overheard!"

"When? Who did you overhear?"

"Ms. Sabeen talking with Dr. Osgood in the Solarium. I was supposed to be in Data Analysis, but I left early. They're plotting something, Needle—something bad."

"I knew it!" he says and paces a few steps before turning back to me. "Lumina and Gaze have been seeing some strange things going on, too."

"Like what?"

He sits on his bed, opposite me, and leans forward, elbows on his knees, but gesturing with his hand and mechanical appendage as he explains.

"You know how the Gapes are often brought in whenever there's a client Ms. Sabeen is trying to impress or a grant she's trying to get funded?"

"Yeah. They're practically celebrities."

"Well, that means they end up spending a lot of time in her offices and the conference rooms where all the AI business takes place. Sometimes they overhear things… and sometimes they see way more than anyone imagines."

"What do you mean?"

"I'm about to tell you something, Galaxy, that you have to promise to keep absolutely secret. Do you understand?"

More secrets! Great! But I nod my head.

"Gaze and Lumina and the other Gapes… well, sometimes they can see through walls."

I sit up straight.

"What? Really? And what do you mean 'sometimes'?"

"I mean they can't detect everything, but if there's an active HCS in an adjoining room, the photons from the hologram illuminate the space making it possible for their advanced eyesight to detect images—even through a wall, if the wall's thin enough…. The walls around Ms. Sabeen's office are thin enough."

"Wow! I had no idea."

"No one does, Galaxy—not even the researchers themselves. This was an unexpected side-effect and something the Gapes have kept completely to themselves… until today."

"So, why did they tell you now, then? And why are you telling me? What did they find out?"

"Just that Ms. Sabeen has been on the HCS a lot lately—with U.S.E.C. Supreme Head Anshar. The Gapes can't hear the conversations, but they can see whatever she sees… like plans—images of AI as it will appear after they're in control of it. Lists of names of CCs—and People, too—who they consider threats. Galaxy, Absalom has not been involved in any of these meetings. In fact, his name and image was at the top of that list."

My throat feels dry. It's hard to swallow, hard to breathe.

So… when Dr. Osgood said he answers to the "top," he wasn't talking about Absalom. He was talking about Anshar.

Oh, no! That means Absalom isn't in on any of this! And, if he's not, then he's in danger, too!

"I think they're going to try to take over AI, Galaxy," Needle says. "I just don't know when."

"It's tonight, Needle," I say, almost choking on the words. "They're going to do it tonight."

I run down the hall to the elevator as fast as I can. Needle is rushing the other direction. He's looking for Gash and Gauntlet. I'm not sure what he's planning to do, exactly, but it has something to do with what I told him about how Dr. Osgood is rendering all the Warriors 'inoperable' tonight.

As I round a corner, I see several AI staff members entering the hallway, leaving the small CC Residence Maintenance and Order Office where they work. Their shift has ended and they're going home, but I doubt anyone will be coming to take their place.

"Lisa hasn't come in yet," I hear the lady complain to her male counterpart.

"Oh, didn't you look at the schedule?" the man responds. "It's been changed. She's not coming in tonight."

"What? That must be a mistake. These young CCs can't be left to their own devices all night long."

"Well, my shift is over. So, not my problem. I'm done babysitting for today." He slips his arms into his suit jacket and hits the elevator controls.

The lady pulls a device from her pocket.

"Well, I'll just text Ms. Sabeen to let her know what's going on. She can deal with it."

"I'd wait 'till I got home to send it," he says with a chuckle. "Otherwise she might ask you to stick around until Lisa shows up— whenever that may be."

She smiles and slips the device back into its place.

"Good thinking!"

The elevator arrives. They get on. Turning, they see me, but don't offer to share their ride and zip out of sight. It's okay. I'm going the opposite direction anyway.

It doesn't take long for another elevator platform to appear in the chute. I step from the brightly lit corridor into the cylinder and in moments it spits me out into darkness.

I feel around for the light panel next to the elevator shaft. A tap illuminates a series of mood lights on the walls and overhead. The room is still cast in shadow, but at least now I can see enough to navigate Absalom's maze. I scan the room but do not find him. He must be sleeping.

My heart sinks a little. I was hoping to find him in the main room. I hadn't imagined going into his private bedchamber—a room I've barely glimpsed, let alone entered—and disturbing his sleep. But this is urgent. His life could be in danger. His life, my life, Needle's....

I cross the jumbled space and enter the hallway, arriving at his massive, decoratively scrolled, wooden door. I swallow hard and raise a fist to knock.

A flash of motion and Absalom is standing before me, robe hanging open over pajamas, hair disheveled. He is as surprised to see me as I am to see him.

"What is it?" he asks.

"I, um... I... I...."

What was I going to say again?

He doesn't wait for me to figure it out. He pushes past me into the main room.

"You can tell me in here," he says.

I follow him. He moves through the obstacle course of furniture and crates. He is looking for something.

"What time is it?" he asks without looking up.

"It's… it's about 7 o'clock." I watch him for a while. He scours surfaces, pushing things around, looking behind them. "What are you looking for?"

"You'll see," he says and continues his search. "What did you want to tell me?"

"Superior…" He glances up at me. "I mean, Absalom, I overheard some things and… well, I… I think you might be in danger."

He stops then and looks at me.

"In danger from whom?"

"Ms. Sabeen… and Dr. Osgood… and even from Supreme Head Anshar himself."

"Then little has changed," he says, and moves to a chest in the far corner of the room. He kneels down, opens the lid, and starts taking things out, dumping papers, odd devices, and empty pill boxes on the floor. Then he stops. "Ah, there it is," he says, his voice softer, almost a whisper.

He lifts his hand from the bowels of the old chest. Dangling from his hand is a chain. And, as he draws the chain higher, I see a triangular shaped, metallic pendant suspended at its base.

"Then you know?" I ask him.

"That Ms. Sabeen is undermining me every chance she gets? Yes."

"Then, why keep her on?"

Absalom, who had been staring at the pendant, fingering the symbol on one side, stops and looks at me.

"Because sometimes it's best to welcome that which is inevitable."

"I don't understand."

Absalom stands and moves to his chair. He sits and taps a control panel. The pixelated fire flares to holographic life in the fireplace. By the glow of the red orange light against his profile, I see that the skin on his forehead and cheeks must be beginning to peel. Absalom returns to examining the pendant, but waves me closer.

I sit across from him in an empty chair that matches the one he normally occupies. Though the chairs match and are likely the same age, mine is in much better shape. The upholstery less faded, less worn. The padding is still full and the seat does not sag. But, for some reason, Absalom never sits in this one.

"Absalom," I press him, "they're going to do something to the Warriors. Dr. Osgood has modified their programming somehow so that, sometime tonight, they'll all become inoperable."

Absalom stops looking at his necklace and looks at me. His eyes aren't wide with surprise nor filled with rage—either of these reactions I would be ready for. No. They're just sad. Sad and resigned.

"So it begins," he says.

Is that it? Is that all he has to say to me? He's just going to give up? Let them destroy everything he's built—including me?

"Absalom! They'll kill you! Don't you understand?"

I'm yelling at him. I've never yelled at him. I've never even imagined yelling at him. I can feel my fists gripping the armrests, my throat tightening, the rage inside my chest beginning to churn. I feel sick all over—from emotion, the drugs, I don't know which. But I have to make him understand. I have to make him hear me.

"I understand," he says at length.

"But… aren't you going to do something? If you knew this day was coming, then… why didn't you prepare for it?"

His expression changes then. He leans slightly forward and looks deeply into my eyes.

"Oh, I have."

"What are you talking about?" I'm in a rage now. I can't stop the words tumbling from my mouth. "You're just going to sit there and let them destroy you? Destroy me? How can you do it? And what about the other CCs? What about Needle and Luster and Decoy? The Gapes? What about them? They depend on you, Absalom, don't you see that?"

I'm choking, trying to get the words out. My throat isn't cooperating. I feel like I'm crying, but the release of tears is again denied me.

"Some sacrifices will have to be made." He reaches a hand out toward me. "But you, my Galaxy…."

I'm angry, and the skin on his arm is diseased, cracked, and peeling. I pull back.

I see from the look in his eyes that I've wounded him, but I don't care. I want to hurt him. I want him to suffer. I hate him.

A swoosh indicates that the elevator has been activated. Absalom jumps to his feet and moves his chair so that it faces the elevator with the high back to the holographic flames.

"Get down," he orders, directing me to my knees behind his chair.

I obey, crouching low, out of sight. My rage instantly morphs into panic. My breath comes in gasps, and I am relieved that the fake fire also makes a crackling noise that covers the sound of my desperate breaths.

From the sound of their boots, I estimate that about half a dozen soldiers have entered the room. I lower myself closer to the ground. I see their legs from beneath the chair. Black pant legs with dark green accents. These soldiers are from the same group that stormed our classroom and seized Miss Abilene—U.S.E.C. military special forces.

"Are you Absalom, owner of Absalom Industries?" One of them asks. I recognize the voice. It's the captain of the U.S.E.C. Special Forces—the man from class. The man with the scar on his chin.

"I am," Absalom replies.

A loud, electrified shot is accompanied by a flash of blue light. Absalom cries out—a sound I've never heard before. I see his knees first, hitting the floor hard. Then a hand. It's covered in blood.

I clamp my hands over my mouth to keep myself from screaming. My chest is heaving and I feel like I'm going to explode. I lean back and close my eyes, using all my strength to control myself.

The elevator door slides open again. The soldiers leave. Their business here is done. I hear Absalom crumple all the way to the ground. They've killed him.

I allow myself a whimper, then a cry, and then I'm screaming and I can't stop.

"Galaxy...."

He's still alive!

"Absalom! Absalom!" I move from my hiding place and I'm by his side. He is lying on his back, one hand covering an ugly, bloody place on his chest—a spot that keeps growing as blood soaks through his pajama top. "Just stay here! I'll get help!"

I go to move, but he stops me. His stained left hand on my arm.

"No. There is no one who will help me now. We both know this."

"But... but, I've got to try," I whimper. "Maybe Needle can do something. He's very good with injuries."

"Just... stay," he says, fighting to talk. "Take... take the necklace."

I nod, my hands gripping his free one.

"It's one of six...." he says, but a choking cough cuts his words.

All I can think of is how much I hated him a moment ago. How I yelled at him.

"I'm sorry," I say. "I'm so sorry, Absalom!"

Absalom's cough subsides. He swallows and takes a breath. Turning his eyes on me, he smiles. "Oh, no, no, my Galaxy. No. It is alright now, don't you see?"

I shake my head. Nothing is alright. Nothing will ever be alright again. His breath comes and goes with a liquid-like rattle and he begins to shudder.

"No, Absalom! Please! Don't die! I need you! I don't understand any of this!"

Absalom takes in a ragged breath.

"I dwell in darkness. But you, my Galaxy… you are the light of a billion stars."

Absalom's eyes shift as if they are no longer focusing on my face. His breath comes out in a long wheeze. And then nothing. No movement in his eyes. No rise and fall of his chest. No pulse beneath the skin of the hand I hold.

Absalom is dead.

IX

The glass has finally broken. I'm falling. Falling. Nothing can stop my wild plummet toward the earth.

I lay on my bed, holding the metallic pendant Absalom gave me. The pendant and chain that are still stained with his blood.

I wait for the soldiers in black and green to appear out of the elevator chute and drag me away. But they don't come. The waiting is driving me crazy. What did Absalom say? Sometimes it's best to welcome that which is inevitable. They will come for me. Eventually they'll come. It's inevitable.

So why aren't they here yet?

I watch the sun sink lower on the horizon until it drops out of sight. I watch the lines of light streaming through my glass walls crawl higher and higher, thinner and thinner, until they fade altogether.

I haven't heard from Needle or any of the other CCs. I imagine they have already been bound and marched from the building. The Warriors will be no help. They are inoperable by now. I'm not even sure what that means. Perhaps they are all dead.

I think of Gash and Gauntlet, Badge and Signet. I see them lying unmoving on the ground... like Absalom.

Is Absalom still there? Have they come for his body yet? As I think of him, the pain in my chest seeps into the rest of my body. I feel it in my stomach, in my neck and shoulders, creeping through my extremities. I feel it rising in my throat, coming to rest along the bridge of my nose and recline behind my eyes and forehead.

The last rays of the sun are gone. The stars are beginning to poke through the expanse of inky black. One, two, three.

And, for some reason, I remember the song he used to sing to me. I've never sung it myself before. But tonight I do.

Alone in the darkness looking for light.
Then she stood with me to force down the night.
One heartbeat searching for another one true.
Two lovers circling as lovers will do.
Two lovers circling as lovers will do.

Nothing is wrong and yet nothing is right.
Letting her go, I'm unwilling to fight.
Seventy letters are all turned away.
Never again will love come my way.
Never again will love come my way.

But as one life ends, a new one is found.
Two became three; the third underground.
Now that I've found you I'll make you my light.
Soon you will conquer this horrible night.
Soon you will conquer this horrible night.

I open my eyes and realize I had been asleep, still wearing my uniform from yesterday. It's too dark to see, but I know that, like Absalom's necklace, I am still stained with his blood.

"Galaxy, are you there?"

"Needle?" His voice is coming from the HCS, but there is no display.

"Oh, good! You're okay!" He sounds relieved. "Sorry about the lack of display. We've been tampering with the system and it's not fully accessible yet."

I let my mind skip over his admission of committing such a serious crime. After all, Absalom is dead. What we do now, or do not do, hardly matters. Like Absalom once said, we're all dying.

I lay my head back on my pillow. "They killed him, Needle." My throat hurts when I talk. My lungs ache when I breathe.

Needle sighs. "I know, Galaxy. ...I'm sorry."

"They just asked him his name. And then they shot him. It was that man from class. The captain of the U.S.E.C. Special Forces."

"I'm sorry."

"You said you knew. How?"

"Like I said, I've been working on the HCS system for the last several hours. I have the Gapes and some of the Wits helping me. We've been doing everything we can to hide the CC files. We've also been overhearing every message they've sent over the HCS… and interrupting others. Ms. Sabeen's team has been overhauling the entire HCS system. We've been tracking their changes and reprogramming behind them. I didn't think we'd be able to adjust fast enough—especially when the entire system began to glitch out. I thought that, if we could identify and override the precise frequency and identify the code they used to—"

"What time is it?" I ask, interrupting his techno-babble. I have no idea what he's talking about.

"3 a.m.. But, we don't have much time left."

"What are you talking about? Time for what?"

"Come down here and I'll show you. Once you get out of Absalom's quarters, the elevators and hallways between you and me are clear—for now. Come to the CC Education Center Computer Lab and Testing Center on the 40th floor. I want to show you something."

I say nothing. I don't feel like going anywhere.

"Galaxy," he prompts, "will you come?"

"I'll come," I say, but don't move. He can't see me anyway.

"Good. See you soon. And hurry."

I feel sick. The nausea from last night's higher-dose injection has yet to wear off. Standing up causes the pain to take up residence in my head. It's disorienting. I feel like I'm locked up inside my own body. My heart beats slowly but loudly. My breath rushes noisily in and out, thick in my ears. I find myself focusing on taking the next breath, and then the next.

I turn on the light in my room and see Absalom's blood on my uniform, my hands, smeared across my cheek. Red on white skin. I strip and activate my shower—a device that rises from the floor, surrounds me, and douses me with soap and hot water until I am clean. Only this time, I don't feel clean afterwards.

After dressing in a fresh uniform, I move to the elevator controls to summon a platform. My hands shake as I lift them to tap the command to take me back to the place I watched Absalom die. As the tube whisks into the empty space of my room, a small glimmering reflection in its curved side catches my eye. I turn and see the cause still lying on my bed.

The necklace.

I can't leave it here, out in the open. Absalom gave it to me. I don't know why he gave it to me but I don't want anyone else to have it. I can't leave it in my room, or someone will find it for sure. The same thing will happen if I leave it somewhere in Absalom's quarters. No doubt they will soon search every square inch of that place. My suit is practically skin tight, so I can't hide it on my person… unless….

I wipe the blood from the chain and the metallic surface of the pendant using my bedsheet. Then I flip my hair to the side and slip the chain down the back of my suit, leaving the pendant itself exposed and suspended against my upper back. I feel the cold chain dangling against my skin almost to my belt, but when I move my hair back into place, it completely covers the pendant. Checking my reflection in the walls, I make sure my secret is completely hidden.

When I step into Absalom's quarters, the room is fully lit up. He is gone. Only a large blood spot remains. I can't remember the last time I've seen that room devoid of shadows. The dust is much thicker than I imagined.

I see no one else, but hear voices approaching from the hallway and more voices emanating from the breakfast room. I swiftly change elevators and whisk from the room.

I'm a little dizzy as I leave the second elevator and head down the dimly lit hallway in the CC Education Center. My head feels heavy and too big for my scrawny neck. The rest of my senses have dulled. Sounds are distorted. Images out of focus. Maybe I feel this way because it's still the middle of the night, but the shower I took didn't really help.

As I approach the computer lab on the 40th floor, I hear voices coming from that direction. I approach the doors—doors with large windows in them—and look in on what looks like a full-scale resistance operation. About four dozen Wits of all ages are hard at work, sitting before HCS displays, sifting through streams of algorithmic data—most of it highly classified, more likely than not. Gaze and Lumina are there, too. It looks like they're helping run the show.

Everyone has gone insane.

Needle, standing next to a female Wit and pointing to a line of digital information emanating from her HCS display, looks up and spots me at the door. Despite the noise from all the talking and shuffling about, Needle always knows when I'm nearby.

He waves me over and I activate the doors.

"What's going on here?" I ask him, staring at the lines of rebels working toward our mutual demise—for that is the reality of what I am seeing.

"We're organizing," Needle says, pulling me over to a relatively private corner of the room. "I'm hoping to get more AI CCs on our side, but communicating with them all is not only difficult—with the HCS malfunctions and all—it's also risky." He glances back at the working

CCs. "The Wits and Gapes were easy to persuade. They're illegals. But some of the classes might have better chances under Ms. Sabeen and U.S.E.C.."

I understand why it was so easy to convince the illegals to join Needle's little resistance movement. They won't last long once U.S.E.C. gets wind of them. Now I begin to understand a little of what Needle had been saying about re-coding the CC files. The only way to protect the illegal CCs is to delay U.S.E.C. from discovering precisely which ones are illegal and what their enhanced abilities entail. Of course, Dr. Osgood and Ms. Sabeen would know most of this information. Still, U.S.E.C. will want searchable, documented evidence. Needle is making sure they won't get it.

But, again, why delay the inevitable? And why does he think I'd be okay with any of this? After all, I'm not an illegal. Maybe I'd have better chances going along with U.S.E.C., too....

"...and so, we managed to find the frequency by examining Gauntlet," Needle says, and I realize I've been tuning him out. I try to focus on what he's saying. "...and the Wits found the code, but then the HCS relays started to overload, so I had to reboot them one by one before I could enter the new algorithms. By then four or five more would—"

"Wait," I say, one hand up. "I'm sorry. What are you talking about?"

A female Wit overhears and looks over at us for a moment before returning to her display.

"Haven't you been listening?"

No.

"I'm talking about waking up the Warriors," he says.

They're still alive?

"To put it simply, I think I can do it through the HCS system by attaching the correct code to a carrier wave along a certain frequency that the HCS can emit."

That's not putting it simply.

"All the Warriors have auditory implants which allows them to receive orders remotely. Dr. Osgood programmed it to emit a noise that knocked them all unconscious. But I can use the HCS to access it and wake them all up at once."

"Oh... OK."

Am I supposed to think this is a good thing? I mean, it's not like I want U.S.E.C. to get ahold of them, but what does Needle expect the Warriors to do? Fight back? If they've been unconscious this whole time, they don't even know about Needle's attempt to organize and rebel, let alone decided to join up with his tiny band of rebels. It's ridiculous.

"I can see you don't understand," he says.

"No, I understand—well, I sort-of understand. I just don't think it's going to work."

"What part?"

All of it—any of it.

"Needle, what do you expect is going to happen here?" I ask him. "Even if you wake up the Warriors, how do you know they'll resist U.S.E.C.?"

"I don't." He admits without apology, looking me right in the eye.

I raise my hands in question... in defeat.

"But don't you think they deserve to make the choice?" He asks.

I don't know. Maybe it's better for them to die in their sleep. Or, if awakened in time for incineration—which is more likely—at least, they would know when death was to come. Needle's way, nothing is certain.

By the look on Needle's face, I can tell he's disappointed in me. He wants me to just go along with all of his crazy ideas like I always do.

"Things have changed for me, Needle. No one stands between me and them now. I don't... I don't know what to do anymore."

"Things have changed for all of us, Galaxy. It's more important than ever that we start fighting back."

"What are you talking about? Fight for what?"

The Wit looks over at us again, but I don't care what she thinks of me.

"For our lives, Galaxy."

"But we have nothing! We are nothing!"

I don't know why I'm getting so hysterical. None of this should matter to me. I'm a CC. I'm nothing. I shouldn't care if I live or die. If there have to be sides, why should I care what side I'm on? CCs never win.

"We have each other, Galaxy," Needle says, putting his good hand on my arm. "And we're more powerful than they've ever dreamed."

I'm still not sure what Needle is planning or what my role is expected to be. He sits me down in a chair next to his. Before us is an HCS display from which he's been tapping into the surveillance feeds from all over the building and even the streets surrounding AI Tower.

"I think Ms. Sabeen and U.S.E.C. are hoping to have a new chain of command in operation by 9 a.m.," Needle explains. "That's when the shifts change. AI is working on a skeleton crew now. When their replacements arrive, the next shift of employees will discover a screening station at each entrance. The employees will be evaluated and a decision will be made about whether or not they'll retain their positions, be fired, or worse... arrested. Any employee coming or going will have to pass U.S.E.C.'s inspection."

"I bet Dr. Osgood won't like that," I say.

"What, didn't you know? I checked his file. Dr. Osgood is a model citizen."

"Of course. Payment for services rendered, I suppose."

"Precisely. No one will have any idea what he's been up to. ...Oh, here we go. Look," he says, pointing to the video feed from the parking garage where we met the female CC, Bangle. The one whose finger was given to Luster.

"What are they doing?"

"See those transport vehicles?"

I nod. There must be twenty of them either parked or parking. As they come to a stop, the side doors slide open and, despite their size, only four special forces officers step from each one.

"Why are they nearly empty?" I ask, but realize the answer even as the question leaves my mouth. "Oh...."

"Yes," Needle says. "It's already happening. They've come for us."

He drags another video feed to the forefront of the display. This camera is angled toward the elevators and the security station. I immediately see that Gauntlet is not at his post. Security Guard Allen Cage is there, though, looking exhausted and helpless. One of the U.S.E.C. soldiers is speaking to him. The soldier has removed his helmet.

"Zoom in on his face," I say.

Needle obliges.

The captain has short-cropped, brown hair, graying at the temples. A narrow face, hard brow, and small eyes. A white scar crosses his chin.

"That's the same man who arrested Miss Abilene and killed Absalom!"

"Really? How can you be sure?"

"The scar on his chin. I noticed it when he scanned me."

"Just a sec." Needle runs a quick HCS search and says, "His name is Captain Gerard Watt."

We keep watching the feed. Allen looks nervous. He fidgets as Gerard Watt, captain of the U.S.E.C. Special Forces barks at him. Still, he makes them wait while he double-checks the orders on his HCS inside his glass security kiosk.

Captain Watt does not wait for an answer, but waves the rest of his men on toward the service elevators. "What are they saying?" I ask.

"Here, let me see if I can tap into the audio."

Needle pulls up a small holographic menu for the surveillance system, locates the correct section, and scans for the precise audio receiver.

"Open this door!" Captain Watt's gruff voice comes over our speakers. He gestures toward the steel security doors that prevent access to the service elevators.

"I have to get clearance from Ms. Sabeen first," Allen says. His words are firm, but his voice shakes. He raises one hand in a calming gesture.

"You already have clearance!" Watt shouts. "Open them now."

Other U.S.E.C. soldiers make their way past the security kiosk and fall in line behind their leader before the steel doors. Each of them carries an energy rifle—like the one used to kill Absalom.

I suck in my breath. My head still hurts.

"Well, I did, but now my HCS seems to be down. I'm always supposed to double-check orders."

Needle snickers.

"What?"

"Watch this," he says.

The captain is yelling that Allen open the doors now or be arrested as a Subversive. Finally, the security guard gives up trying to check his console display and hits a button. The steel doors slide open, but stop short, leaving a gap of only about a foot wide. Watt looks back at him in annoyance. Allen hits the button again. The doors snap shut, almost catching the Watt's fingers. Now he's really mad.

Needle snickers again as he opens the doors all the way and then, just as the soldiers take a step forward, slams them back, nearly taking off noses.

Allen raises his hands in defeat. "I'm sorry. It's not me. The system has been glitching out for the last few hours. I... I'll call maintenance."

"You do that!" Captain Watt turns toward the smaller elevator chutes. "For now, we'll take these, but the service elevators had better be working within the next fifteen minutes, or you and I are going to have a problem!"

"Y-Yes, Sir."

We watch as the soldiers begin taking the smaller elevators, a few men at a time. Needle's smirk turns into a frown. He turns around in his chair and addresses one of the Wits working in the row behind us.

"Trig," Needle addresses a skinny boy of about seven, "how close are we to emitting the carrier wave?"

"We still need more time," the boy says, swiveling in his chair. But though he's talking to Needle, his eyes are on me. "Synapse and Clarity are working on it, too." He indicates the two Wits on either side of him.

"How long?"

The young woman of about twenty-five, sitting next to Trig, reacting to her name, turns to join the conversation.

"I'm working on the carrier wave code now, and—" Her eyes land on me and she stops mid-sentence. "What is she doing here?"

Needle glances at me and then back at her.

"I asked her to come," he says.

"But she's one of them. You know you can't trust her."

"She's one of us, and yes, I can. I do."

I swallow. Why is this woman singling me out? What have I ever done to her? How does she even know who I am?

"She'll betray us."

"You don't know that, Clarity," Needle defends me. "She's one of us."

Now all the Wits near us have turned to listen to the debate. I don't like the way they look at me, the way her words make me feel, and that I can't defend myself. …Because I'm not sure Clarity is wrong.

X

"She was just Absalom's pet. We all know that," Clarity continues, eyes like daggers. "She has never really been one of us."

"But that doesn't make her one of them," Needle says and glances at me.

I meet his gaze. I want to reassure them, but I don't know what I would be promising. I don't even know the plan. Or if there is a real plan. Right now it just looks like a few rebel CCs, with Needle in the lead, are just messing with Ms. Sabeen and U.S.E.C.'s takeover. What ultimate purpose could it serve?

"Right, Galaxy?" Needle says, blue eyes gazing at me. His sandy blond hair draped across his forehead and curling under his ears from a lack of combing.

"I... I... I don't know—"

"See! I told you!" Clarity snaps. She spins in her chair back to her console, angrily sweeping through her data files to continue whatever work she was doing a moment ago.

I can see disappointment in Needle's eyes.

"I just mean, I-I don't know what is expected of m-me," I stagger across the words. "I want to help, but I just don't know what... what I can do... to... to... help."

"It's okay," Needle says to me, a half-smile on his face, but the passion has left his words. "I'll explain everything."

"Better not," Synapse, an middle-aged man with a scar above his right eye says. He, too, had been listening to the exchange.

"Perhaps the less she knows the better," Trig agrees, green eyes looking at me apologetically.

"Look," Clarity says, turning back to Needle. "Maybe you're right about her." She gives me a glance. "Maybe she won't betray us all to our deaths in the incineration chamber. But, really, what can she do? What is she good at?"

Needle looks at Clarity, to me, and then back at Clarity. He wants to protest, but he's having trouble disagreeing with her. I'm having trouble disagreeing with her, too. I can't manipulate the HCS like a Wit. I can't fight the U.S.E.C. special forces like a Warrior. I can't see through walls like a Gape. I can't even charm anybody like a Pristine. Why did Needle ask me to come?

"It's okay," I say, rescuing my one friend from an impossible situation. "She's right. I'm not good at anything. I have no real skills. I'm just a valueless CC. I'm just in the way down here."

"Galaxy, that's not true," Needle says, looking at me now.

I rise from my chair. "Yes, it is. You know it. I know it."

"Galaxy—"

"It's okay, really. I... I'll just go back to my room and let you get back to whatever it is you're doing." I back away. "I hope it works. Really, I do. I hope you stop them—if that's what you're trying to do... or delay them, even. But I'm just in the way here. Don't worry about me, though. If you need me you'll know where to find me."

But we both know he won't need me.

I turn to go and take fast strides down the aisle of working CCs. They watch me as I leave. I slip around the corner and head to the door, but suddenly Lumina steps into my path, looking up at me from her child-like stature. Her head too large for her body.

"You're wrong, you know," she says. She's looking at me in a weird way. Like she's looking through me the way she can look through a wall.

"What are you talking about?"

"You're far from valueless."

Needle must have some kind of plan to thwart Ms. Sabeen or U.S.E.C. or both, but I can't see how he could ever succeed—even if all of the AI CCs were working with him, and they aren't. Even if they manage to take over AI Tower, how long would they be able to hold it?

Still, I can't see what harm can come from trying. If what I've been hearing is correct, nearly all the AI Warriors, Technics, and the other AI special CC classes are illegals. They won't be sold; they'll be incinerated. At best, they might be kept around just long enough to be experimented on. If they're caught, well... death by energy rifle couldn't be much worse.

Maybe Needle isn't trying to take The Tower. It sounded like he was just trying to hide or doctor the CC files to keep the illegals from being discovered as illegals. Messing with the U.S.E.C. soldiers and hacking into the surveillance system was probably all just a way to stall Ms. Sabeen's team long enough to clear all traces of illegal activity from the records. Doing so would at least give the CCs a fighting chance to be reassigned instead of incinerated. Those with illegal abilities would just keep them secret if they can.

But, then… why wake the Warriors?

I make my way back down the empty hallway to the elevators and whisk back to Absalom's quarters. I don't really care who I run into. It's unlikely any of the U.S.E.C. team is ready to confiscate the harmless Naturals like me. They're too busy trying to round up the unconscious Warriors and get them to the transport vehicles without the use of the service elevators. I'm the least of their worries.

But Absalom's quarters are deserted when I get there. The lights are still on. They must have completed their preliminary search for anything of interest and moved on to other tasks associated with their hostile takeover—whatever those might be. I try not to think about it as I return to my room.

I strip the bloodied sheets from my bed and lie down. It's comfortable enough, and I rarely use covers anyway.

What did Lumina mean when she said that I'm far from worthless? Perhaps she was just being nice. Most of the CCs I've known are pretty nice to each other. Not to me, usually. They just ignore me most of the time, but now that I no longer have Absalom to set me apart, maybe they'll want to be my friends.

It's an interesting thought. I find the idea appealing, if a little late.

But the look on Lumina's face wasn't one of friendship. It was more… more like… interest.

Of course, the Gapes are a little weird.

I roll over and glance at the HCS. It reads 4:14 am. I close my eyes. I should try to sleep. I'm so tired. And I still feel sick, wasted. But my mind keeps going over and over everything that has happened… everything that could happen.

I dream, but I know I'm dreaming. I don't feel like I'm really asleep, but I see Needle at his HCS, zipping through streams of data. I see the Warriors waking up. I see a line of soldiers with Ms. Sabeen at the head. She orders a charge. An energy rifle is fired. It's heading toward the Warriors, but then Needle is there. He's shot in the chest. The same place where Absalom was shot.

Needle's hand is covered in blood. And then I'm covered in blood.

I open my eyes. The sky is still black. I sit up. I feel fully awake. My heart is pounding.

The HCS reads 4:43am. Hardly any time has passed. I'm worried about Needle. I have to find out what's going on, but I don't want to go back down to the computer lab. It would be embarrassing to show up there and have Clarity and the other Wits just chase me out again.

I open my HCS. Maybe I can use it to find out what I need to know....

Twenty minutes later, I swipe it off in frustration. I'm blocked out of everything! Even the information I could usually access—like Needle's location—reads "CLASSIFIED." My password is useless.

I sigh out a groan of frustration. I wish I knew how to manipulate the system like Needle does. But if you don't know something, you just don't know it! I have no choice but to give up. I guess Steven was right about me.

Maybe I should've paid more attention in class. We took a computer programming class once, but I missed most of it and slept through the rest. I don't think I ever did any of the homework.

...I wonder what happened to Miss Abilene. She and I never got along, but for some reason, I really hope she's okay. ...Needle liked her.

How long has Needle been planning all of this? He's been tracking Miss Abilene's subversive activities for the better part of a year, but he didn't seem sure until fairly recently. Of course, he might've shared his suspicions with any number of CCs. They're all his friends. And the Wits might have also been following it.

I wonder if Needle shared all Miss Abilene's stolen files. I'm sure he did—at least all the stuff they could use, like her secret password.

I sit up straight in bed.

Her password! I saw it, too! It was on the illegal outline Needle showed me. I can almost remember what it was. It's there... floating around in my mind. I had found it interesting because I've never seen a Person's secret password before. It's unheard of for CCs to access that kind of information. But I saw it!

It's... it's.... I sigh.

It started with her initials. "A" for Abilene, and... what is her first name? Dara! So the number started with "DA" and then... There were a couple of ones in there somewhere. A prime number and a two, I think. Thirteen was the first one... and then....

I close my eyes, trying to see the number in my mind. DA13.... DA13.....

DA1321! I think that's it!

I sit up again and reactivate my HCS.

I just hope they haven't wiped all her codes from the system, with all that's been going on lately. I know her AI files would have been wiped—

by Needle—but he wouldn't have deactivated her entire account. Ms. Sabeen would do so, but there would be no rush, since the only Person who's supposed to have access through Miss Abilene's account is Miss Abilene—and she's gone. Ms. Sabeen has been busy plotting her takeover, so maybe....

I find the correct code panel and enter Miss Abilene's code. It works! Immediately, I have full access to everything Miss Abilene did!

"Take that, Steven!" I say aloud, smiling.

But then I swallow and take a deep breath, looking around the holographic display that hovers all around me as I sit on my bed. There is so much information here! Where do I begin?

I need to find Needle.

I enter his code into the tracking application. It shows him as still being in the computer lab. I breathe a sigh of relief. If he's still there, then he's probably okay. But it sure would be nice to see what's going on.

I swipe through the various access ports. I'm amazed that Miss Abilene—a mere teacher of CCs—had access to this much AI information. Laboratory data, personnel records, even information on security systems. I frown. I think Miss Abilene probably wasn't supposed to be accessing all of this. But she was.... Who would give her so much unchecked freedom?

I enter the security systems access port and pull up the surveillance section. If Needle can use the cameras and audio feeds to find out what's going on here, maybe I can, too.

For obvious reasons, the camera and audio feeds to the computer lab have been deactivated, but so have the feeds for the entire CC Education level—everything along that one relay is inoperable. Smart. It just looks like a system failure for an entire section, rather than a deliberate attempt to hide one room. And this way, the CCs can come and go within that area without fear of detection.

I move on to the staff offices feed. Ms. Sabeen is in her office in front of her HCS. She's working on something, but I can't tell what from the camera's angle. Interesting that Miss Abilene was able to listen in on anything going on in the staff offices, though. She was definitely a Subversive.

I scan through the feeds and view the one in the conference room next to Ms. Sabeen's office. I smile. Several Gapes sit around the table, but none of them are talking to each other. They are all looking the same way—toward the wall the conference room shares with Ms. Sabeen's office. Or, more precisely, through the wall.

"Well, they'll know what she's up to," I smirk.

Out of curiosity, I search for Absalom's quarters—the top twelve stories, including my spire room. As I had always believed, none of them shows up as having either visual or audio surveillance. Absalom was one of the few in the nation who enjoyed genuine privacy. Me, too, I guess. For some reason, that makes me happy.

The Solarium is one of these rooms. No wonder Ms. Sabeen and Dr. Osgood met there to talk about their plans. They knew no one would be listening in—well, they thought no one would be listening in. They hadn't expected me to be there.

Next I sift through various images of empty hallways, vacant personnel stations, and silent classrooms until I notice activity in the images coming from outside AI Tower.

The streets surrounding The Tower are lined with U.S.E.C. vehicles. Soldiers and men and women in suits come and go, lit up by the street lights and the light that always emanates from the structure itself. AI Tower was designed in such a way so that, when the sky goes dark, it glows.

I turn my attention to the parking garage video feed. It looks like all of the transport vehicles have arrived. I count 25. They stand empty, wide, sliding side doors open, exposing rows of empty seats. The guard is still at his station. He's alone. He's playing with his ear and dinking around on his HCS. He looks nervous, distracted.

The steel service elevator doors are open now. It looks like they finally managed to override Needle's "glitches." More likely, he let them. Perhaps to keep himself and the other Wits from being discovered.

Security Guard Allen Cage whips his head back. He's looking at the service elevator. The platform comes into view and lowers until it is level with the ground. It is full of soldiers and gurneys bearing other individuals I can't yet make out. I reach into the holographic display and turn the audio on.

The first to disembark is Captain Gerard Watt. He stands aside and oversees the others leaving the platform, rolling the gurneys toward the waiting vehicles. As they leave the elevator, I get a clear view.

Signet is on one of them. Gash is on the next. Padlock. Some oversized female I don't recognize. An older male Warrior. Badge. Last, Gauntlet comes out. He walks out under his own power, though, fully conscious, wrists bound by massive, high-tech metal handcuffs. My whole body could slip through one side of the cuffs, but they bind his hands tightly together behind his back. Four guards flank him, two on each side. Still, he towers above them. They look like children next to him.

The guard looks at Gauntlet. Gauntlet stares back at him, unblinking. Allen vigorously rubs the back of his neck.

"For some reason, this one managed to remain conscious," Captain Watt explains to Allen, as they near the security kiosk.

"I don't... I don't see why you have to take this particular CC," Allen says, gesturing at Gauntlet. "He's always been a service to AI and works in Tower Security with me. I assure you he can be trusted." His voice sounds weak, pleading.

Watt stops next to the kiosk, Gauntlet and his captors behind him.

"Oh, you assure me?" The beady-eyed captain gives a short, humorless laugh. "All the more reason for me to take him! U.S.E.C. is revamping the entire security system here at Absalom Industries. Of course, soon, they won't be calling it that anymore, now that Absalom is dead with no heirs to take his place."

"Well, surely he had a will or something to—"

"Nope. No will, no instructions, no nothing. Trust me, I helped search his quarters myself. So, U.S.E.C. has full legal authority to confiscate all AI holdings and properties, including these CCs. But, don't worry. I expect you'll see some of them back here again. After they are screened and tested at a secure U.S.E.C. facility, the ones who pass may be reassigned to this building. After all, they know their way around." He glances up at Gauntlet. "Of course, it's unlikely that you'll see this particular CC again. He's an illegal for sure."

They start to move away. The other soldiers are already loading the transport vehicles. Not all the Warriors will fit easily in the same one, so they are dividing them up. Still, there are plenty of open seats left. I wonder who will fill them. Another elevator full of soldiers and unconscious Warriors arrives.

"What will they do to the illegals?" Allen asks.

"What do you think? They'll be disposed of. Incinerated."

"But-but he's never done anything—"

"Look!" Captain Watt is losing patience again. "You shouldn't let yourself get attached to CCs. Don't forget; they're disposable."

Gauntlet jerks. I follow his eyes. Four soldiers, standing next to the open door of a nearby transport, have accidentally dropped unconscious Gash to the ground. Even through the audio feed, the sound his head makes at it hits the concrete floor puts a sick feeling in my gut.

"Hey, what are you doing?" One of them says to the one whose corner of the gurney buckled, but then laughs. "Oh, don't worry about it. It's not like this one's going to last long anyway."

They bend to try to lift him, but the four of them can't do it alone. Before they can call for assistance, however, we all hear a great cry of anger. Gauntlet is moving almost faster than I can see. I had no idea he could move so fast. He pushes past the captain, knocking him over, and smashes a corner of the security kiosk as he heads to Gash's side. All of the glass of the kiosk shatters at the same moment, sending a cascade of shiny, crystal shards around the AI guard. He ducks shields his head with his arms.

"Code Red!" Watt yells.

Immediately all the soldiers in my view pull their weapons, but Gauntlet has already barreled into two of the U.S.E.C. soldiers next to Gash, sending them flying upside down through the air until they crash against the far wall and slide down, unconscious. The other two duck and run for cover, cowering behind a transport.

Gauntlet's normally smooth black face contorts in anger and exertion. With a strength of force I can only guess at, Gauntlet strains against his cuffs. I hear a metallic crunch and then a loud pop as one side bursts open.

XI

With his free right hand, Gauntlet grabs the remaining shackle and rips it off like one might tear a piece of fabric. He drops it with a loud clank to the cement floor.

Everything is happening so fast that the U.S.E.C. soldiers are still scrambling to find a safe place from which to level their energy rifles on him.

"Shoot! Shoot now!" Captain Gerard Watt yells, rising to his knees and then to his feet. He, too, draws his weapon.

A blue blast shoots past Gauntlet, barely missing his right shoulder. He's moving again. He runs up against a transport vehicle and pushes it up and over onto its side. I can't see them, but at least two soldiers have been crushed beneath it. I hear their screams. One of their rifles goes off in the wrong direction, destroying the entire back end of another vehicle. The tank erupts in a blaze of fire and noise.

Gauntlet ducks, avoiding an onslaught of discharged weapons. Still, a blue stream of plasma-like energy finally meets its mark, hitting him in the back.

"Oh, no!" I yell into my empty room, heart pounding. "Gauntlet!" I reach toward the holographic image, but my fingers merely move through it. I can do nothing for him. Gauntlet goes down, an ugly wound marring his back, just under his left shoulder blade. He disappears behind a transport vehicle.

Soldiers surround him, I hear weapons recharging. Watt is on his feet, running forward, weapon drawn.

Suddenly, another high-pitched sound echoes through the audio. It's a terrible noise. I put my hands over my ears. All the soldiers in the parking garage hear it, too. Only, for them, the sound is debilitating. They fall to their knees. Some of them drop their weapons so they can cover their ears as well.

The sound doesn't last long—not long enough to completely incapacitate the soldiers, but it has an amazing effect on the Warriors.

They're waking up.

"Needle, you did it!" I gasp.

I watch as the Warriors in the transport vehicles begin to show signs of life. Those still strapped to gurneys try to sit up, but find themselves restrained. Spur, from class, is among them, a white, 16-year old CC with brown hair and brown eyes. I see a few others I recognize but don't know well—Barricade—an adult CC with salt and pepper hair, Fuse—an adult, redheaded female with bulging muscles, and a child of about four—I think his name is Blast—heavily muscled for his age. I see them in the CC cafeteria from time to time.

They look confused, disoriented. Another energy rifle is discharged, this time in the direction of a transport vehicle. The blast was intended for whoever was trying to exit. But they missed.

The faces of the Warriors change. It's like they're listening to something—something I can't hear. And, then, the Warriors on the gurneys start breaking through their restraints, snapping them like old rubber bands.

Before Barricade is free, a soldier levels his rifle and shoots. The blast hits Barricade in the arm. He cries out in agony.

More shots are fired, peppering the transport vehicles, the walls, and zipping past the security guard who is cowering in his destroyed cubicle, trying to find shelter between the desks and equipment.

The Warriors no longer look confused. They know what's happening and they've begun to organize. Gash is awake, seeming no worse for wear, even after having been dropped roughly on his head. He has moved to Gauntlet's side, taking cover between vehicles and clearing the area of soldiers.

I see a soldier in black and green, mask smashed in, fly through the air from Gash's position, bounce off a transport vehicle bumper, and land in a heap on the concrete. Another soon follows, screaming the whole way.

"Fall back and regroup!" The captain yells. "Fall back and regroup!"

My eyes move back to where little Blast was tied to his gurney. He has disappeared. I spot Fuse ducking behind a low, concrete wall. A head pops up next to her.

"There you are," I breathe out in relief. Blast is safe... for now.

Signet has escaped her vehicle. It was she who the soldier had been shooting at to keep her locked inside the transport. What he didn't expect was for her to punch a hole in the opposite side and go out that way. Suddenly, one of the heavy transport doors, having been ripped from its hinges, flies through the air, clearing the top of the transport, and lands on the soldier. I hear an "Ugh" escape him but nothing more.

All the soldiers who had been near the vehicles when the Warriors woke up are either dead or unconscious.

The rest, following Captain Watt's orders, gather into a defensive line, weapons drawn. They rain down a constant barrage of fire upon the vehicles and any Warrior who is caught out in the open. Barricade is shot in the back of the head as he flees the gurney and runs for cover. He collapses and doesn't move.

I clap a hand over my mouth. I want to scream but I can only whimper in horror. And that's when I realize it.

I've chosen sides.

The CCs must win this battle. I don't care what happens later. Right now, we must win!

From this camera angle, the transport vehicles and the low wall are hiding the Warriors from my line of vision. I have a full view, though, of the backs of the U.S.E.C. soldiers. They are advancing, not caring whether or not they destroy their own vehicles. All they want is to kill the Warriors.

I sweep through a few more HCS windows until I find a better view. This camera provides a side view of the fight. I can see in between the vehicles. Spur and Signet are together, crouching to avoid being hit by energy blasts. Gash kneels beside Gauntlet. Gauntlet is moving! He's badly wounded, but he's alive!

"Yes!" I cry, fist clenched.

And then I see something. Dropped energy rifles lay all about the Warriors, but none of them are picking them up to use them against the U.S.E.C. soldiers.

"Look!" I say at the image of Badge, whose left knee is right next to one of the weapons. "It's right there! Use it!"

Instead, he brushes it out of the way as he ducks another shot, this one from the captain himself. That's when I remember something I heard once, about U.S.E.C. weapons. They are coded for the individual user, so only the Person or CC issued the weapon can use it. It's a security measure that prevents just anyone from picking up such a powerful weapon and using it. In fact, I think it was Absalom's idea—or maybe his father's—I can't remember.

Again, anxiety fills me as I consider the dire situation the Warriors are in. They are fast and strong, but not impervious to energy fire. The exits have been sealed with three-foot thick, magnetically sealed doors. Even Gauntlet wouldn't be able to crash through that. And a row of about fifteen U.S.E.C. Special Forces, constantly laying down streams of energy blasts, stand between them and the elevators that could take them back up into AI Tower. They're trapped.

I watch in horror as the seconds tick by. Blue streaks light up the space, even as lighting elements are destroyed by the blasts. The soldiers advance, pushing the Warriors further and further into the corner. The Warriors haven't given up, though. They're working together to make a path for Fuse and Blast to escape their places behind the wall—a location that will soon be swarming with U.S.E.C. soldiers—and join the rest of the CCs behind a barricade of transport vehicles.

Spur and Signet have overturned a second transport and stacked it on top of the one Gauntlet overturned earlier. Badge and Gash use a third one as a shield, creating a path for Fuse and Blast to join them. The other Warriors are tearing doors off transports to use as portable shields and removing seats and panels to launch at their attackers.

From the corner of my eye I see movement. I turn back to the first camera feed to see that the service elevator has been activated.

"Oh, no! Not more soldiers!"

But I am not at all prepared for what I see. As the platform lowers to the ground, a single occupant comes into view. A massive, white, snarling polar bear!

Immediately, the bear barrels into the midst of the U.S.E.C. soldiers, teeth bared, thick, sharp claws swiping at them, only barely missing. The soldiers, even more startled than I, scatter in all directions. Several of them cry out in terror. The forgotten security guard, Allen Cage, still cowering in his broken kiosk, climbs under the desk and positions the chair in front of him.

I'm so intrigued by the polar bear that I almost miss what is being shown on the second feed. The bear does not seem to surprise any of the Warriors. They must have begun moving as soon as the platform came into view, because they are already halfway across the garage floor, using transport vehicle doors as shields, heading to the service elevator.

I hear cries of sheer terror coming from the U.S.E.C. soldiers as the bear continues his wild attack. Before the soldiers have time to stop them, the Warriors have boarded the elevator. Gauntlet is with them, leaning on Gash.

"Decoy!" I hear someone yell from the elevator. The bear immediately stops his assault and turns back. An energy rifle is fired at the bear as it retreats, but though it was aimed to hit the bear in the right haunch, it passes completely through the animal without slowing it down.

"It's not a bear!" I breathe in amazement. "It's Decoy!"

Though a bear that size would not have fit in the service elevator with all those Warriors, this one manages it without any problem. The holographic bear disappears, leaving a skinny Indian boy in its place.

"Get them!" Captain Watt yells. He aims his energy rifle at the service elevator. The other U.S.E.C. soldiers finally realize what happened and re-aim their weapons.

The captain squeezes the trigger and a blue wave of plasma-like energy leaves his weapon.

"No!" I cry, helpless to stop him.

But in that same moment—just before the burst of blue flames reach the CCs in the elevator—the thick steel doors snap shut.

"Who did that?" Watt cries, small, bloodshot eyes blazing in fury. He turns to the security kiosk.

I follow his gaze.

Allen is there, no longer cowering under his desk. He stands at the HCS, finger still on the holographic elevator door button.

"You!" The captain rages. He raises his energy rifle.

"No! Please!" Allen cries.

Watt shows no mercy. One squeeze of the trigger and Allen Cage is blasted through the heart. He is dead before he hits the ground.

It won't take long for the U.S.E.C. soldiers to get those steel doors open again. I search the surveillance feeds to see where the Warriors and Decoy have gone.

My heart beats wildly and my hands shake as I swipe through one holographic image after another. The service elevators let out on nearly every floor, except my spire room, of course. I don't understand the system well enough to determine precisely where it went.

I have kept one image open, though—the one that shows me the parking garage. I keep an eye on the soldiers even as I search for my friends… I mean, for the other CCs.

I hope they're okay.

"Oh, no! No!" I cry.

After kicking aside the dead body of Allen Cage, Captain Watt has accessed the HCS. The steel doors have opened and the soldiers who can still walk are entering the elevator. As the steel doors slide quickly shut I see the captain speaking into the HCS embedded in the sleeve of his uniform—getting information on the whereabouts of the Warriors who escaped, no doubt.

Several minutes pass as I desperately search feed after feed, looking for them. But, before I can figure out where they've gone, the display suddenly shuts off. Everything disappears, sucked back into the now unresponsive device embedded in the foot of my bed. No amount of tinkering will make it respond.

"Now how will I know what's going on?"

Needle probably did this. To help the Warriors hide. It would make sense. No doubt he has another way of communicating with them. It must've been him giving the Warriors orders during the brief battle in the parking garage. That's why they were able to organize so quickly after they became conscious, and why they knew the polar bear was Decoy—a child of fourteen hiding in the center of bear-shaped cage of light and color. Even I didn't expect that. I've seen holograms all my life, but none so real as that bear.

Amazing. Absalom spared no expense.

I look toward the east. The first rays of the sun are coming over the horizon. Morning is breaking through the darkness. The city and the farmlands and pastures beyond look so peaceful.... And yet, somewhere, below me a battle is raging. People could be dying. CCs could be dying. And I have no way to find out without ending up in the middle of it myself.

I lie down on my back and then—

"Ow!"

I flinch at a sharp pain in my back. I reach back and pull out the triangular pendant Absalom gave me, still attached to the chain draped down the back of my uniform. I'd forgotten about it in all the commotion. I pull it out and examine it again. Both sides are metallic, but the back is a darker shade. It is nearly smooth, except for some randomly spaced points—small, indented squares of a different kind of metal.

The front has some kind of swirl in bas relief going across it in gold and silver, but the image makes no sense to me. Just a decorative design of sorts, I suppose. I can't imagine what importance it might have had to Absalom. Perhaps his illness—the unnamed disease that caused him to lose weight, his hair to fall out, and his skin to develop a peeling rash—had also affected his mind or memory. I've heard such things can happen in the late stages of some diseases. He certainly did not seem himself when he took my hand... called me "my Galaxy...."

I swallow, drop my hand to the mattress, and look toward the sky. I don't want to think of him now.

But his face fills my mind.

Sometimes it's best to welcome that which is inevitable....

"Is that true, Superior?" I ask into the sky all around me. "Is that true, Absalom? We all die. Should we welcome that, too?"

I don't want to die... but I'm not sure I want to live, either.

I open my eyes. The morning is still new, but the sun is higher in the sky than it was a moment ago. I must have dosed off.

But something has awakened me. A noise. A whooshing sound like wind. It's getting louder.

I stand and look out from my wall of glass onto the city streets below. The city is alive with new activity.

At first I see nothing. Then, suddenly, rising from beneath my feet, a helicopter rises before my eyes, just outside the walls of my spire room. I gasp and step back, but there's nowhere to hide in my room of glass.

The pilot wears dark glasses. He looks at me and talks to an HCS-generated hologram projected from his control console. He is so close, I can see it clearly. The hologram is of Ms. Sabeen.

The passenger section of the helicopter carries about a dozen members of U.S.E.C.'s military special forces. They all hold the same military grade energy rifles. For a moment a cry of panic erupts in my throat. I am certain they're going to aim their weapons at me, and I will die in a flash of blue and red. But they don't. Instead, the helicopter banks to the right and flies off. It leaves me alone for now, but with no reason to stay here. I have to find Needle. I have to find someone.

I take a deep breath and tell myself it doesn't matter who I run into. If it's a CC, they might help me or they might not. If it's a U.S.E.C. soldier, I'm going to have to face them soon enough anyway. At this point, they'll either ignore me or arrest me… or shoot me…. I try to push that thought out of my head, but I can feel a trembly sensation starting at the base of my throat when I think of those blue streams of energy and light and fire.

Again, I hide my pendant under my hair and enter the elevator chute.

I can't believe Needle's rebellion has gotten this far! What is Needle's plan? I thought he was just trying to wipe some files—make it look like a computer glitch—but a full-scale rebellion?

I swallow and activate the elevator. In a brief moment it deposits me in Absalom's quarters. Someone is here. She turns around and looks me right in the eyes.

Ms. Sabeen.

I was wrong. It does matter who I run into. It matters.

XII

"Ah! There you are, Galaxy." One side of her mouth curls up in a smile.

I don't like the hungry way she's looking at me. Usually she just glares at me—like one might glare at a rival—or she pretends not to see me at all. Now that Absalom is dead, things are different between us. I'm no longer a rival. I'm at her mercy. I know it. She knows it.

"I was just about to send someone to look for you. It was nice of you to come to me."

I just look at her.

She moves closer, puts her hands on the fronts of her thighs, and leans down until she's eye to eye with me—speaking to me as she would a small child.

"Maybe you could help me with something."

"What?" I ask, surprised. I don't know what I expected her to say, just not that.

"You spent a lot of time up here with Absalom." She straightens and turns from me as she speaks, looking about the room. "You know more about him than any of us, I suppose. Perhaps enough to know where he liked to hide things?" She glances back at me. "I'm looking for something, Galaxy. It's something that belongs to me. I loaned it to Absalom once because he found it interesting, but now I'd like it back."

"What is it?"

She turns to face me. "It's just a trifle, really," she says. "It's not valuable—except to me. For sentimental reasons. It was... given to me by my grandmother many years ago."

She's lying. Why is she lying?

"It's a necklace. It has a metal, triangular pendant of gold and silver. Have you seen it, by any chance?"

"A necklace? N-No. I haven't seen any n-necklaces."

The smile leaves her face to be replaced with a hardened stare.

"If I find out you are lying to me, Galaxy, you will regret it. But, if you somehow manage to find the necklace and give it to me, I'll spare you. Do you understand what I'm saying to you?"

I nod.

"No. I don't think you do." She draws closer. Too close. "You're not exactly a Wit, but you do understand what's happening, don't you? Absalom is dead. AI belongs to U.S.E.C., and guess who they've put in charge? That's right. Me. I get to decide who stays and who goes. And if a CC goes, you know where they'll go, right?"

I swallow hard.

"To the incinerator, Galaxy." She smiles. She's enjoying this. "Have you ever seen a CC burned alive? Of course, you haven't. Absalom sheltered you as if you were a Person…. I've seen it, Galaxy. Let me assure you, it's a horrifying way to die. Their screams can be heard all across the compound. So… if that's something you'd like to avoid, I suggest you start looking for that necklace."

"And… and what if I find it? And give it to you? What then?" I feel panic rising in my chest.

"Well, you'll be spared, of course. You'll continue to live here at AI as you always have. Little will change for you."

"And what about the others?"

"What others?"

"The other CCs? Will they be spared, too? What about the Warriors and Technics?" I feel desperation driving me, but I can't stop the feeling—the fears rising in my mind.

"Well, some of them are illegals, Galaxy, but… I might be able to make some exceptions."

"You would have to spare Needle, too. In exchange for the necklace… I mean, if I find it, that is."

"Needle?" Something in her eyes changes. She's discovered something. "Oh, Needle, too, of course. I promise."

I find the CC Computer Lab dark and deserted. None of these HCSs appear to be working, and the only light comes from dim emergency lights running in thin lines along the ceiling and in the floor, providing just enough light to keep me from bumping into things.

Where could they be?

I quickly search the floor and then move through the nearby floors, making sure to first search the ones I know to have been blacked out to the surveillance cameras—just in case U.S.E.C. still has access. I find no one.

Where would Needle go?

Possibly to his quarters… or to some electronic station where he might still access the HCS, of course I have no idea where that might be… or to find the Warriors….

I try to think where the Warriors would go. They weren't on any of the first 38 floors when I was searching the HCS in my room before it cut off. I just finished checking floors 39 through 41—the first three floors of the CC Education Center. Floors 42 through 44 contain the School of Technology, 45 through 47 are the Trade School, then the next three contain the Technic Development Center….

The School of War!

Floors 53 to 57 contain the School of War! And, if memory serves, floor 56 is where the weapons are stored!

I step into the elevator and am about to press 56, but stop myself. If that's where they've gone, I might land right in the middle of a full-scale battle. I tap 57 instead. It's the Weapons Training Facility—a room full of practice target ranges and an unlikely place to stage a resistance effort. I can take the stairs from there.

I step off the elevator into silence and breathe a sigh of relief. It doesn't look like anyone has been here recently. There are no windows in this part of the building. All the ranges are dark and silent. Fake enemy soldiers stare back at me from their posts at the end of long aisles—many of them bearing some form of blackened wound or missing an appendage from battle practice. The whites of their painted eyes catch the dim light, making them look eerily interested in me.

I cross a short space to the stairs, making sure to tread lightly and keep an eye out for motion in the shadows. I find the stairwell dark and silent, but as I round the bend, halfway down, I see that the lights on the next floor are on. I swallow hard. Someone has been here.

I creep down the steps, taking one step, listening, and then taking another. No sound, nothing. I move forward toward the thick, stairwell door. I look through the window in the door to find a fully lit but deserted hallway. I open the stairwell door and step into the hallway.

Blood! Splatters and smears of blood mar the floor. Boots have tracked it onto the white tile from the open room.

There are several rooms on this floor, including a storage locker for small weaponry—guns, energy rifles, knives, and the like. Usually locked and bolted, the thick, metal door has been ripped from its hinges and discarded further down the hallway to my right, lying in a twisted heap.

I move to the left and pass an abandoned guard station and several darkened rooms. I round a corner and spot a door that appears to be open. Light streams into the hallway from that direction.

A hand! Someone has fallen just inside the room, their hand sticks through the open doorway. It's a man's hand—a normal sized male—not a Warrior.

Needle? I suck in my breath at the thought.

But, no. It can't be him. This is a right hand and Needle doesn't have one. I feel relief at that thought, but my heart still pounds wildly in my chest. I move ahead slowly, trying to avoid stepping in the blood.

As I near the entrance, the body of a man—a U.S.E.C. soldier begins to come into view.

Noises! I stop short.

Energy rifle bursts. Shouts. But the sounds are muffled, distant. They seem to be coming from… the floor beneath me.

I step into the entrance and gasp in shock, one hand flying to my mouth. There are bodies everywhere.

Warriors and U.S.E.C. soldiers lie about the room, some in puddles of blood, others partially hidden behind overturned tables or equipment stands. I count at least six U.S.E.C. uniforms among the dead. But the Warriors lost members, too.

A male and female Warrior I don't recognize lie to my right. And then further on, the body of a younger CC is turned away from me. He looks… he looks like….

"Spur?" I speak into the room. "Spur!"

I run over to him and, with great effort, am able to turn him from his side onto his back. He feels stiff, cold. His brown eyes stare unseeing beyond me. No air escapes his lips. An ugly wound covers his chest, exposing his ribcage. He had been shot directly in the heart.

"Oh, no…."

I withdraw my hands from him and sit back staring. Spur is dead. He was only sixteen. Just a year older than I am. Dead. For years I'd been in many classes with him, seen him in the cafeteria, passed him in the halls. But, until that night in Needle's room, I never really thought of him as anything more than just another CC. And now I'll never get the chance to know him.

The thought makes me feel bad… guilty. Like I missed out on something special. And now it's too late.

"I'm sorry, Spur," I whisper. "I'm sorry."

I hear another shot and a scream from beneath me. The battle is not over. More CCs could be dying right now.

My hands tremble. I stand and feel suddenly dizzy and nauseous. I turn away from Spur's empty stare. I can't look at him anymore. The floor feels like it's moving beneath my feet, and the light starts to dim.

I stumble back a few feet and then turn back toward the door. A great deal of blood and death lies between me and it. I only make it halfway before I have to bend and vomit.

This is too much! I can't take this!

I feel spent, wasted. I cross to the door, but have to brace myself against the hallway wall just outside the room of death, lest I lose my balance.

I've stepped in blood. It's on my shoes. I've knelt in blood. It's on the knees of my suit. I've brushed up against blood. It's on my right thigh and sleeve.

I stumble back toward the stairwell. When I open the door, I hear the noises from below more clearly now. I hadn't heard them earlier—there must have been a break in the shooting—but now the sounds of gunfire, shouting, small explosions, are clear.

I should leave. I should go back to my room—wait for them to come to me. Or I could hide. AI Tower is a big place. Needle has shown me lots of panels in the walls I could hide behind. I might be able to last for a long time that way. But something compels me further down the stairs. The cries. I feel I must follow them. I must know what's happening.

I move down the steps, again taking them one at a time. I make it to the halfway mark where I can see the door to the 55th floor—the Combat Training Facility, an entire floor of obstacle courses and training battlegrounds.

"Galaxy. Shh!"

"Needle?" I whisper back.

"Stay down!"

I round the corner. Needle crouches at the stairwell door, looking in on the battle scene. Blue flashes light up his face every few seconds. Seeing him makes me feel a little bolder. The nausea in my gut lessens. I move up behind him. The shots and yelled orders grow louder.

"I didn't want this," Needle says. His voice is tight. He's been crying. "I just wanted to protect them. Give them a fighting chance. But they're dying."

I come up next to him and look into the room. A contingent of U.S.E.C. soldiers, still led by Captain Watt, are attacking from a line of low walls and blast-resistant barriers. The Warriors have been pushed to the far side of the room, but are shooting back. They've secured weapons and are defending themselves well. I see only two bodies. Both of them wear U.S.E.C. uniforms.

"They would have died anyway," I whisper back. Seeing the force of the resistance, I no longer have any doubt that the AI Warriors, if they didn't resist, would have gone straight to the incineration chambers. There is no way U.S.E.C. would allow them to live, knowing what they are capable of. They are just too powerful. "This is a better way to go than the incineration chamber."

"Hey, are you hurt?" Needle asks, indicating the blood on my uniform.

"No, it's not mine."

He nods, relieved, and turns back to the battle.

I spot Gauntlet among the resisters. He is fighting back, no longer appearing weak from the earlier energy blast that hit him in the back—a shot that would have instantly killed an average man. Warriors heal quickly, I've heard. It took two shots to kill Barricade, and Spur had been shot right in the heart.

Suddenly, a flash of red hair rises above a wall. Fuse launches something—a grenade! It lands among the U.S.E.C. soldiers. They only have seconds to react before it goes off. The explosion sends a ricochet of force throughout the room, shrapnel and bodies fly from the space. Men cry out in agony and then go silent. The blast pushes the heavy stairwell door open for moment. Needle and I are knocked off our feet and land with a thud on our backsides.

"Fall back! Fall back!" I hear the captain yell. I can no longer see him, but I recognize his voice. "New orders! Retreat! Retreat! Group A, take the elevators! B, the stairs! Go, go, go!"

"We have to move!" Needle says, no longer whispering. "Now!"

He grabs my arm with his left hand and forces me back up the stairs. The stairwell door flies open, banging against the wall, just as we duck beneath the low wall around the bend, on the upper half of the stairwell. Heavy boots pound concrete, echoing off the stairwell walls. I crouch low with Needle beside me. I cover my head with my arms, fearing discovery at any moment.

But the sounds move away from us, dissipating. The soldiers are heading down the stairs, not up.

"Shh... It's okay. They're going," Needle whispers, and I realize I'm whimpering in sheer terror.

He is hunched down beside me, left arm around my back and robotic arm in front, encircling me, protecting me. I feel his breath against my ear. I can't remember the last time someone has held me. Most likely, it was someone from the CC Childcare Center, but I can't remember.

I turn and look in his eyes. Blue eyes. Frightened eyes.

I reach around him and hug him tight.

"Come on," he says. "They've gone. Let's go see what we can do for the Warriors."

Entering the battle zone sounds like a dangerous idea. What if the Warriors mistake us for the enemy? But, of course, Needle has that covered. He activates the HCS device embedded in his robotic arm and speaks into it.

"Needle here. I'm in the stairwell," he says, voice low. "Galaxy is with me. We're coming in."

"Roger that," Gauntlet's voice comes back at us.

The smoke hasn't cleared yet, but we step inside the room, our feet crunching across tiny pieces of rubble and shrapnel as we make our way to the Warrior's position.

"Hey," Gauntlet says to Needle. He nods at me. "We're going to need some medical attention."

He turns to indicate the rest of his team, but I get a view of the blast mark on his back—an ugly, red wound. Still, it's not as bad as I thought it would be, given the injury Spur sustained. Spur must have been shot at point-blank range.

"Fuse got shot in the arm," he continues. "And, I think Padlock has shrapnel in his legs. I haven't had time to look yet."

This side of the room, too, is strewn with debris. Blackened, charred bits of ceiling tiles and rubble from crumbling cement barriers cover the floor. The room was structured to withstand running, tumbling, and practice battles using harmless lasers; it was not designed for the detonation of grenades, energy rifle discharges, nor the use of live ammunition. Now that the smoke is beginning to clear and the 'all safe' signal has been given, the Warriors are coming out from their hiding places.

"What about Blast?" I ask, looking for the small boy I had seen on the camera feed.

"Oh, he's okay. Fuse made sure of that." Gauntlet answers, but then turns to me with a curious expression. "How did you know he was with us?"

"I saw your garage battle over the HCS," I say, suddenly self-conscious. "I'm glad you're okay."

Gauntlet nods, a half-smile of thanks on his lips, but then his eyes grow sad. "Not all of us are okay."

"I know…. Spur. I'm sorry."

He takes a deep breath. "They train us to expect losses like that. We're not supposed to let it affect us. But, I guess…. Well, I'm not done with my training."

"Spur was your friend," Needle said. "He was my friend, too. I think seeing a friend die should always affect us—no matter how well-trained we are."

Needle moves past Gauntlet and addresses the others. "Have there been any more casualties since the fight in the Armory?"

"No," Gash answers, looking around, counting comrades.

"Then we should make it to a safer place and secure some medical supplies."

"When will they be back?" Blast says, standing up from behind a low, cracked cement wall.

"Why did they leave so suddenly?" Padlock wants to know. He moves toward us, limping and dragging his weapon. "What called them away?"

"They'll be back, mark my words," an adult Warrior speaks up. I think he's one of the trainers. His black hair is slightly graying, and he has an old scar across his left temple.

The only adult CC Warriors at AI were those kept to train the others. Fuse works in bomb construction. Barricade works in combat training— at least, he used to. He's dead now. I don't know what this man does, and he wasn't in the first battle. In fact, I see several other Warriors who must have only just joined the rebellion. But there are a lot more—mostly children—who are not here.

"They were losing," the scarred Warrior continues. "They were out-manned and out-gunned. But they have a much larger army waiting in the wings. I know. I used to work with them before I got reassigned back here. They could swarm this place with soldiers if they wanted to."

"Then what should we do?" Gash asks.

"There's not much we can do. But we can't stay here. We'll need to get all the weapons we can and find a place where we have access to food and water. Then we should—"

"Hey, what's that noise?" Needle asks, raising his hand and turning his head so that his robotic ear aims at the stairwell.

"I don't hear anything," Signet says.

"Me either," Padlock agrees.

A moment passes.

"Wait...." The scarred Warrior looks toward the stairs. "I think I hear it."

Then I hear it, too. An electric, high-pitched whirring noise. It's getting louder. Closer.

"Get down!" the Warrior yells. "Take cover! Now!"

XIII

The room bursts into motion, Warriors ducking in every direction. Needle grabs my arm and pulls me further away from the stairwell door toward a broken bit of wall. As he pulls me, I look back.

Suddenly, the glass of the stairwell bursts apart and a small, metallic object shoots into the room. But it stops mid-air. It's a metal ball about the size of Gauntlet's fist that hovers and spins, using little jets of air as propellants.

We duck down, but I peak around the side. The device, still hovering in the center of the room, sends out a red beam of light from a lighted node on one side. It's scanning the space. It's looking for us! I pull back before the light reaches me, pressing my back against the wall and making myself as small as I can. Needle is beside me, doing the same.

The ball whirs again, making that horrible high-pitched noise. It's moving. I hear it moving off to my right. I peek out again. It spins as it goes, making the red light look like a red ring circling its middle. It finds Padlock. I hear a little hiss. Padlock cries out, but then falls over. He doesn't move.

The ball moves again, this time toward Badge. A hiss. Badge goes down. The Warriors are scrambling to keep away from it, but there's little to hide underneath, and the ball follows them.

"Shoot it! Shoot it!" the adult Warrior cries, and he pulls the trigger on his energy rifle.

The ball is extremely agile though. It easily dodges the stream. It's headed toward Blast. Blast cries out in terror.

"No!" I cry.

But I'm too late. Even Fuse is too late. She tries to move in front of him, but the ball maneuvers around her. A hiss. Blast falls limp in her arms. Then she is hit and they crumple to the ground together.

The ball continues its wild attack, but the Warriors are fighting back. As the hovering dart shooter nears Gauntlet, a large wall panel flies through the air, knocking the ball out of position. As it tries to right itself, an energy blast from the adult Warrior's weapon blows it to pieces.

But we have no time to celebrate.

"More!" Needle cries. "More are coming! They're all over the building!"

A moment later, three more appear, noisily entering the room from the stairwell. Warriors use energy rifles and throw debris to knock them out of the air, but the balls dodge in and around both CCs and obstacles so nimbly, they are nearly impossible to hit. They zip around, shooting darts into the necks, backs, arms, and legs of the Warriors. Signet manages to destroy one, but then gets a dart in the shoulder from another. The scarred Warrior finally succumbs to one that catches him in the thigh. Gash and Gauntlet fall next.

"It's coming!" Needle says and, as the words are leaving his mouth, we come face to face with one of the swirling balls. It floats on air-jets for a mere moment before I hear a hiss.

"Needle!" I scream, reaching for him.

I feel a pain in my chest and everything goes black.

Sounds. Voices. Something clanks near my head. A jumble of words. Two voices. One male. One female. Gradually they begin to make sense.

"...on that tray. Pass me the scanning device."

"Here. Are you going to clean up this one's wounds first?"

"Those are the orders. It will help us make accurate diagnoses about their abilities."

"I'll start getting the shrapnel out of his leg then."

The voices go silent for a moment. I feel myself drifting off again. I hear metal on metal, scraping, clinking, but the sounds seem distant... part of another world....

"Seems odd that we're healing them when there's so little chance they'll be retained," the female voice says.

"Like I said, it's so we can determine the extent of the alterations. ...If we only had the files, this wouldn't be necessary."

"Odd, that. How does that much information just go missing?"

"They're not sure. Could've been a system malfunction. ....Or the CCs did it."

"Well, I wouldn't have believed it if it weren't for what I'm seeing right now. There hasn't been a CC rebellion in I don't know how long!"

"I know. Crazy. I don't know what they were thinking," the male says, his voice followed by a loud clank.

I can't seem to move. Even my lids feel heavy. I have to concentrate to force them open.

"Maybe they just wanted to live."

"More evidence that AI was subversive. CCs aren't supposed to care about that."

I see white tiles and lights above my head. I'm in some kind of hospital room. I detect the sterile sent of antiseptic mixed with the acrid stench of some chemical or mixture of chemicals.

"You, know," the male voice says. "I'm going to have to call in a team of engineers to figure out what's going on with this one. They didn't train me for this."

I turn my head to look in his direction. A brown-haired man in a doctor's smock stands at a metal table to my right. He wears a mask that covers his nose and mouth. He's holding Needle's robotic arm.

"No! Needle!" My voice sounds gravelly, foreign. I try to move, sit up.

"What is she doing awake?" He says, looking at me with hard eyes.

The female doctor moves into view from a table where the unconscious body of Padlock lays, bloody legs exposed. She grabs something from a tray as she comes.

"She must not have gotten a full dose," she says just before pushing me down with her body and sticking me with something.

"Isn't she the one we're supposed to skip?" the male doctor asks, as the lights begin to blur.

"Yeah. No need for a diagnosis here. This one's a Natural, and Dr. Osgood says Ms. Sabeen has special plans for her... now that Ms. Sabeen has gotten what she wants from it."

They've moved me again. The hospital room is gone. I see only gray walls from where I lay. My head is spinning. My jaw feels tight and sore. I'm lying on my stomach, the right side of my face pressed against the hard, stained cement floor.

I try to move. It's difficult at first. My arms don't want to cooperate, but I manage to turn onto my back and, with some effort, sit up.

I'm not alone. A large black girl, her back to me, lies on the floor to my left, unconscious. She wears a cornflower blue AI uniform. Signet.

We're in a jail cell. Four cement walls. No windows. A door of bars bearing a thick, electronic or magnetic lock. No bed. No chairs. Only a bucket in the corner.

I move toward her on my knees. I've always been scared of her, but she's all I've got.

"Signet!" I whisper as loudly as I dare. "Signet, wake up!"

No response.

"Signet!" This time louder.

Still no response. Not even a flinch.

"Signet, wake up!" I say, putting a hand on her shoulder and shaking her.

Nothing.

Even when I roll her over and slap her in the face while calling her name, she does not hear me. If it weren't for the rising and falling of her chest, I would think she was dead.

I give up and examine my surroundings. In the cell opposite me, lays Allure—the twelve-year-old, Asian Pristine, her pink hair splayed across the ugly cement floor like a mop. She's on her back, one hand on her stomach, looking as though she hasn't moved since she was dumped there.

She's not alone. I see a hand through the bars, the rest of the body is behind the wall. But, there's something strange about the skin on that hand. It shimmers and shines. But one finger doesn't react precisely like the others. It shimmers, but the rhythm is off. Luster.

I push myself to my feet, but I have to steady myself against the wave of dizziness that accompanies the effort. I balance myself, hands on my knees until the sensation goes away. I make my way to the bars. I'm in one cell of many. The hallway moves away from me in both directions, cells lining both sides, but I have no idea how many of us are in here. Though I can see some doors, my line of vision is restricted from seeing inside any of the other cells.

"Allure!" I call.

No response from her, either.

"Allure!" I scream.

Nothing.

"Luster! Luster, it's me, Galaxy! Wake up!"

She, too, remains impervious to my voice. I try a few more times to get their attention, but Allure and Luster are lost beneath layers of tranquilizers. I push on my cage door, but it doesn't budge, and I find no handle on either side of the lock. I'm trapped.

I still feel weak, so I sit again, leaning one shoulder against the bars. I examine the ceiling in the hallway. Lights run down the length of it and, just outside my cell, a pair of holographic imaging cameras aim in opposite directions—one toward me, the other toward Allure and Luster's cell. There's one inside our cell, too, up in one of the corners at the back wall, locked behind a cage of thick plastic—probably unbreakable, even bullet-proof.

Someone is watching me. Someone sits at a desk somewhere, amused by the tiny holographic girl with white hair who is trapped like a mouse in a cage.

Still, I feel utterly alone.

"Is anyone else awake in here?" I ask into the void.

"I am."

I startle at the voice. I did not expect a response. It's a boy's voice, and he's close. It's coming from the cell to my right.

"Who's there?" I ask, suddenly frightened.

"My name is Rocket."

"Rocket...." I try to remember a Rocket. There were so many CCs at AI I'd never bothered to talk to.... "I don't think I know you."

"No, you wouldn't. Not if you're from AI, anyway."

"Where are you from?"

"CC Tech."

"Oh." He was talking about Commodity Class Technologies, Absalom Industries' greatest business rival. Though AI easily tops the market both in product and reputation, CC Tech has recently been undercutting our business by providing high-tech CCs at a cut-rate price. The rumor is their products tend to be cheap, but for the price, few can argue.

I hear a humorless smirk.

"Does that mean we can't be friends?" he asks.

"O-Of course, not," I stammer. "I can use all the friends I can get."

I don't know why I'm being so honest with him but since we're all probably about to die, I see no reason to hide anymore.

"Good," he says, voice soft. "Me, too.... 'Cause this guy's not good for much."

"Wait... Who's in there with you?"

"I don't know him. Maybe you do. He's from AI, anyway. He's got an arm missing. A robotic arm, I would guess. And one of his ears is—"

"Needle!" I cry. "Needle, it's me, Galaxy! Wake up, Needle!"

"Hey! Whoa!" Rocket says. "He's not going to wake up anytime soon, trust me. In fact, I don't know how you're awake already."

"Is he okay? Is he breathing?"

"He's fine. Just knocked out, like the rest of these guys."

"What about his arm? You said his arm is gone?" I remember now—the doctor with brown hair.

"Yes, it's missing, but he's still got the attachment piece. It's not like he's bleeding all over the place. Relax. He'll be fine.... Well, no he won't, but then neither will the rest of us, so...."

I feel the panic rising in my chest. My heart, already beating rapidly, pounds in my ears. I have to gasp to catch my breath.

"How can you be so... so... flippant? So heartless? He's going to die! We're all going to die!"

The weight of the situation we're in descends on me like a collapsing building. I'm whimpering, crying—that useless, pathetic, tearless cry. I wrap my small body in scrawny arms and hold myself as tightly as I can, but the feeling doesn't go away.

"Hey, shh...." Rocket says, his voice soothing. "I'm sorry.... Um, Galaxy, right? I shouldn't have said that. I'm sorry.... I guess I've just been in here so long—waiting for the end—that I almost welcome it now. I mean, get it over with already!"

I can't contain the cry that escapes my chest. How can he talk that way? I don't want to die! This can't be the end!

"Okay, that's not helping.... Uh—maybe we should talk about something else, okay, Galaxy? Why don't you... tell me about your life at AI? What's the food like over there?"

I can't stop weeping. I can't stop the wild, helpless feeling.

"The food, Galaxy.... Tell me about the food."

"It... it was...."

"Take your time.... What was the food like?"

"It was r-really g-good... but only for m-me." I sniff. I take some deep breaths, but I can't keep the choking sound from my words.

"What do you mean, only for you?"

"The o-other CCs. They didn't get what I g-got."

"That's interesting," he says. "Go on."

"They treated me differently."

"Why, Galaxy? Why did they treat you differently?"

I hear genuine interest in his voice, but I don't like this story anymore. It's not right. It never used to bother me that I was treated better than the other CCs. I liked it. It made me feel powerful, special. But that was all an illusion. Where did it get me? I'm locked in a cell along with the rest of them. And they're not even my friends—not really. Except for Needle, I barely noticed the them. I felt they were beneath me. I didn't care about them. I only cared about myself. Now I wish things had been different.

"Hey, Galaxy," Rocket prompts. "You still in there? You didn't escape and leave me behind, did you?" He chuckles. He's trying to lighten the mood, but I don't see any humor in this situation. "Won't you tell me why they treated you differently? Who treated you differently?"

"Absalom," I say, my voice dull. I feel suddenly very tired, spent, "the staff, the other CCs, everyone... everyone, except Needle."

"So this guy's special, huh?"

I sniff. "I wish I could see him for myself. I wish I could be sure he's okay."

"He's fine, I told you... Here, I'll check him again, if you like."

I hear motion. A metal on cement scrape. A short gasp of effort.

"Yep! He's good," Rocket confirms. "Breathing is steady. Good pulse. Just asleep. He's probably even dreaming. Maybe about you."

I laugh at that. "No. He wouldn't be dreaming about me."

"Hey, well, I finally got you to laugh! So, tell me. Why wouldn't he be dreaming about you?"

"Because Needle is friends with everyone. I'm just... I'm just one of many."

He's silent for a moment, considering.

"But he's special to you, though, isn't he? He's not one of many."

I sigh and let my head rest against the unyielding, steel bars of my cell door. "No. He's not. He's special. He's like my... my...."

"Boyfriend?"

"What? No!"

I've heard People talking that way about each other. Tricia and Steven always have some gossip to share about one of their girlfriends or boyfriends. Steven is living with some girl he always complains about, and Tricia gets a new boyfriend nearly every weekend. The things they talk about make my skin crawl. It's disgusting, the way they carry on. I never want to have a boyfriend if it means acting like them.

"Then a brother, maybe?"

I turn my head slightly in his direction.

"Yes. Yes, that's it. A brother."

CCs don't have brothers or sisters—at least, none that we will ever know about. And we don't have boyfriends or girlfriends. It's strictly forbidden... although sometimes I get the feeling that Ravish and Luster have something going. Once or twice I even hoped Ravish might look at me the way he looks at her. He never did.

Of course, such things are never openly discussed.

"So tell me more about why they treated you differently, Galaxy," Rocket says. "Are you special somehow? Maybe a Technic or a Wit? A Gape? I hear they're pretty special. I've only seen pictures, but...."

"No, I'm not a Gape. I'm nothing. I'm not special at all."

"A Natural, then."

"Yes."

"Then why....?"

"I don't know," I sigh, and move my head to stare at the gray ceiling. I find a dark stain spreading from a tiny crack, evidence of an old leak. "It was Absalom's doing."

"The Absalom?"

"Yes. I was his... his...." I don't like the word I'm about to use, but it's the only one that fits, "his pet."

XIV

Hours pass before Signet shows the first signs of life. I spend that time leaning against the cell door, lying on the concrete floor, pacing my cell. The whole time, Rocket engages me in conversation. I've never talked to anyone for this long—not even Needle. But I like it. It helps pass the time.

I tell him about my childhood—the earliest days I remember spent in the CC Childcare Center, days interrupted by medical treatments and illness, Absalom giving me anything I asked for—but me being too afraid to ask most of the time. I tell him about Needle and how he gets on my case for being late to class all the time, nags me to get my injections, and makes me feel... needed... known. I tell him about the other CCs— what little I know of them. Gauntlet's huge body and big heart. Decoy's amazing ability to become a giant polar bear. Smudge's smiling face when he hands me a plate of the best the cafeteria has to offer. The other CCs' jealousy.

Eventually, I realize I'm doing all the talking.

"What was life like at CC Tech?" I ask.

"It was very business-like," he says. "But we CCs managed to make friends anyway." From the sound of his voice, I believe he's smiling as he says this.

"I bet you were like Needle—always surrounded by friends," I say, certain I am right.

"Oh, I don't know.... Needle sounds like a pretty special guy. I hope I can meet him someday...."

I allow myself a chuckle, imagining him staring at a sleeping Needle. I imagine Rocket as a tall, good-looking blond boy about my age. Or maybe he has creamy black skin like Gauntlet. That would be nice, too. But he probably looks a little bit like Ravish... with perfect features, soft green eyes, a strong body....

Rocket laughs, encouraged by my response. "I'm kidding. It won't be long now. I'd give them another hour or two and they'll start to come around. Just in time for dinner."

"Dinner?"

"Yes, you hungry?"

"Um...." I feel that I shouldn't be hungry, given how horrible our situation is... but I am. I realize I haven't eaten all day, and the mention of food puts a knot in my stomach.

"Me, too," he fills in for me. "But, don't get your hopes up. You're not going to get any of your chicken chi-mangas—whatever those are— in here, I can guarantee.... But, let's see. Where were we? Oh, yes! Friends. I suppose I have lots of friends. Of course, the best news is that none of them are in here."

"Then, why are you?" I ask.

He sighs out a groan of sorts. "Well, I'm not supposed to be telling anyone. But given our current situation.... I guess it would be okay. Of course, I should warn you. It's a long story."

"Good," I say. I want our conversation to keep going. I can't see Rocket, but I like him. He's making me forget my surroundings, the horrible events of the last two days, my fears. He's keeping me from being alone.

He chuckles. "Well, it all started the day I was conceived...."

"What?"

He laughs at me. "Just kidding! It all started about three months ago."

I smile.

"Well, I was in the Technic Development Laboratories, and—"

"Wait," I say, interrupting. "You've not told me. Are you a Technic?"

"Uh... sort-of."

"What do you mean?"

"Well, I don't fit easily into one class."

"Neither does Needle. ...So, what are you then?"

"I guess I'd be considered a Warrior... and a Technic."

"I thought that was illegal."

"I'm not sure. I only know I'm the only one like me they ever made. Anyway, like I said, I was in the Technic Development Center and Sprig was there, causing trouble like she usually does, and—"

"Who's Sprig?" I ask, interrupting again.

"Keep your suit on, I'm getting to that," he says, chiding me for my bad manners.

"Sorry."

He laughs. "Sprig is a beautiful girl with soft blond hair and clear blue eyes. She has an infectious laugh and she likes to hold my hand whenever we're together. She especially likes it when I hold her and let her kiss me. I'm telling you, this girl can't get enough of me. She's always following me around, wanting me to spend time with her, talk to her, help her with something or other...."

"So... I guess you have a girlfriend, then," I say. The words put a sour feeling in my gut and a knot in my chest.

"Please, Galaxy," he says, "don't be gross. Sprig is only three years old."

I laugh, trying to hide the relief in my voice. The sick feeling leaves. Rocket laughs, too. He's toying with me, I know, but I like the attention.

"So what happened, then?" I ask. "In the Tech Lab?"

"Sprig was in there. The lab techs began working on her." His voice changes as he tells this part. His words come more slowly. He's not laughing anymore. "She was crying and then... screaming. They were hurting her. I had been working in the storage room, organizing it for the head technician. I came out of the room and saw them standing over her. One of them had a knife. She was scared. I don't know what came over me. I just... I just snapped. I... I shot the technician holding the knife in the left shoulder. The others turned on me. I shot another one in the leg before they tackled me to the ground. One of them raised his fist over my head. He was holding something—I'm not sure what. ...And then lights out. The next thing I remember I was here in this cell. I've been here for three months."

"I thought you said it was going to be a long story," I said, trying to lighten the mood for him as he had done for me.

I hear a humorless chuckle.

"I'm sorry," I say. "I'm sorry that happened."

"Well, I guess I know a little something of what it's like to have a sister. I bet Needle feels the same way about you... And, I tried, right? Stood up to them, for once. Same goes for you, from what the guards have been saying. You had the courage to try."

"Not me... not really. I just got caught in the middle. Needle's the one who tried to help. And the Gapes and the Wits. The Warriors... and Decoy—they were amazing."

"Hey, it's better to go down fighting, right?"

"Maybe... except I might've saved him. I might've saved Needle, if only—" I grab the back of my neck, remembering the necklace. My one bargaining chip. "Oh, no! It's gone!"

I frantically feel the back of my neck and all down my suit, just in case it slipped inside. But I don't see or feel anything. It's gone! Absalom's necklace is gone! The conversation from the hospital bed begins to come back to me. Something about Ms. Sabeen getting what she wanted. No need to evaluate me for any abilities. She already knew I had none. She just wanted the necklace—and she got it!

"What's gone?" Rocket asks.

"Oh, no, oh, no!"

"What is it, Galaxy?"

"She took it! She took the necklace—the one Absalom gave me!"

"Was it valuable?"

"No... I don't know. I just know that Absalom wanted me to have it, and Ms. Sabeen took it!"

"How do you know it was her? Any number of doctors may have looked at you while you were uncon—"

"I know it was her! She wanted it. She told me that if I gave it to her she'd spare my life. My life and Needle's. I even overheard the doctors talking about it, but now—" My voice breaks.

"Galaxy, you can't expect to keep anything from them. In the end, they take whatever they want."

"I know, but I should've hidden it better... tried harder.... Maybe, if I had it now, she might let us go."

He laughs at that.

"No, Galaxy. She would never let you go."

"I don't mean that we'd be free—just that we could have gone back to our lives at AI and—"

"That would never happen, Galaxy, can't you see that? People can't be trusted when it comes to what they say to a CC. Not ever. If they believe they don't owe us life, do you think they believe they owe us the truth? They hold all the chips, Galaxy! You can't bargain with someone who holds all the chips!"

"But, but...."

"Look... I'm sorry you're in here. I'm sorry she took your necklace. But you can't blame yourself for any of it. You were never in control. She was. There was nothing you could've done."

"Where are we?" Signet says as she regains consciousness and sees me.

"I don't know," I tell her, "some U.S.E.C. jail, I think."

At first I had thought we were still on AI property, but Rocket has assured me otherwise.

"We've got to get out of here," she says, standing.

She manages to rid herself of the dizzy feeling much more swiftly than I had. She walks over to the cell door and shakes it. Then she fiddles with the lock with no success. Next she attacks the box surrounding the security camera—something I can't even reach. But, as I feared, the box cannot be broken, not even by a girl with her superior strength. Finally, she gives up with a growl of frustration.

Banging her fists on the plexiglass in front of the camera, she yells at it, "Let me out of here! Let me go! You can't keep me here!"

I sink lower into the corner of the room, trying to stay out of her way.

"Uh, yeah, they can," Rocket says from the safety of his cell.

"Who said that?" Signet yells, marching to the cell door again and trying to peer down the hall in Rocket's direction.

"Name's Rocket. Nice to meet you, Signet."

"How do you know my name? Did you put me in here?"

"Of course, not," Rocket says, unperturbed by the force of her rage. "I'm a prisoner like you. I've been here for three months. I admit I'm glad for the company, but I'm sorry you're stuck here. This is not a good place."

Signet spots Allure, still lying unconscious.

"Hey, Allure! Wake up!" she orders. "Allure! Wake up, now!"

To my surprise, I think I see Allure move, but she's far from conscious.

"You!" Signet says, turning to me. "Who else is in here?"

"I don't know," I say. "Luster is in there with Allure and Needle is in with Rocket, but other than that, I don't—"

Signet lets out a hard, mocking chuckle of frustration. "What good are you, Galaxy? What good have you ever been to anyone but yourself? I despise you, you know that?"

"Hey, whoa!" Rocket says from the adjoining cell, but Signet ignores him.

She's coming closer, face contorted in rage, eyes blazing. I can't back up any more. I'm already up against the wall as far as I can go.

"You never thought about anyone but yourself! And now you can't even tell me where the other Warriors are! Why did I have to get stuck in here with you? If Gauntlet or Gash or nearly *anyone else* were here with me, we might be able to bust out of here!"

She's right in my face now, fists clenched. One blow would be the end of me. I close my eyes and put my arms over my head. I expect an attack any second.

"You make me sick!" she says.

I hear steps moving away. She's returned to the door. I try to catch my breath.

"Gauntlet, you there?" She cries. "Gauntlet!"

"Signet, is that you?"

It's Gauntlet! He's awake and he's here! His voice comes from somewhere beyond Rocket's cell.

"It's me! I'm here!" Signet cries, genuine joy on her face. "Who's in there with you? Another Warrior?"

"Uh... no...." Gauntlet's voice sounds groggy. He's still a little disoriented from the drugs. "It's one of the Gapes. I don't know his name. He's still asleep."

Signet swears under her breath and mutters to herself. "They did this on purpose! Separated us! They knew if they put two Warriors together that they wouldn't be able to hold us!"

"Gauntlet, who is across from you?"

"Uh... it's Trinket and Siren. They're out. Oh, and Trinket's left hand is missing."

"You, Rocket," Signet says. "Who's in the cell in front of you? Describe them to me."

Why didn't I think of asking him that?

"Uh... okay. A big guy and a little guy. The little guy has funny skin."

"What do you mean 'funny?'"

"Well... it's like his skin is reflective or something. It just looks weird."

"Abracadabra," Signet says, more to herself than anyone. "I thought he might've been able to hide. I guess not. Those tranquilizer balls must work on infrared." She turns her attention back to Rocket. "Describe the big guy. Is he white or black?"

"White. His legs are all bandaged up."

"Padlock!" She cries. "Wake up! Padlock!"

After several minutes of Signet screaming at everyone, we start to get some responses. The Warriors wake first. Then the Technics and Wits, followed by the Naturals and the rest of the classes. The Gapes wake last.

I listen to the different reactions as the other CCs wake up. The Warriors talk of nothing but escape, drawing some of the Technics into their dialogs about possible wall-thickness and lock mechanisms. The Pristines weep and commiserate with one another, but are resigned to inevitability of their fate. The Wits and Gapes say very little, reminding us from time to time of the presence of the surveillance equipment and that any plan we make now will fail.

But not everyone is here. Badge and Lumina and Bandy, for example, aren't among us. Neither are Granite, or Ravish, or Decoy. There must be another holding cell somewhere else. Perhaps nearby, in a room next to ours, or they might be in another part of the U.S.E.C. compound or in another facility altogether.

When I hear Needle making the first noises of consciousness, I dare to creep from my corner to the door of our cell. Signet has taken up a place on the floor several feet away, but glares at me as I move.

"I think your friend is coming around," Rocket tells me.

"Needle? Are you okay?"

"Galaxy, is that you?"

"Yes, it's me! How are you? Are you hurt?"

"My arm… it's gone. They've taken my arm!"

"But are you hurt, Needle?"

"Uh… no… no, I don't think so."

"He's fine, Galaxy," Rocket says. "See, I told you."

Needle has a lot of questions and I try to answer them the best I can, but like Signet said, I'm pretty worthless. I know very little. Rocket ends up explaining most of our situation for me. After a while, we sink into silence.

A good deal more AI CCs than I know personally are here among us, putting in their comments and sharing their woes. I prefer to stay out of it, keeping to my corner and avoiding eye contact with Signet. It's been a while since I've heard from Rocket. He stopped talking to me shortly after Luster woke up and stepped up to the iron bars of her cage where he would be able to see her.

Figures.

What I was thinking trying to wake Signet up earlier? It was so much nicer when everyone was unconscious.

I close my eyes and lean my head against the cement wall. It's so uncomfortable here! What I wouldn't give to have my bed right now.

Five days. Five long days in tiny cement cells. They feed us twice a day—and it's never enough—but I've started giving Signet some of my food. It's well-known that Warriors require more sustenance than the rest of us. I begin to wonder if that's the real reason they've mixed us up—making sure to put a Warrior in nearly every cell.

The lack of food is bad enough, but by the third day the hunger pains are nothing compared to the stench. None of us has bathed and our toilet buckets haven't been emptied yet. I assume they'll only come for them when they're full.

Of course, it's hard to decide what's worse—the smell or the aches in my muscles and joints. Trying to find a comfortable sleeping position on a damp concrete floor is impossible.

I often see Signet rubbing her hips and arms. She is much heavier than I and sleeps on her side. She is probably covered in welts under that AI suit of hers. Each morning, I, too, feel like I've been beaten with an iron rod. None of us slept at all the first night—except for Rocket, of course. He says we'll get used to the hard ground in time. But by the fifth night, I'm sure he's making things up.

It's late—at least, the lights have been off for several hours, and I'm so sore from lying on the ground that I can't sleep. I sit up on my only slightly less sore, meatless butt cheeks and lean my aching back against the cement wall. I can only stay there for a minute or so, and then I have to stand to give my body a break from hard surfaces. But I'm so tired I decide to brace myself against the bars.

"Galaxy." I hear my name whispered from Needle and Rocket's cell. I'm not sure who it is until he speaks again. "Is that you, Galaxy?"

"It's me," I whisper back.

"Can't sleep again?" Rocket asks.

His voice is close, but I have yet to glimpse the boy who belongs to it. We've not had any private conversations since that first day. I've overheard him talking to the other CCs, though. Needle, Gauntlet, even Signet... but mostly to Luster. She's so beautiful and her distress is like a beacon to all decent human beings everywhere—CC and Person alike—especially to the male variety. It's not like I can blame him.

"No," I say, trying to suppress a groan of exhaustion. "Why aren't you sleeping?"

"I don't know. I guess I'm not used to having so many roommates." He gives a brief chuckle.

"Me either, actually."

"Missing your crystal palace?" If anyone else had said it, I would've thought they were trying to rile me. But not Rocket.

"I'm just missing my bed right now." I yawn. "I'm trying to take my mind off of it, though. I doubt I'll ever see it again."

"Then tell me something."

"What?" I ask.

"Tell me something about you."

XV

A loud clank at the far end of the passageway quiets all the voices at once. Someone is coming—no, several People are coming. I hear a noise like wheels on stone. It's the dinner cart. Our one meal is here at last! I'm so hungry. My suit, once skin tight, hangs on me around the waist and thighs. Signet, at first full of fight and fire, after six days with nearly nothing to eat, usually just sits on the ground, leaning against the wall. But she's not as weak as she appears. AI Warriors are conditioned for this sort of thing. She's just biding her time, waiting for them to get sloppy, conserving her energy. And she considers dinnertime her best opportunity to escape.

They stop at the first cell.

"Dinner!" a man's voice echoes down the hall. Metal slides across concrete—a metal plate being slid under a cell door. They keep coming, stopping every six feet or so to serve the next set of prisoners. After sliding Rocket and Needle their food, they find Signet up against the bars, glaring at them.

"Back up!" one of the men orders. The guards wear different uniforms than the U.S.E.C. Special Forces. Theirs are white with a blue belt and blue stripes on the sides of the slacks. Blue strips of cloth cover the shoulders and cuffs, too. An insignia with the U.S.E.C. Military Police symbol decorates the left breast. These aren't regular guards—more highly trained than that—but they're a step down from the soldiers we fought—I mean, the other CCs fought—at AI Tower. "Back up, now!"

Signet refuses. She's waiting for them to get close enough so she can grab them, but they are ready for her. One of the guards grabs a metal stick from his belt and taps her shoulder with it. Immediately she is thrown to the ground in a convulsion, agony marring her otherwise reasonably attractive face. Foam appears at the corners of her mouth as she writhes in pain. She makes a choking, gagging sound.

"No, no!" I cry, but am powerless to help her.

"You just never learn, do you?" The shorter guard says. This same scenario happens every night. And Signet isn't the only one who gets tagged by their electric shock sticks. Several of the Warriors and a few of the Technics have buckled under its force.

One of the guards—a dark-skinned, barrel-chested, bald man—opens our cell door using some kind of magnetic strip in his sleeve.

Why is he opening the door? They never come in the cells. What is he going to do to her?

"No, leave her alone, please!"

He smirks. "I'm not here for her."

He crosses to me, stepping over her body, and grabs me by both arms, lifting me from the cell floor. I flail my legs but am powerless against him. He deposits me in the hallway where another guard slaps handcuffs on my right wrist, wrenches my arms painfully behind my back, and attaches the remaining cuffs to my other wrist.

"Where are you taking her?" Needle demands from his cell. He's at the door, his one hand gripping a steel bar.

"She has an appointment to keep," the bald guard answers him.

As they drag me past the food cart back the way they came, I get my first glimpse of Rocket. I see a pale, gaunt-looking boy with black hair. A quarter of his face is covered by an implant bearing a cybernetic right eye. His thighs end in metal fixings, marking the place where legs should be. And I can't be sure, but he might be missing an arm, too.

The guards take me to a conference room. A long, single table occupies the center of the room surrounded by cushioned chairs on wheels. There are no windows from which I might be able to gauge my location, only white, paneled walls bearing a few pictures in black and white of U.S.E.C.-owned properties. This place is lifeless, dull, sterile. It suits Ms. Sabeen perfectly.

"Just put her there."

The guards set me down in a chair. One of them uncuffs my left hand only to secure my right hand to the chair armrest. I'm not going anywhere without taking the chair with me. But, finally getting to sit in a chair is a lot more comfortable than the concrete floor of my cell.

Ms. Sabeen dismisses the guards. They close the door behind them, leaving me alone with her. She stares at me, unblinking. I almost wish they would come back.

She approaches from the far end of the room, wearing her usual, tight mini-skirt suit. She moves slowly, eyes never leaving my face. When she gets within only a few feet of me, she stops and reaches into her pocket. Ms. Sabeen slowly draws her hand back out. At first I see only a chain suspended between her fingers. Then out comes my pendant.

She leans down, and lets the metal, gold and silver triangle dangle in front of me. I do have one free hand, but it would do no good to try to rip it out of her claw-like fingers.

"Remember this?" she says, eyes hard. "You said you'd never seen it. But guess where it was found. On you, Galaxy. You lied to me. You had it all along."

She straightens and moves behind my chair out of my line of vision, high-heels ticking on hardwood.

"Remember what I said would happen to you if I discovered you were lying to me? I said you would regret it."

My heart thumps in my chest, hatred and fear rising in me. I wonder what she might do that could be worse than putting me in an incinerator. I don't like the images that come into my mind. People are nothing if not creative.

"But, I might be willing to give you another chance—even now, Galaxy," Ms. Sabeen continues, her voice coming from above and behind me. "If you're finally willing to cooperate, I still have the power to return you to AI. You would like that, wouldn't you?"

Yes!

"Needle, too," she says. "I might even be willing to spare some of the others...."

She's saying exactly what I want to hear... but there's something about her voice.... It's smooth, slippery. She's trying to bait me. But, why? What does she want?

"And I see you've made a new friend since you've been with us," Ms. Sabeen continues. "Rocket, right? Too bad about him, though.... He's scheduled for incineration tomorrow."

Oh, no! No!

"But, if you help me with this little problem I have, I might be able to pull some strings...."

"What problem? What can I do? I'll do anything!"

"Oh, it's not much. Not much at all." Ms. Sabeen moves around my chair and again takes up her position, standing in front of me, eyes leveled on mine. "Just tell me what you know about the necklace, Galaxy. And, if what you say helps me, I'll let you and your friends live. That's simple enough, right?"

"But I... I don't know anything about it. I'd never seen it before that night—the night Absalom was killed. I don't even know why he gave it to me. He-he just handed it to me as he was dying and said I should take it.... That's all I know."

Her eyes have grown harder.

It's not working! I haven't told her enough! She's not going to save us! She's going to send us all to the incineration chamber! Me. Needle. Rocket....

Ms. Sabeen clicks over to the doors to my left and opens one.

"Come in. You can return her to her cell."

No! I feel panicky. Desperate. I have to think! *Think, Galaxy!* And then I remember something.

"Wait!" I cry.

Ms. Sabeen turns her head to me and then waves the guard back and closes the door.

"I remember something Absalom said... about the necklace," I tell her, nearly choking on my words.

"Well?" She walks back toward me.

"One of six," I say.

"What? What is that supposed to mean?"

"It's what he said about the necklace when he gave it to me... that it's one of six."

She just stands there staring at me. Oh, no! It's not enough. That's all I know and it's not enough.

But as I watch, her eyes move away from me and she straightens up a little taller. She lifts the pendant and examines it closely, turning it over in her hands, and I watch the slow spread of realization crossing her features.

"One of... six...." she mutters, no longer talking to me. "Absalom was one of the original six.... Six U.S.E.C. members, six pendants. And here," she moves a thumb over the edges of two of the triangle's sides. "...nodes."

"Absalom was a U.S.E.C. member?" I ask.

She looks at me as if she has just remembered I'm still here. "No, you stupid girl!" She laughs. "The Absalom you knew was never on U.S.E.C.! I'm talking about the first Absalom—Absalom's grandfather—the one who founded Absalom Industries nearly a hundred years ago. This was his pendant, I'm certain of it! They were all supposed to be destroyed, but here it is...." She holds it up and looks at it like a woman might look at a diamond. "He must've hidden it and passed it on to his son, who passed it on to Absalom, the third."

"But U.S.E.C. has ten members, not six," I say, still not understanding.

She shoots me a piercing, penetrating look, and I realize speaking was a mistake.

"U.S.E.C. has ten members now—you ignorant CC—but the original commission only had six members. Six members, six pendants." She looks me up and down with disgust and then returns her gaze to the pendant. "And this is the last one…. No wonder he wants it so badly…."

An uncomfortable moment passes as I watch her gaze at the necklace and examine its odd gold-against-silver design, the nodes on the back, and the nodes she discovered on the edges.

"Ms. Sabeen…" I venture to speak, knowing this is my only chance to rescue my friends. "Is that what you wanted to know?"

"What?" She looks at me, seeming to have again forgotten I'm in the room with her.

"Is that enough? The information I gave you. Is it what you wanted?"

She smiles. "Yes, Galaxy. It's perfect. You have helped me a great deal."

I sigh in relief, and even allow myself a small, hopeful smile.

"Then, when will we be going back?"

"Back where?"

"To AI? The other CCs and I—and Rocket—when will they take us back? Today?"

Ms. Sabeen slips my pendant back into her pocket.

"Oh, very soon," she says. She straightens and yells, "Guards!"

I land on the hard concrete floor of my cell with a thud, scraping up the palms of my hands. The guard slams the door shut again quickly, keeping a sharp eye on Signet who watches like a tiger from her position against the back wall where they ordered her to stay.

Something doesn't feel right about the way they're treating me. Ms. Sabeen said she'd let us go back to AI. Why am I back in a cell?

"Well," Signet asks. "What did they do to you?"

"Nothing," I say, pushing myself up to a seated position and examining my hands.

"They wanted something. What was it?" she demands, getting up to stand over me.

"They already have what they want," I say, not looking at her. "They just wanted to find out what I know about it."

"Galaxy, be straight with me! What are you talking about? What did you tell them?"

"She said she'd let us go," I say, standing up and facing her, but keeping as much distance between us as I can in our small cell.

"What?"

"What did you say, Galaxy?" It's Luster. She's at her cell door, copper hair and shimmery skin only slightly less gorgeous for her having been caged like an animal for a week. But she's lost some weight, just like the rest of us.

Allure comes up behind her. Alone any one of them is stunning. Together they utterly fascinate. AI is an expert in all areas of CC development, but it's their Pristines that are the real gems in the crown. I can only imagine what Rocket must be thinking right now, as he again has a full view of them.

"Galaxy, are we getting out of here?" Allure practically pushes Luster aside in her attempt to get closer to me, her white-knuckled fists gripping iron bars.

"That's what Ms. Sabeen said, but...."

"We're getting out! We're going home!" Allure is ecstatic. She and Luster are practically jumping up and down.

"Galaxy," it's Needle's voice. "What happened?"

"Yes, tell us everything," Signet says. She's too close. And she smells. Of course, I dare not say so.

Several of the other CCs who are in earshot chime in and urge me to explain.

"The guards took me to see Ms. Sabeen. She has something of mine—I mean, something of Absalom's." CCs don't own anything. I have to be careful of the way I speak around them. "It was a necklace—a triangular pendant on a chain."

"What does that have to do with anything?" Signet demands, clenching her right fist.

"Just give her a chance to explain," Needle says, and she shuts up and backs off a couple of paces.

I will never understand how he does that!

"She had asked me for it before," I say and then falter. I shouldn't have said that. If they find out I could've given it to her before and saved them all, they'll hate me! I might've prevented Spur's death! But I didn't. I didn't want Ms. Sabeen to have the satisfaction of owning something Absalom had given to me.

"Keep going," Needle urges. His voice is gentle. Like Rocket's.

"Just before Absalom died he gave me a necklace. He just told me to take it and that it was one of six."

"One of six?" Needle asks. From the sound of his voice, he must be close to the bars of his cell.

"Yes. I didn't know what it meant either. In fact, I almost forgot he said it. I had it on me when we were knocked unconscious. Ms. Sabeen has it now. She asked me if I knew anything about it. She said that, if I could tell her what the pendant did, she'd let me go—she'd let us all go, even Rocket. She said she'd send us back to AI."

"What does the pendant do?" Needle asked.

"I don't know. But I guess it's worth something," I say. "When I told her what Absalom said about it—that it was one of six—that meant something to her. She said Absalom the first—our Superior's grandfather, the one who started Absalom Industries—was one of the founding members of U.S.E.C. and that back then there were only six members. For some reason, they each had a triangular pendant like the one Ms. Sabeen took from me, but they were supposed to have been destroyed a long time ago. Apparently, Absalom the first, instead of destroying his like he was supposed to, passed it on to his son, who passed it on to our Superior."

I take a breath. Signet hasn't taken her eyes off of me since I started talking, and the rest of the cell block has gone still.

"But what would Ms. Sabeen want with it now?" Needle asks. "And why would she promise to let us go just for some information about it?"

"I… I don't think Ms. Sabeen knew anything about the pendant until recently and, even now she knows very little. I think someone else asked her to get it for them, but she wants to know what she's handing over first."

"Who?" Signet asks. "Who asked her to get it?"

"I don't know… but she said, 'no wonder he wants it so badly.'"

"But when are they going to let us out?" It's Luster. She's still at her cage door, jockeying for space with Allure, eyes trained on me.

"I don't—"

"They're not!" It's Rocket. "Can't you see? She was lying. You are never going back to AI! Why else would they have thrown Galaxy back in here?"

"But… but maybe, maybe they just put her here to get the transports ready," Luster insists.

Rocket laughs. There is no humor in the sound he makes.

"Look, you!" Now Luster is angry. "Stop being such a downer! Galaxy is at least trying to get us released! You should be grateful. She said she even bargained to get you out of here! And you're not even one of us!"

"Oh, I would be grateful, except that I told her not to bargain with them! It's a waste of time, and now they have what they wanted! Information about a necklace that, apparently, has quite a lot of value to them!"

What? He's mad at me? How can he be mad at me when I just tried to save his life?

"Hey, she was just trying to help," Needle says.

"Help?" Rocket is livid. "She just ended all of your lives! Now there's no reason to keep any of you!"

XVI

"I'm sorry."

I open my eyes. Someone is whispering.

"Galaxy… I'm sorry."

It's Rocket. Once again everyone else is asleep, or nearly so. But I have nothing to say to him. Nothing matters anymore. Not him. Not the pendant. Not even our freedom—assuming there's any possibility of it. I put an arm over my ear to block out the sound of his voice.

But he doesn't stop. He keeps pestering me. Apologizing. Pleading with me to answer.

I start to feel bad.

Rocket has been here longer than anyone. He has more right than any of us to flip out. Besides that, he's probably right about Ms. Sabeen. About my foolishness to trust her. And if it wasn't for him, I wouldn't have made it through that first day.

I sit up and scoot over to the cell door.

"I'm here," I say.

"I'm sorry, Galaxy, really. I don't know what I was thinking to attack you like that. It wasn't fair."

"Don't worry about it," I tell him, leaning my head against hard steel. "After all… you're probably right. We may never get out of here now."

"We wouldn't have anyway," he says, "whether you told her or not."

I sigh. I'm so tired, but sleep continues to elude me.

"Are we still friends?" he asks.

I raise my head.

Friends. Are we friends? CCs aren't supposed to have friends. But I'm far beyond worrying what a CC is supposed to do and not supposed to do.

"Of course. Friends."

He's silent for a moment and then says, "Thanks, by the way."

"Thanks? For what?"

"For asking for my life to be spared. No matter what happens. Thanks for that."

I close my eyes. I can feel a lump rising in my throat.

"Galaxy?" he says. "You still there?"

"Yes," I mutter, my voice catching.

"What's the matter?"

"It's just that... that...." I can't continue.

"What is it?"

"It's just... if you're right, then...."

"What, Galaxy? Just spit it out."

"Then tonight is your last night in this cell," I say, forcing the words out in rapid succession. "You're scheduled to be incinerated in the morning."

I bury my face in my arms and hug my knees to my chest. Rocket says nothing. The night returns to silence, interrupted only by an uncomfortable groan of one of the CCs rolling over in their sleep, searching without success for a more comfortable position.

And then Rocket chuckles.

I lift my head. He chuckles again.

"Well, then," he says. "I'm finally getting out of here, after all. It's about time."

I know it's morning when the lights in the corridor between the rows of cells come on. I push myself up from my back using bruised muscles.

Today's the day. Today's the day we'll find out the truth. Either Ms. Sabeen will honor her promise to me or she won't. If they come for Rocket, she was lying. And if she was lying, we'll be next.

My stomach makes a weird noise. I must be hungry. I let Signet have my meal last night. I was too upset to eat, and food has lost its comforting qualities. Plus, if Ms. Sabeen was lying to me, Signet is my best chance of escape. She needs to keep her strength up.

I scoot across the floor and lean against the cement wall. I don't feel well. I don't feel well at all. I've been noticing a change in my constitution over the last few days—a weak, sick feeling that comes and goes. Of course, no one has felt particularly well since we got thrown in here, so I knew better than to complain. But this morning I feel particularly nauseous, spent. My head aches. It's like the darkness of my cell has closed in on me. The lights in the hallway help, but they're not enough.

Perhaps I'm having a relapse—a return of my childhood illness. Nurse Marlene used to say that if I didn't come in for my regular injections, I could get sick again. I haven't had an injection since the day they killed Absalom. That was over a week ago now.

I don't know how long I sit here, leaning against the cement wall, but I think I must've dozed off again. When I open my eyes Signet is up at the iron bars of our door trying to angle herself to see down the hallway. I hadn't heard her move nor noticed the voices of the other CCs until now, but there had been a noise. A loud metal clank of a door opening.

Footsteps.

I'm instantly wide awake, trying to force myself to my feet. They're coming! They're either coming for all of us or just for Rocket.

Oh, no! They're not stopping at the first cell. If they were coming to set us all free, wouldn't they start at the end of the hallway and work their way down? Wouldn't they just start opening cells and marching us all out?

The footsteps get closer. Signet is blocking my view. They stop outside our cell. Outside Rocket's cell.

"Move back!" the guard says. "Move now!"

Is he talking to Needle?

Signet shifts and then moves, revealing our regular guards just beyond her, standing in the corridor. The bald guard has his electric shock stick pointed at her. She steps back.

"Up against the back wall! You know the position!"

She moves back further. He unlocks our door and moves inside.

"What's going on?" I ask him. "Does Ms. Sabeen want to see me again?"

"I see a week in prison hasn't cured her of her insolence yet," the other guard says. "That's what you get when you spoil a CC!"

One guard keeps a close eye on Signet, holding his weapon toward her while the other enters and grabs me by the wrist.

"Leave her alone!" Signet yells. She moves toward me, but the guard hits her with the electric shock end of his weapon and drops her to the ground convulsing.

"No, please!" I cry as I'm dragged from the cell.

They're taking me a different direction this time. They carry me past door after door and I realize I'm passing other rows of cell blocks, just like ours. No doubt the other AI CCs are in there, waiting to discover their fate.

"Where are you taking me?" I gasp.

"Shut up!" the short guard says and jerks my arm so hard it feels like he's pulled a muscle. I cry out in pain.

We pass out of the building and toward a smaller version of the white transport vehicles I saw at AI. I look up into the bright morning sun. This is the first I've seen of the sky since my last night at AI Tower. They strap me into a seat, locking me in. The driver starts the vehicle and we move from the alley into the main compound. I see the U.S.E.C. symbol everywhere. Lots of austere, cinder-block buildings, few trees.

Perhaps Ms. Sabeen thinks I know more about the necklace. Perhaps she wants to meet with me again. Or, maybe, they're taking me back to AI Tower. Just me....

"Stop! I want Needle!" I cry, trying to force the seatbelt mechanism to release. "Go back!"

The bald guard, now seated in the front passenger seat, turns around and points his electric shock stick at me.

"I said, shut up!"

He pushes a button on the baton and blue electricity, highlighted with red and white sparks, begins to flow between the nodes decorating the end of the stick.

I press myself back against my seat, turning my face away and trying to distance myself from the buzzing, snapping tip. I haven't been hit with one of these weapons yet, but judging from what it did to Signet, I doubt I'd survive.

The guard turns back around. I begin to whimper.

Needle! Needle!

I lean toward the thick glass windows, put one hand on the pane, and watch as we leave the prison building where Needle, Rocket, and the others are still trapped. We make our way onto a road that cuts through the center of the complex. It is peppered with military vehicles and shiny, black cars. We pass a line of large, white transport vehicles heading back the way we came.

At first we move directly toward a large, white building at the center of the compound along a wide, main road. As we draw toward it, we pass several smaller, less impressive structures, and I begin to recognize my surroundings. I have often overlooked this complex from my spire room at Absalom Industries. It is a hexagon-shaped compound with the main U.S.E.C. command center in the middle and six, equidistant roads moving away from the center toward the streets beyond the compound, cutting the hexagon into six equal, triangular sections.

Leaning closer to the window, I catch a glimpse of AI Tower, just before we pass behind an ugly gray building that blocks it from my sight. A sob catches in my throat.

We draw close to U.S.E.C. Central Command, a tall, white-brick building with four white pillars in the front, offsetting two oversized, two-story high doors. Though I can't see it from this angle, I know that the top of this building proudly displays the U.S.E.C. symbol. I've looked down upon it often from my bedroom.

I expect the drivers to come to a stop here, but they cut to the right and travel parallel to U.S.E.C. Central Command before heading away down another one of the main roads. I lean back and watch buildings pass by my window. Some look like small office buildings. Others appear to be apartment complexes designed for the staff. Some are military barracks or warehouses. I see uniformed or suited People everywhere, getting in and out of official-looking vehicles, moving up and down wide, stone staircases that lead to impersonal, brick buildings, or walking with brisk steps as they talk into the HCS devices in their sleeves.

We pull into a large but nearly empty parking lot and come to an abrupt stop.

We are on the opposite side of Central Command, and I can only make out a wall of white brick and wide windows from where I sit. Soon, the shorter guard opens my door and unlocks my seatbelt. He grabs me again roughly by the arm and pulls me out. The second, bald guard comes around from behind and grabs my other arm.

They lead me around the vehicle, and I get my first glimpse of our destination. I recognize this building immediately. It's the only building on the compound that is not built in squares or rectangles. It is a perfect hexagon, made mostly of glass, with a glass ceiling. Its shape mirrors the shape of the compound itself. But though I've seen it often from above, I have no idea what it is.

Though they continue to pull me forward, I look back over my shoulder and again get a view of AI Tower. As I watch, the morning sun pierces the clouds and strikes the tower so that the entire structure bursts into a beacon of light. I've never seen it in its entirety from this distance nor realized the effect of its design. It is stunning in its beauty and majesty. Like a burning sword rising to the heavens from the center of a mess of jumbled, inferior structures.

Absalom....

It disappears as they pull me inside the hexagonal, U.S.E.C.-owned structure. I go from staring at the brilliant beauty that Absalom managed to create to staring into the black eyes of Ms. Sabeen.

"Welcome, Galaxy," she says. She's excited about something. "I've been looking forward to this day for a very long time."

She stands before me wearing a new, white suit. My necklace dangles from her neck. Suddenly I recognize what the symbol on the pendant is. It's this building. The hexagon on the triangle represents this hexagonal structure which is at the center of a triangular section of the compound—another hexagon. Six triangles make up a hexagon. My necklace was one of six....

It all comes back to this place, to U.S.E.C., to the first Absalom—a founding member of the new government. A committee of geniuses who believed they knew better than the People.

Ms. Sabeen follows my gaze and reaches for the pendant. She slips it inside her blouse, hiding it from sight. She nods at the guards and they release my arms but remain, one on each side of me. Ms. Sabeen turns and indicates that I follow. We walk past a security station and into a hallway. Again I see the compound and AI Tower beyond through a long wall of windows that line the hallway to my left. To the right we pass several closed doors built into white brick.

"Do you know where we are?" Ms. Sabeen asks me as we round an angled corner and proceed down another side of the structure.

"We're on U.S.E.C. grounds," I say.

"Of course, silly child, but do you know what building this is?"

"No. But I've seen it often from The Tower."

Ms. Sabeen glances out toward AI. "Ah, yes, of course you have. Interesting, though, that Absalom never told you what it is. After all, his grandfather built it and he personally remodeled it about ten years ago."

We come to a set of wide, double doors. Four U.S.E.C. Special Forces soldiers stand before it. Captain Gerard Watt, who murdered Absalom, is not among them. They wear the black and dark green uniforms with the U.S.E.C. insignia emblazoned over their hearts. Recognizing Ms. Sabeen, they move aside, and one of them obliges her by activating the security panel to the left of the doors, causing them to slide open.

We move forward down a wide hallway of more white brick and enter a giant room with a glass ceiling. We're in a large, single room at the center of this hexagonal building. But what I see dotting the space confuses me. I'm not sure why, but my throat tightens and my pulse speeds up.

"Now do you know where we are?" she asks. Her voice is smooth, but her eyes dance as she surveys the space. She's nearly giddy with excitement.

"It's... it's...."

I can't breathe. I can't breathe.

The hexagonal room contains a series of rising platforms, each constructed as a hexagon with a small hexagon stage in the middle, directly beneath the center of the wide, crystal ceiling. Six rows of narrow stairs cut from the base to the top, dividing the shape into six equal sections, just as the roads of the U.S.E.C. compound divide it.

Before me, crystal, cylindrical tubes dot each ascending level, not unlike our cylindrical shaped elevators. Only, these aren't elevators, and the material they are made with appears to be alumina-reinforced, like the walls of AI Tower. Vertical strips of a steel-like superalloy and ceramic run around the sides of each cylindrical tube, about two-feet apart. Built into them, facing the inside of the tube, are small jet-like protrusions.

As the platforms rise toward the center, fewer and fewer cylindrical chambers line the levels until they reach a hexagonal platform so small it will only fit one chamber. And that chamber, like all the others, is the perfect size to comfortably fit a single human being.

My breath comes in gasps. I feel constricted, weak, panicky, dizzy. Though the sunlight in this room is brilliant and powerful, darkness passes before my eyes for a moment, threatening me, tempting me to lose consciousness.

"Come on, Galaxy," Ms. Sabeen prompts, relishing each word. "Don't be shy. Tell me what this room is."

I swallow and close my eyes. I take a deep breath.

"It's… It's the incineration chamber."

Ms. Sabeen laughs and claps her hands together in excitement.

"Yes! That's right! And guess what? Today you get to see how it works!"

XVII

I have no time to react. As the words leave Ms. Sabeen's mouth, the guards grab my arms and drag me forward.

"No! No!" I scream but am powerless to stop them. They lift me by the elbows so that my feet only barely brush the ground, no matter how hard I kick or struggle.

"I've reserved the best place for you, Galaxy," Ms. Sabeen says, following. "The place of honor. Isn't that what you're used to?"

"You said you'd let me go! You said you'd let us all go!"

She laughs. "I lied, of course, Galaxy! Did you really think U.S.E.C. would let all of those illegal CCs just go back to AI—like nothing ever happened? After their rebellion? After People died? After Needle broadcasted your little resistance movement all across the nation?"

Needle did that?

"You must be out of your mind!" she continues. "You and all the AI CCs will become the first wave of CCs who help us fulfill U.S.E.C.'s new CC Population Reduction Act. It's the first of June and a decision on it was scheduled for today. The commission met first thing this morning—just as the first rays of the sun touched the horizon. The bill passed unanimously. We must now reduce the CC population in our country by a third... starting with you and your friends."

"No! Please! I'm begging you! I haven't done anything! And I told you everything you wanted to know! I'm no threat to you!"

We're nearly at the top now.

"Galaxy, of course you're no threat! That isn't the point! I have a job to do. A duty to fulfill. You wouldn't understand that—you never have. But today, Galaxy, I'm going to make an example out of you. By giving you the place of honor—and letting all the nation, and ninety-nine of your friends," she gestures to the other incineration chambers, "watch you go first."

The bald, dark-skinned guard opens the door of the center chamber and together both guards shove me inside. They slam the transparent door closed again, trapping me behind glass and locking me in. I bang on the tube and scream for them to let me out, but the sides of my cage don't budge. They don't even shudder beneath the force of my fists.

I search for a way out—anything I might do to open the door—but the inside of the tube bears no handle, no control panel, no weakness of any kind.

Ms. Sabeen turns and leads the way back through the massive crystal room, the guards following behind. They disappear from the room, and for a brief moment, I am alone. But then a series of doors open all along the sides of the hexagonal walls. U.S.E.C. Special Forces soldiers filter in, line the wall, and take up positions along the platforms. Again, Captain Watt is not among them. Once in their assigned positions they stop, stand with feet shoulder-lengths apart, and cross their wrists behind their backs, waiting for further instructions.

I pound on the walls of my cage again and scream at the soldiers, but not one looks my way. It's as if they don't hear me at all. But I know they do, for I clearly heard Ms. Sabeen's laughter as she left, and I remember how Ms. Sabeen described the screams of a CC who was being burned alive. She said the screams could be heard across the compound....

"Let me out! Let me out of here!"

No matter how hard I fight my cage, I succeed at nothing but exhausting myself. Finally, I give up and lean against the curved side, leaning my head back and closing my eyes in defeat.

This is it. This is the end. This is how I will die.

I guess I always knew I might end up in an incineration chamber. It's common practice. Even if I had been allowed to grow old, living out my days at AI Tower, one day they would deem me no longer useful—too old, too weak—and send me here.

We all start off worthless. We all end up worthless.

Of course, I've always been worthless... of no good to anyone... anyone except myself....

I always justified my selfishness by telling myself that I was only a CC anyway and a Natural, at that. No real skills, no exceptional abilities, not even particularly bright. What could I offer? But Needle somehow knew different. Yes, he has unique abilities, but that isn't what makes the other CCs like him... love him. He is kind. Thoughtful. He puts others before himself. I never have.

I'm not sure how much time passes as I stand in my crystal prison. I find myself staring up into the sky, watching the sun moving ever so slowly upward on the horizon, stretching toward the highest heavens.

As I wait for death, I realize something strange, ironic. The illness that had begun to plague me more and more the longer I stayed in that dark cell has finally subsided. The nausea is gone, my headache is ebbing away, the aches in my muscles and bones from days and nights spent on hard concrete are less bothersome. I feel stronger, more alive here standing in the sun than I have in a long time… just in time to face the end.

"Absalom, you were right," I whisper into the sun beams that stream into my crystal prison, lighting up the space in radiance and beauty. "Sometimes it is best to welcome that which is inevitable. It's… it's freeing somehow."

It's nearly noon before the main doors open again. I can tell because the sun is directly overhead and the guards have been fidgeting and sweating for a long time now. Obviously, this procedure is taking far longer than anyone expected.

I turn toward the doors as they open. Captain Gerard Watt enters, followed by a row of U.S.E.C. Special Forces. At the beginning of a line of CCs, Gauntlet enters, bound by three sets of heavy-duty cuffs and surrounded by six guards. By the looks of them, he did not come willingly. Three of them have visible wounds on their faces and a fourth walks with a limp.

Next I see Lumina, then Allure, Bandy, and Decoy. I watch one after another of the AI CCs as they are forced through the double doors and handed over to the U.S.E.C. Special Forces who grab my would-be friends and force them into incineration chambers, one after another.

"Needle!" I cry and he looks my direction as they lead him toward me up the narrow stairs and shove him into a chamber on the level just below mine.

It looks like Ms. Sabeen has reserved a place for him close to me… so he can watch me die, hear my screams, and not be able to do anything about it. And then he will be next.

He stands looking at me, his one hand on the glass as though trying to touch mine. His eyes are saying goodbye. Even he cannot figure a way out of this.

Another chamber nearby remains empty, until Rocket—carried in by soldiers—is dropped into it. Even now he is provided no dignity. Robbed of his legs and an arm, he watches me, horror on what remains of his face.

Though I had managed to calm down somewhat as I waited for the end, now that I see Needle and Rocket, Gauntlet and the others, I begin to feel panicky again. The time is almost here. The chambers are filling up. As soon as the last CC steps into the final incineration chamber, the soldiers will activate mine. Burning plasma will shoot through the many jets that line my cage and I will be burned alive. My hair and clothing will catch fire first. The flesh will melt from my bones. The screams will be cut off in my throat. And Needle, Rocket—all of the AI CCs—in fact, all of the United States, will watch as I burn to death in a nationally televised event.

Now only one chamber stands empty. One of the soldiers at the door motions for the last prisoner to be brought in. This one is not coming quietly. I hear her angry cries before I see her face. And then she is there, struggling, having to be dragged the same way they dragged her from our class.

Miss Abilene!

I'm not the only one surprised to see her. Many of the CCs turn to watch as the soldiers shove her unceremoniously into the final chamber and slam the door closed as she screams obscenities at them.

To be a Person and to be incinerated along with a bunch of CCs must certainly be the lowest form of punishment U.S.E.C. could imagine for her. She must have done far worse than simply doctor a few classroom outlines.

Finally, I watch a line of twenty or so spectators being ushered into the room and shown to a row of seats, followed by a full camera crew bearing high-tech, holographic cameras and several reporters. A hush falls over the room as they enter. Ms. Sabeen is among them looking proud of herself—like a giddy hostess at a fancy ball. Like her, everyone has dressed for the occasion—suits and ties or suit dresses, not a single stray or unruly hair.

As desperation again fills me, I scan the newcomers, hoping I might find at least one friendly face—someone who might take pity on us and have the power to do something about it. After all, the men and women in the suits look important. In fact... the man in the middle actually looks familiar.... Supreme Head Anshar! I recognize him from the times I've seen him speaking with Absalom through the HCS—projected into the space in tiny particles of colored light.

"Supreme Head Anshar!" I cry. "Please! Help us!"

He looks my direction. In fact, everyone looks my direction. The cameramen heft their devices and point them at me. Reporters start babbling about the unusual CC child who dares beg for her life from the very man who ordered her destruction. But I don't care what they say. I don't care what they think about me. This is my last chance—my last chance to use what little influence I have to save Needle, Rocket, and the other CCs.

"You know me, Supreme Head! I belonged to Absalom. He was your friend once! I was special to him! Please! For his sake, don't do this! Save us!"

Anshar rises to his feet and looks at me, intrigued. He's a tall man. Black hair shows only the earliest signs of gray at the temples. Masculine face. Smooth features. Despite how angry he made Absalom, I had often felt Anshar seemed much more reasonable in temperament. More patient and thoughtful. Perhaps he might be more merciful as well.

"Who is this small thing who knows my name?" he asks Ms. Sabeen who now stands at his elbow looking embarrassed.

She leans in and whispers something to him that I can't hear, but the light of recognition spreads across his face as she speaks. He waves her away.

"I remember this child," he says, to the great interest of the reporters and cameramen gathered about. "She was often with Absalom before he died."

"Will you spare her, Supreme Head?" one of the female reporters asks, thrusting a narrow microphone before him.

Ms. Sabeen's eyes have grown wide. Concern that her grand celebration may come to a disappointing end.

"Spare her?" Anshar says. "Why would I do such a thing? It was she who killed Absalom. And the rest of these CCs are known rebels and illegals."

"No! No! You're lying! It wasn't me!"

Anshar is no longer listening. He takes his seat again and motions to a soldier who stands near a control console across the walkway. Red warning lights flash from each of the six corners of the room. A loud beeping accompanies the flashing light, and I feel the ground beneath me shudder.

We all feel it. The furnace has been lit.

I pound on the glass and scream. Anshar looks on, his face hard. Ms. Sabeen is smiling with anticipation. None of them will help me. None of them care.

I turn to Needle. He looks at me, blue eyes wide with terror. He's saying something—screaming my name—but a rush of sound, like wind pushing through pipes, drowns him out. The shuddering from beneath is growing stronger, closer.

The fire is coming!

The jets come alive. A great blast of power hits me from all sides. I am instantly surrounded by light and heat. I try to brace myself, closing my eyes and covering my head. I scream in panic and desperation.

A rush of new sensations fill me. I open my eyes. I am amazed at what I see. I stand in a blaze of fire—fire so thick I can barely see past it to Needle's desperate, pain-filled face as he watches me, Rocket's look of shock.

I'm burning. I'm on fire. But I feel no pain. In fact, it is the most delicious sensation. Like an over-hot shower, I want to crawl inside the burning streams of plasma and soak my entire body.

How can this be happening? How is it that the fire rages about me, but my eyes, my skin, my hair, even my blue corn-flower suit, do not ignite?

I'm glowing!

I bring a hand to my face and see that the fire is not just outside me anymore. It's inside—beneath my skin, moving through my veins like rivers of lava. I'm not just on fire. I am fire!

Is this what Lumina saw in me? Is this the illness Absalom was so desperate to cure? Is this why I dream of chasing through burning rooms, seeking a woman, never finding her, but never myself getting hurt?

Not a singe. Not a welt. Not a single blister.

I throw my head back and let myself absorb the heat and the light and the energy. I have never felt so good! So strong! So powerful! I let the blazing streams flow into me, fill me, cover me. I consume them as a man dying of thirst might consume a drought of fresh water.

"Shut it off! Shut it off now! She's overloading the system!"

I open my eyes to see a commotion of activity. The soldiers are backing away from my chamber. Anshar, Ms. Sabeen, and their elite group of friends are on their feet, looks of horror, shock, and fear on their faces. They fear me.

They should.

XVIII

"Shut it down! Shut it down now!" It's Anshar. He's yelling at the soldier manning the control console.

"I can't! I can't shut it off! She's pulling power!"

The air is clearing up. My chamber no longer contains a cloud of flame. I don't know how, but I'm pulling it into myself too fast for the flames to build up. I can see everyone now. The CCs and Miss Abilene stare at me in amazement. The soldiers and U.S.E.C. personnel stare at me in terror.

People scurry about. Captain Watt tries to assist the man at the console. Most run from the room. A few remain rooted to the ground, mesmerized by fear and fascination.

I hear a loud bang and feel another shudder from somewhere beneath me. Whatever mechanism produced the flaming plasma is no longer putting out. I've taken it all.

I feel as if the power surging through me has transformed me. I am no longer myself. I am no longer human. I am no longer Galaxy. But even as I think these things, Absalom's words return to me. *I dwell in darkness... but you, my Galaxy... you are the light of a billion stars.*

He knew. He knew I was different. He knew everything. In fact....

No! It can't be true.

Absalom, tell me you didn't do this to me!

But I immediately know the truth. I was never sick. I was being altered, transformed, manipulated. Absalom took a child, pretended to care for her, but all the while he was turning her into a weapon—turning me into a weapon.

"No!" I cry out, suddenly feeling great pain—but not from the fire—from the truth.

He did this to me! On purpose! He did this to me!

I can no longer contain my hurt, my loss, and my rage.

With a cry of pure anguish, I force out all the energy I just absorbed. I hear a crash above me. Glass breaking and falling. Screams of terror. Cries of agony.

I let the blaze rage. I take my time with it, relishing the power I've discovered, the outlet for all my pain and loneliness and fear. The screams die away.

But then I hear another voice.

"Galaxy, stop! Galaxy, you have to stop!"

It's Needle. I'd forgotten about him. I'd forgotten about everyone. Only Absalom and my pain occupied my thoughts.

I open my eyes and realize I'm no longer inside my chamber. The walls of the chamber—indeed, most of the building is gone. Only the charred remains of the once white wall and the other chambers remain— chambers designed to withstand a great deal of heat and pressure... but now they, too, have begun to melt, as mine did. Dark clouds of smoke mix with the fire, billow from the earth into the sky.

"Galaxy, you have to stop now! Please!" Needle cries again. He has backed up against the far side of his chamber, as far away from me as he can get, but the flames still burn hot, pouring from my body like fire from the sun.

"I can't stop it!" I cry, rage melting into panic as I realize the overwhelming force of my actions. "I can't stop!"

"You have to! Please. Just calm down! Back it off!"

Calm down! I have to calm down! I have to stop this!

I close my eyes again and try to reverse the direction of the flames once again. I focus on absorbing the energy, pulling it back inside myself.

It's working! The air begins to clear again. The heat and light return to me. Smoke still rises from a few hot-spots, but breezes from the open sky begin to dissipate the black clouds.

I pull my arms in toward my chest, soaking in the energy and willing my heart and breathing to return to normal. My skin, once ablaze, begins to dull. What was once an inferno becomes a river of lava... then a brilliant glow... and then only pink skin.

"You're okay, Galaxy. You're okay," Needle says, no longer shrinking away from me. "It's going to be okay now."

"Galaxy, over here!"

It's a different voice. It comes from behind. I turn to see Gauntlet smiling at me.

"You did it, girl," he says. "You did it! I can't believe it! That's the most amazing thing I've ever seen in my life!"

Like Needle's chamber, Gauntlet's is also nearly melted through. A few more moments and none of the CCs would have made it out alive. But Gauntlet is all smiles. One punch and he has broken through his chamber. It doesn't take long for him to bust open several more, and he and the other Warriors and Technics get to work releasing the rest of the prisoners.

They're safe! They're okay!

Relief floods me as Needle approaches. He looks at me tentatively, like he's not sure if it's safe to come any closer. But I'm so glad to see that he's okay, I move forward to give him a hug. Needle takes a step back, not letting me get close.

"It's okay," I say. "I won't hurt you. I've gone back to normal again."

He reaches his good hand toward me and tentatively taps my outstretched hand. Then, smiling, he rushes to me and hugs me as tight as he can with one arm, his little head on my shoulder. I hug him back. It feels good.

"Man, that was so awesome!" Gauntlet is still freaking out about what just happened. "Girl, you're incredible! Anything you need, you got it, Galaxy! I mean it. Anything."

"That was some trick."

I turn to see Miss Abilene moving toward us on what remains of the stairs—only exposed ceramic now. "I never thought I'd say this, but you've impressed me, Galaxy."

I don't know what to say to that, so I say nothing.

"But we can't stick around here," she continues. "The whole world will know by know what happened. They'll be coming for us."

"They already are," Needle says. "I hear trucks moving this way… and a helicopter."

The ground is littered with the black, charred bodies of soldiers, reporters, and the elite guests who did not make it out in time. I don't know if Anshar or Ms. Sabeen is among them. All the bodies look the same now—crumbling, smoldering figures which are quickly turning to ash.

It takes us a while to figure out what to do. Signet looks at me and asks, "What now?"

Why is she asking me? How should I know?

Even Needle and Gauntlet and the few adult CCs among us are completely without ideas. I look about the group at the sheer number of CCs. If Ms. Sabeen was right about the number of other chambers, we number one hundred in total. But I know there are more of us on this compound. AI has—had—at least a thousand CCs in training at any given time. And some adult CCs lived and worked there, too. Of course, many of the CCs were likely confiscated and reassigned. It's impossible to know how many still remain at the U.S.E.C. prison.

"Come on," Miss Abilene says, taking charge, blond hair spilling haphazardly around her shoulders. "We're going to get back in those transports and get to a safe place!"

"But where will we go?" Signet asks, her former bravado gone.

"I know just the place, but it will take some doing to get there without being followed." Miss Abilene looks around the group. "You are all going to have to use whatever skills you have to help us get out of here. Do you understand?"

We all just stare at her, unblinking.

"Hey! There's no room for hesitation! If you want to survive, you'll do whatever you have to do—kill whoever you have to kill—to get out of this place! If you get caught here, they will kill you! Tell me you understand!"

"We'll do it," Gauntlet says and turns to the others. "We'll do whatever you say, won't we, guys?"

We all nod and a few of them voice their assent.

"Alright," Miss Abilene says. She does not look like a military leader to me, with one fist clenched in front of her, barely reaching beyond her massive bosoms. "Follow me!" But she certainly sounds like one.

Miss Abilene takes off toward the place we came in. The double doors are gone, reduced to smoldering rubble we easily step over. We pass through what remains of the brick wall, avoiding puddles of steaming, melted glass and more blackened bodies—these only slightly less charred than those in the main room. The smell is horrific, overpowering. We choke on it as we run, heading directly toward the transport vehicles. But I stop short, seeing someone I recognize lying face down on the charred ground that had once been a lush lawn of green grass.

Ms. Sabeen.

She must have escaped the main blaze, but even this far away from the building, the heat had been too much. Her once nice clothing is scorched, holes burned into it on her back and arms. Red, ugly blisters cover her once perfect, brown skin. Her smooth black hair, too, has burned. Tiny wisps of smoke still rise from her head. I cover my nose at the smell.

"Come on," Needle says, limping up to me and taking my elbow.

"Wait," I tell him. "She has something of mine. I want it back."

I reach down and find the chain at the back of her neck. Pulling hard, I'm able to wrench it free. The metal of the chain has weakened and breaks. But the pendant, hidden beneath her body, appears to be unaffected.

"OK," I tell Needle, gripping my pendant tightly in my fist. "Let's go."

Several of the transports are inoperable. The tires of those closest to the building have melted into the pavement. I had no idea the blaze I created reached this far. Thankfully, we find four vehicles that still function, and the Wits easily hot-wire them. It will be a tight fit but, now that there are no soldiers taking up room, we should be able to get everyone inside.

As I stand next to Gauntlet and Needle, waiting for my turn to get inside one of the black-scorched vehicles, a helicopter appears above us, zooming toward us from the center of the compound. As soon as the pilot is in range, he opens fire.

"Get down!" Gauntlet yells and pushes me toward the ground near the transport. He covers me with his body.

I hear bullets bouncing off concrete, several cries of pain, screams of terror from young CCs. And then the sound of metal ripping. I manage to peak around Gauntlet's massive arm and see Gash holding a door he just ripped from one of the damaged transport vehicles. With all his strength, he launches it into the sky, just before a bullet rips through his right shoulder.

The door misses the main body of the helicopter, but slams into the spinning blades, causing them to choke and falter. The helicopter tips and begins to spin wildly. We watch as the pilot desperately tries to regain control. The soldier who had been shooting at us can now only hang on for dear life. The helicopter banks right and then left, tipping at an extreme angle before crashing into the pavement. We duck as shrapnel from the crash flies past us.

"There are more coming," Needle yells. "We have to get out of here!"

I slip from beneath Gauntlet's protective embrace. I spot a line of military vehicles heading our direction.

"Come on, we've got to go," I say, touching Gauntlet on the shoulder, but he slumps away from me, groaning. Two ugly red bullet wounds in his upper back dribble blood in lines running down his side. "Gauntlet! Oh, no! Gauntlet!" I cry, drawing Gash's attention.

Gash, ignoring his own bullet wound, runs over and grabs his friend.

"Come on, buddy. I've got you," he says, and hefts the giant teenager, helping him into the vehicle. "You!" he addresses a boy I don't recognize who occupies the seat next to Gauntlet. "Put pressure on these wound—push your fists into them as hard as you can—and keep pressing! Got it?"

The boy nods furiously and complies, having to straddle Gauntlet in order get in the correct position.

Gash turns to me. "He'll be okay. He's strong. We just need to get him and the others out of here."

"But you're wounded, too," I say.

"I am?"

"Your shoulder."

Gash notices the wound then, touching it and looking at the blood on his fingers. "Yeah, that hurts."

"Let's go, let's go, let's go!" Miss Abilene cries, pushing CC kids toward the transports. With her other hand she directs some of the Warriors to help those who have been shot. Three more are down, groaning on the ground. One of them I recognize. Arbor, the Wort girl from the cafeteria. With leaf-covered hands she grips a red-stained place on her upper thigh. Padlock rushes over to her, scoops her up as she cries and disappears with her into one of the vehicles.

"Decoy!" Miss Abilene says, spotting him among a group of huddled kids. "Come here!" Decoy obeys. "And where is Abracadabra?"

Abracadabra appears out of thin air just to her left.

"Oh, there you are. And Fuse, I'm going to need you, too," Miss Abilene calls them over.

"Needle, Galaxy, and Badge—you, too." We join the small gathering group around our teacher "OK, now listen up. Fuse, see that small military truck over there?" She gestures to a vehicle parked on the far end of the lot. It looks to have escaped the blaze. "We're going to need it. Hot-wire it and bring it to me."

"No problem. I'll be right back," Fuse says and dashes off.

Miss Abilene turns to Decoy and Abracadabra. "Boys, you two are coming with me. Decoy, I'm going to need you to tap into Abracadabra's disappearing abilities and project them across the road to hide our departure from those trucks that are coming."

"What? But I don't know how!" Decoy protests. "I've never done anything like that before."

"But you can do it. I've read your files. I know it's possible. Just trust me and do as I say."

The boys, though wide-eyed, nod.

She turns to the rest of us. "Badge and Needle, you need to lead all of these transports back to the prison. Break inside, get the rest of the CCs out of there, and find the room where they stored the Technic's arms and legs and such. We're going to need them. Take Galaxy with you. Use her if you have to, but don't let her blow the place up."

I cringe.

"We'll meet at the far eastern exit, by the office buildings—furthest away from the military quarters. Now, go!"

XIX

As we drive away, leaving only Miss Abilene, Fuse, Decoy, and Abracadabra behind, I watch through the back window of our transport vehicle. Miss Abilene, walks the boys into the middle of the main road and has them join hands. She's talking to them. I see her put a hand on each of their shoulders. They stretch out their free arms, and I watch in amazement as Abracadabra blinks and disappears. A shimmering forcefield of light rises from Decoy's body, covering the entire road, extending from his body like a blanket of energy.

The U.S.E.C. military convoy pulls over to the side of the road. Several of the soldiers get out of the vehicles, confusion marking their body language. But then a building hides my view of them.

"I hope they'll be alright," I mutter.

"They will be," Rocket says.

Only now do I notice him sitting nearby, sharing a seat with Blast, the four-year-old Warrior who got caught in the middle of the AI rebellion. Rocket has to hold onto the seatbelt strap to keep himself in the chair. The lack of legs and an arm makes him look precarious to me, but I'm glad to see him. I'm glad to see both of them.

"We're going to find your legs and arm," I tell him. "Needle's arm, too."

He smiles, looking at me. I feel color beginning to rise in my cheeks.

"It will be nice to be whole again," he says with a chuckle. "Then I won't have to look up to everybody anymore."

He can always make me laugh. Even when nothing is certain.

We pass several other buildings, moving swiftly. Then we take a sharp right and are heading back toward the prison. Again I spot AI Tower gazing down upon us from its imperial position in the sky. It's like Absalom is watching us… watching me… and smiling.

We pull up in front of the prison, but immediately draw the attention of a contingent of security guards and a few U.S.E.C. military soldiers assigned to this post. They run to block our path, each of them carrying energy rifles aimed our way.

"Miss Abilene didn't tell us what to do about them," Needle says.

We have stopped just out of range, but the line of men moves forward. About twenty-five armed men and women march toward us, and we are forced to back up to keep away from their weapons' fire. We aren't driving military-grade vehicles. We have no shields or offensive weaponry. If one of those energy blasts hits us, there's no telling what it might do to the transport vehicles, let alone to the occupants. We have no way to defend ourselves.

One of the soldiers runs forward and shoots. A blue blast of energy and plasma surges from his weapon and hits one of the other vehicles in the front, causing sparks and smoke to rise from the front end. One of the lights blows out, shooting glass and metal debris across the road. Screams of frightened CC children and youths reach us.

"What are we supposed to do against those energy weapons?" Bandy asks Badge, our driver.

Wait... energy... plasma....

I jump from my seat and try to push my way to the door.

"Galaxy, what are you doing?" Needle demands.

"Let me out of here! I have to get out there!"

"No, you can't! What are you thinking?"

"I have to get out!" I cry, reaching for the door controls, fighting past CCs who aren't sure they should let me pass.

"Wait! Let her go!" It's Rocket. "She can help."

At that, Needle stops protesting and nods, but his face still clearly displays his concern for me. The CCs in my path stop blocking me and help me get the door open.

I'm trembling as I take my first steps from the relative safety of the vehicle and the company of the others, but I can't turn back now. I take a deep breath and walk out in front of them, taking a position in the middle of the road.

The soldiers pause, curious about this new change of events, but they don't wait long. They approach, confident that they can take this petite, white-haired girl who foolishly stepped into their path. Perhaps they think I'm asking for mercy. They are not about to give it. Though their helmets cover most of their faces, blocking their eyes, several of them smile as they raise their weapons to take aim.

Three of them fire at once with two more quickly joining them. Others attempt to fire past me to hit the vehicles, but the streams of plasma are pulled out of trajectory as I focus on pulling the energy into myself.

Again I feel a warm, soothing, powerful force filling my body, rushing through me, turning my body into a boiling pool of molten lava. It's a delicious sensation! Though overwhelming at first, I relish it, soak it up, bathe myself in the raw power of the sensation.

I hear loud pops followed by cries of terror and pain as the energy rifles explode in their arms. I have sucked out the energy and overloaded the weapons' internal mechanisms. Several more soldiers, reacting rather than thinking, empty their weapons into me, but they only succeed in giving me more power.

I move forward.

"Hold your fire! Fall back!" the captain yells, finally realizing the hopelessness of their attack. This is a different man—not Captain Watt. Watt must be dead. I must've killed him in the inferno at the incineration chambers.

Good.

So far, I have managed to maintain my physical form without bursting into a raging ball of fire and light. I am simply absorbing the energy, storing it within myself. But now, as if by instinct alone, I throw out my hands toward the new captain. A stream of blue and white light flows from my hands, catching him in the chest. It passes completely through him, knocking him off his feet and dropping him to the ground. He does not move again.

Seeing this, the other soldiers and guards drop their weapons and run. They do not escape. I strike them all. I am able to take down several at a time just with a mere thought. All the firepower they poured into me, I now send back upon them. Not one escapes. The fire and energy passes through their bodies, burning holes into their middles, killing them as they try to flee. One after another, I drop them where they stand, catch them as they run, eliminate all chance of survival.

They all lie dead before me, littering the ground like so much garbage. My attack at an end, I stand trembling, shuddering, as I survey the destruction—the loss of life—I have wrought. And I am filled with horror. Horror at what I have done. Horror at what I am.

I sink to my knees and bury my face in my hands.

Footsteps approach from behind, but I don't turn around.

"You did what you had to do, Galaxy," Needle says, his voice coming from just above me.

I'm weeping. For the first time in as long as I can remember, I feel myself crying. I feel my eyes welling up, tears slipping from my eyes and down my cheeks. I shake with sobs.

I'm a killer. I killed those People back at the incineration chamber—but that was an accident. I didn't know what was happening to me or what would happen to them. But I killed these People on purpose. What have I become?

"I d-don't even know w-who I am anymore, Needle!" I cry, unable to stop the convulsions.

"But I know who you are," he says, his voice soft. I feel a hand—tentative at first—touch my shoulder and squeeze. "And I know it'll be okay. You saved us, Galaxy. But our work isn't done yet. There are more CCs inside who need our help."

I raise my head and look at him.

Amazing... Needle is actually asking for my help.

He smiles at me, but then his expression changes. "I'd wipe away your tears for you, if I didn't think they'd burn through my hand."

"What?" I lift a finger and swipe one of my tears onto my finger. It's a tiny, tumultuous drop of liquid fire. Soon my skin absorbs it, a steamy wisp rising from the surface of my finger.

It doesn't take long for Gash and Padlock to force their way inside the prison doors. Ripping the doors from their hinges, they use them as shields against the few guards remaining inside. I follow Needle to search for his missing arm while several of the Wits head to the control room to release the locks on the cell doors.

"There!" Needle says, excitement in his voice, spotting something through windows into an interior room. "In there!"

We enter and find shelves full of various metal arms, legs, and cybernetic attachments. Needle searches the shelves, attacking them with a frenzy until he finally holds up his prize.

"Here it is!" he cries with a shout of joy. He activates a mechanism in the base of his robotic arm and attaches it with a snap to his empty, right appendage. Testing it, he causes several of the tiny tools to appear, swirl about, and then snap back into place again. "Yes!"

"What about the rest of these?" I ask, surveying the junkyard of stolen technology.

"We'll take as much as we can, starting with this pile here," Needle says, indicating the shelf where he found his arm. "This looks like the most recent stuff."

We locate two large bags and begin to shove items inside.

"Rocket's legs, I'd bet," Needle says, putting two heavily armored, intricately designed leg attachments into his sack."

"And I think I found Trinket's arm," I say, sweeping my arm across the shelf to knock all the smaller items into my bag. "It's in here somewhere."

"Come on," Needle says, tightening the strings on his sack. "We've got to get out of here."

By the time we leave the building, most of the other CCs have been loaded into vehicles, only this time we're driving military grade trucks. Some of the Warriors have even commandeered a couple of tanks. We'll need them. By now U.S.E.C. will have called in the military—and not merely the ones stationed at the compound. More helicopters are already heading our way.

"Come on! Let's go!" Gash shouts at the last few CCs leaving the building, waving them into vehicles. "We've got to meet Miss Abilene and the others at the eastern gate! Let's move out!"

I pass the bag to Signet and she gives me a hand into the back of a truck. Needle climbs in after me and we're off almost before his foot leaves the ground. He takes the seat across from us.

"Nice work back there," Signet says, looking at me.

I nod, not knowing how to respond to her newfound respect. A few days ago she wanted to put me through the wall. Now I wonder if she would've been able to had she tried.

As if reading my thoughts she says, "Hey… I know we haven't exactly gotten along in the past, but—"

"Look, it's no big deal," I say, cutting her off. "We're on the same side, right?"

"Right," she says looking me in the eyes. Then smiling, "yeah, that's right."

I smile back. "Good."

"Are we there yet?" Needle asks, desperation showing in the strain of his voice. "Because they are!"

A moment later, the sound of heavy blades chops the air just above us. I expect them to open fire, but they don't. Instead, they zoom past us toward the prison.

"What's going on?" I ask.

"They don't know it's us," Signet says, realizing the truth even as the words leave her mouth. "They think we're with them. They've been called to the prison."

"But as soon as they see what happened there, they'll come back," Needle says.

Signet turns to me. "Galaxy, you have to be ready when they do."

"What? What do you mean?"

"Those helicopters carry armor-piercing rounds. They won't do too much damage to the tanks, but they'll cut through this truck like cardboard. You can't let them."

"But they're shooting bullets!" I cry. I feel the panic rising in my throat. "I can't stop bullets!"

"You're going to have to try."

"But I can't! I'm not a Warrior! And-and-and I don't want to do this!" I stammer, feeling panic rising in me. "I don't want to kill! I wasn't trained for this!"

"Galaxy," Needle says, voice calm. "Look at me."

I turn and look in his eyes. He puts a hand on my knee. "When you protected us from the soldiers, I was watching you. You weren't acting from training. You were acting on instinct. You can do this. You don't have to stop the bullets. You just have to stop the helicopters. You can take them out of the air before they have a chance to shoot at us. I know you can."

"O-Okay." I try to believe him, to find the confidence in myself that he seems to have in me. But I dread the thought of taking more lives, seeing more People fall in death at my hands. I close my eyes tight and swallow. "I'll try. ...But Needle, is what we're doing right? I mean, we're just CCs! Do we even have the right?"

"Of course, we do, Galaxy! U.S.E.C., since its inception, promised a new era of peace, enlightenment, and prosperity. But they have delivered nothing but darkness and death! They enslave, sacrifice, and massacre their own! Us, Galaxy, us! We're human beings—no different from them!"

He's right! Of course, he's right! Why has it been so hard for me to see? All this time, we've been taught that we are less, but at the core we are the same. How can it be that some human beings—already born, already in power—have been allowed to arbitrarily assign personhood or non-personhood to others? Where does such power come from? By what right does one human being proclaim that another is not a Person but rather a commodity to be bought, sold, used or destroyed on a mere whim?

"Galaxy...." Needle is looking up. He hears something. And then I hear it, too. The helicopters. They're coming back. "It's time, Galaxy. It's time for the night to end."

I follow his gaze. Reaching for the side of the truck to steady myself, I stand.

"You're right, Needle.... They've killed enough of us already."

XX

Signet rises with me, steps over the legs of the other CCs occupying the back of the covered truck and bangs on the glass separating us from the driver. Bandy, riding shotgun, opens the window to see what she wants.

"We need to stop!" she says.

"What? We can't stop! We'll never make it if we do!"

It's Smudge! He's driving!

"We'll never make it if we don't!" she yells. "We have Galaxy back here. We have to stop and let her out! Then you can keep going. I'll stay with her."

"Galaxy?" I hear Smudge say. "Okay, but you'll have to jump out quick!"

It's a good thing I'm holding on because Smudge swerves suddenly to the left and parks. Signet grabs my hand and together we jump out of the back. As soon as we clear the back, Smudge hits the gas again and they speed away.

The helicopters are nearly on top of us. There are six of them. The dust begins to rise about us. I glance at Signet.

"You can do this, Galaxy!" she yells, seeing the fear in my eyes.

I refocus on the helicopters. I take a deep breath.

"Okay!" I yell to get my voice over the sound of the choppers. "You might want to back up!"

I don't have to tell her twice. She sprints to the side of the road and takes shelter behind a nearby utility shed.

I hope I can still do this!

But I suddenly know I can. I spread my legs shoulder width apart, bracing against the power within me. It's still there, churning. All I have to do is summon it. Channel it. Aim.

I reach toward the lead helicopter. A stream of electric flames bursts from my hand and fingers and catches the bird in the nose of the cockpit toppling it back. A black hole burns through the main chamber and I know whoever had been inside is already dead. My second blast removes the blades from another helicopter. It crashes to the ground in a pile of burning wreckage. But now the pilots of the other helicopters are aware of the danger and they bank right and left to avoid the small girl standing on the ground below.

They circle, flanking me, surrounding me. And then they begin to shoot.

"Look out!" Signet cries, as a line of bullets dig into the ground moving straight toward my position. I duck, covering my head with one arm while pushing back with the other. Another blast of energy and plasma pours out of me, hitting the oncoming helicopter in the gas tank. It explodes in the air. Pieces of it shoot in all directions. One of its blades pierces the cockpit of another helicopter impaling the pilot. It, too, crashes and bursts into flames.

Only two remain now, but they have had enough of me. They shoot past, leaving me and Signet in a cloud of dust.

"Oh, no! They're going after the others!" I cry.

I hear the revving of a motor. Signet pulls up next to me on a red and black motorcycle.

"Look what I found," she says. "Hop on!"

I throw a leg over and Signet pulls me up with one hand. I hold tight to her firm, muscled midsection as she steps on the accelerator and we take off after the helicopters.

"Okay, I'm going to get you close," Signet hollers, to keep the wind from blowing away her words, "but don't blast them until I'm clear, got it?"

"Okay. I'll try."

"You better do more than try!"

Looking ahead, I see the helicopters gaining on the vehicles. One of them opens fire.

"Oh, no!" I cry. "We have to go faster! You have to get me closer!"

"This thing won't go any faster!"

But the CCs aren't without recourse. Whoever is driving one of our tanks has stopped, its massive gun aimed at the sky. A loud bang and the tank jumps. A mortar hits one of the helicopters and blasts it into two pieces which fall flaming to the ground. A second shot is fired at the last helicopter, but misses. This pilot is savvy, banking left and then right. It opens fire, cutting into one of our military vehicles. The disabled truck crashes into another and both spin to a stop at the side of the road.

"Oh, no!" I cry. "We have to help them!"

"We're too far," Signet yells, "and we still have that guy to deal with!" She indicates the last helicopter with a thrust of her chin.

As we speed toward them, the helicopter swings wide to avoid another shot from the tank. I spot motion from inside the crashed vehicles. One of the side doors open and a girl steps out. She has short brown hair and looks to be about twelve.

Granite!

"What is she doing?" I ask Signet, but get no response. Signet is concentrating on dodging helicopter wreckage.

Granite's body suddenly changes—getting whiter and taking on a strange looking texture. She moves to the other side of the vehicle and disappears behind it. But then the vehicle starts sliding back onto the road.

She's pushing it!

The helicopter has spotted her, though. I watch as Granite runs to the middle of the road, providing the helicopter with what looks like an easy target. The helicopter moves toward her and opens fire.

"No!" I cry.

A round of armor-piercing bullets sprays all around Granite. She instinctually covers her head with her arms. Bullets hit her on her arms back and legs, but Granite doesn't budge.

We're nearly on top of them. From here I can see that Granite looks like a girl made of stone. The bullets have done no damage, but she has distracted the helicopter from shooting at the other CCs long enough for Signet and I to reach them.

"We're close enough!" I shout. "Let me off!"

Signet skids to a stop and helps me dismount. She takes off again, putting some distance between us.

I run forward, letting the fire within me build until, finally, as the helicopter swings around to take another pass at the vehicles, I let loose, both hands in front and bracing myself with one leg forward.

The blast engulfs the helicopter in a ball of flame. It swerves haphazardly but then begins to fall, heading directly toward the vehicle that is still immobilized on the side of the road.

"Look out!" I cry but, of course, no one can take cover.

As if by instinct, I brace myself again and take aim. My second shot is a stream of bright energy. It catches the bottom of the spinning cockpit and pushes it to the side, barely keeping it from landing on top of the damaged vehicles.

I race forward, fearing the worst. Signet meets me at the wreckage.

"Is everyone okay?" she asks as the door of the most badly damaged vehicle opens.

"We have wounded," a CC says, exiting. I don't recognize him. "And I think this girl has died."

We scramble to unload the CCs from the damaged vehicle and find room for them in others. We head off toward the eastern exit of the compound. I again ride with Signet on the motorcycle just in case I'm needed again.

We're nearly there! Only another block. But as we approach, we see no sign of Miss Abilene, Decoy, or the others.

"Where are they?" Signet says, frustration in her voice, as our ragtag collection of CC-operated, stolen U.S.E.C. vehicles comes to a stop at a locked and heavily-defended gate. "They should be here by now!"

From the west we see a line of U.S.E.C. vehicles coming our way, and the soldiers manning the gate are ready for us. Giant automatic guns swing toward us and soldiers scurry across the top of the two-story high security wall that surrounds the compound. They take up defensive positions and train their weapons on us.

"We're trapped!" I cry.

"You're going to have to stop them," she tells me.

"What? I don't know what to do! I can't fight them all! Not at the same time!"

"Take cover!" It's Gash. "Pull those trucks in close! Move that tank to the front!" He's waving the other drivers forward and positioning our two tanks at both ends of the caravan to provide a defense at both ends.

Suddenly, a flurry of bullets from above digs into the pavement, spitting up bits of asphalt around our legs. Another helicopter zooms past, having appeared from the other side of the wall. It swings to a stop and shoots again, aiming at the cab of the truck we recently evacuated. I see Bandy fling himself from the passenger side door and slide beneath the cab moments before a series of bullets slice through it.

"Smudge!" I cry.

Signet grabs me, letting the motorcycle fall as she dismounts, holding me under one arm. She carries me to the base of a tank and orders me to keep my head down as the helicopter begins to shoot another round. We cover our heads with our arms.

A loud bang rocks the ground and sends us sprawling. The tank has launched a mortar. It rips through the underbelly of the final helicopter, removing the back end. The helicopter plummets from the sky, spinning wildly, and lands with a crash on the roof of a nearby office building.

Even as all this is happening, I am aware that the soldiers on the wall above the gate have also opened fire, but our Warriors on the ground, evidently having located functioning weapons at the prison, are returning fire. They hide behind trucks and tanks as best they can, but we're outgunned. The weapons on the wall are massive, high-powered automatics. And the U.S.E.C. military caravan on the road has slowed to form an offensive line.

Suddenly I see a missile rising from the midst of our circle of vehicles. It shoots straight up in the air, but then stops, hovering about fifty feet overhead.

No! It's not a missile! It's a CC! It's... It's Rocket!

Rocket, now fully whole again, raises his robotic right arm and opens fire on the soldiers along the wall and defending the gate. He has the enemy ducking for cover, but the two soldiers manning large artillery canons on either side of the gate are still attacking. With an agility and speed I've never before witnessed in a human being, he spins and dives toward them, easily avoiding their line of fire. He kills one soldier with a shot to the chest and forces the second to duck and hide behind the ramparts.

Rocket halts his wild, diving, spinning flight and again hovers before the gate. Just as the soldier again takes aim, panels in Rocket's thighs open and a small series of rockets appear, aim, and fire. Though small, the rockets create a massive explosion, punching a hole in the gate, taking out the heavy artillery and turning a huge section of the wall to rubble. Pieces of brick, bodies of men, and a shower of dust and debris descend from above.

"Galaxy!" Signet cries in my ear. "You have to stop them!"

I return my attention to the enemies approaching from behind and see that they are in striking position. She gives me a push and I find myself facing an army.

Bullets! They're all using bullets! They've communicated with each other and abandoned the energy weapons. I scan the force before me. I have no time to count but there must be over thirty vehicles and several hundred male and female soldiers. I look across this sea of enemies knowing they are determined to kill me—to kill all of us.

There are too many of them! Too many!

I have to do something. I have to try.

I step away from Signet and the tank, moving into the road, knowing I am putting myself within easy range of their guns. Fear and panic creep into the edges of my consciousness. But then Absalom's face again flashes before my mind's eye. I close my eyes. He is here with me. It was his design and intent that protected me in the incineration chamber, making me impervious to the energy weapons. I have to trust that he knew I would face bullets as well. He designed me for this.

I lift my head and open my eyes. I stare directly into the sun overhead. Instantly, the power is back—burning, surging, transforming me from a child-like teenage girl into pure fire, energy, and light.

I shine so brightly the soldiers begin to shield their eyes. Many look away. But they still manage to pull their triggers.

Bullets head for me, flying in—darts of metal seeking a vulnerable target. But, as they near, something happens to them. They melt in mid-air as they near my body. In mid-flight they become mere wisps of molten metal and disintegrate like moths attacking a flame.

I find I can control the heat. The CCs at my back are safe. I do not let the radiation explode from my body as I did in the incineration chamber. This time, I'm in full control, and there seems to be no end to the light and heat I can produce, as if I'm channeling it directly from the sun itself.

I turn my eyes on the army before me. I begin to run.

"Move!"

"Look out!"

"Shoot her! Shoot her now!"

An enemy tank fires a mortar, but the round explodes before it reaches my body. Two more military helicopters swoop in, coming from the city. They are larger than the others. More heavily armored. But it doesn't matter. Their armor piercing rounds cannot pierce me. Even the ground beneath my feet is melting as I go.

The closer I come, the more desperate the orders become until their shouts become cries of fright and then of pain. The first vehicles I reach begin to sizzle and smoke, tires melting, interiors bursting into flames along with the occupants, until the fuel tanks explode. Though the noise startles me at first, I find the additional flames and energy from the explosions empowering. And now that I'm no longer near the other CCs, I let loose—forcing energy from my body and expanding the reach of the burn.

More cries. Thick flames engulf the soldiers, quieting their screams. Military-grade vehicles disappear behind liquid fire. More fuel tanks explode in such quick succession that they rock the ground. I nearly lose my balance. Debris and charred bodies fly into the air amongst the flames. Black smoke collects and rises, blocking the sun—but I have all the energy I need.

I keep moving deeper, pushing forward into the enemy ranks. I let my rage burn hot. Their weapons cannot stop me. The sheer power I exude cannot be stopped. I am invincible!

"Look out! Galaxy, look out!"

The voice comes from above. Just in time, I turn to the massive treads of a tank moving toward me, only inches away. I fling myself to the ground, barely missing being crushed. The tank continues to roll until it is positioned directly on top of me.

What was I thinking? I nearly got crushed to death! If it hadn't been for Rocket, I would be dead right now! Fear pushes back into my mind, forcing out the fire. I begin to fade and tremble. I'm on my back, lying in a pool of melted asphalt and earth, staring up at the thick metal base of the tank's underbelly.

What do I do now? What do I do? They almost got me! Almost....

I try to still the wild pounding in my chest, calm myself, and think. Of course, the remaining U.S.E.C. soldiers are just as desperate to find a solution as I am. As I stare, trying to collect my thoughts, I see the metal just above me begins to glow. I'm still expelling a great amount of heat.

I place both hands on the burning bottom of the tank and focus on intensifying the glow. I hear the metal whine and pop as it warps, bending against the stress and pressure. The glowing spot grows malleable, more flexible as the heat builds. As the metal turns to liquid, great drops of molten steel land on me and sizzle out of existence.

I hear cries. Something crashes. A hole appears at my hands. The main chamber of the tank opens before me as the remaining bits of metal drip away.

I stand up into the glowing metal beast. I find I am alone. The hatch is open, but the bodies of three soldiers remain. They smolder and stink. They have been cooked alive.

XXI

Iclimb from the tank hatch to find the battle over. Rocket and the Warriors have dispatched both the enemy at the gate and those at the edges of the U.S.E.C. Special Forces unit who ran for cover at my approach. And, I see three more helicopters I had not noticed before, languishing in smoking heaps of twisted metal and broken blades. And Miss Abilene is here!

She heads my way but stops short of the steaming liquid that was once pavement. I hop down and cross to her.

"Good work," she says.

"Where did you come from?" I ask.

"We were here all along," she says. "You just couldn't see us." With a nod, she gestures to the gathered CCs, and I spot Decoy, Abracadabra, and Fuse among them.

Something lands with a burst of wind and dust at my side. I turn to see Rocket. This is the first good look I get of him now that he's his whole self again. He's several inches taller than I. His black hair is a bit windblown, but he looks excited—alive with energy and joy at our victory. Though his right arm is robotic from the shoulder to the tips of his fingers and set with panels bearing the guns I saw him shooting a little while ago, the other is bronzed and muscled. His legs are shining steel and chrome, also built with artillery-hiding panels. Blue and white rivers of energy run along their lengths. But it is his face that has me most interested.

The upper left side of his face has been replaced with a cybernetic implant, ending just before his hairline. His right eye is gone, cybernetic eye in its place. But his left eye is black. He has long eye lashes, masculine features, smooth skin. He looks Native American.

"That was amazing," he says. He's looking at me. Talking to me. A smile plays on his lips.

"I-I was j-just about to say the same th-thing about you," I reply. I'm stammering. Why am I stammering?

"You saved us, Galaxy," he says.

"Well... and you saved me. If you hadn't warned me about that tank...."

"Yeah.... You looked like you got a little distracted there for a minute."

Distracted. I was more than distracted. I... I think I lost myself for a while.

"We still have a long way to go," Miss Abilene says. "But none of you is going to get very far as long as those CC tracking devices are still operational." She turns and calls for Bandy. "Flick, too," she says.

I've almost forgotten about Flick, the shy Natural with an amazing gift for creating novel computer programming techniques.

Soon, they join us from the group of gathered CCs. "Boys, I need you to work together to disable everyone's tracking chips. Flick, I know you'll be able to figure out how to do it and, Bandy, your robotic arms are perfectly suited for the task. I'll get Trinket and a few of the other Technics to help."

"Okay," Bandy says and looks at Flick. "Do you think you can do this?"

"I can figure it out," the seventeen-year-old Latino boy says.

"What about Needle?" I ask. "He could help, too."

Miss Abilene turns back to me and hesitates. "I'm sorry, Galaxy. Needle was hit."

"What?" I cry. "Where is he?"

She puts a hand on me to stop me from charging off. "He's okay. It was only his left shoulder. Lumina and Synapse are—ow!" She pulls her hand away from me.

I must be heating up.

"They're treating him now," Miss Abilene continues, rubbing her sore hand with her other one. "He's going to be fine."

I want to run to where Needle is, just to be sure, but Bandy taps me in the back.

"Galaxy, before you go, let me scan your tracking device. I want to get a reading for Flick."

I flip my hair to the side for him, exposing the back of my neck. Bandy waves a scanning device in his right robotic hand over the back of my neck. Then he does it again. And again.

"What's the problem?" I ask, losing patience.

"That's strange. You don't have a tracking device."

"It must've burned up and disintegrated when you turned into that fire monster," Flick says, "like your CC tattoo."

"What?" I say, touching my right temple—as if I could feel it anyway. "It's gone?"

"Yep."

"I guess you're not a CC anymore," Bandy says. "Congratulations."

But, somehow, I think it will require more than that to make me a Person.

Trinket, Synapse, and a few others join us then. In less than a minute they figure out the best way to disable the tracking chips and get to work, spreading out among the other CCs and shorting out the devices embedded beneath the skin at the backs of their necks.

As I leave to find Needle, I hear Miss Abilene shouting orders to the tank operators.

"Start blasting through what's left of the gates. Everyone else, as soon as your tracking chip is disabled, gather into those." She indicates a row of civilian cars and vans in a parking lot a short distance away next to an office building. The building looks abandoned, but more likely the non-military occupants are just cowering inside, hoping the battle is over. "Wits and Warriors at the wheel," she says, since they are the only ones with any understanding of how to operate a vehicle. "We have to make it out of the city. These vehicles will attract less attention."

I rest my forehead against the window pane of the mini-van Miss Abilene drives. It's amazing how quickly feelings of triumph and joy can turn to sorrow and despair.

Smudge is dead. So are about twelve others—caught by enemy fire. Synapse, Siren, and one of the Gapes—a shy boy named Beacon. And we have more wounded.

They tell me Needle is stable for now. But he had been bleeding badly. It's all over his uniform. They bandaged him, using the first aid kits from the military vehicles, but a crimson stain had seeped through the white cloth. Needle has to remain as still as possible. They wouldn't let me ride with him.

It's easy to cry now, only I shouldn't. I might accidentally set the van on fire. I have to make sure I catch whatever tears escape, reabsorbing them back into my skin. It's not easy.

"Only about another hour now," Miss Abilene says.

I'm not sure where we're going, exactly—only that it's a place that used to be called Baltimore before the New Dark Ages hit. Now it's just a burned out city of rubble and charred buildings. Miss Abilene says we'll be safe there—except that getting there is proving difficult. We can't go straight there for multiple reasons. One, we need to head as quickly out of the city as we can, making sure we're not followed. That means getting into the more rural areas where the streets are smaller but navigable. Two, the main roads that lead to old Baltimore were destroyed long ago when the city was bombed out by anarchists.

Trees and green pastures slip past my window. I've never seen so much green up close before. We have managed to get clear of the city by blending with traffic. Thanks to Decoy we even managed to escape with one of the tanks. He is sitting on the top, using his holographic abilities to disguise it as a backhoe. Its noisy, slow progression still draws attention, but the People's reactions are those of impatience and annoyance rather than fear and suspicion. We even escaped discovery when a series of U.S.E.C. military vehicles zipped past us—no doubt on their way to answer the call for reinforcements at the compound. They will not be pleased with what they find when they arrive.

Needle... I hope you're okay....

The wounded are all traveling together with the Wits—who have the most medical know-how. I'm in the lead vehicle. Miss Abilene is the only one who knows where to go, but though she claims the distance between Washington DC and old Baltimore is not great, we must travel slowly to accommodate the tank.

"He'll be alright," Rocket says, leaning close. He occupies the seat next to mine.

I glance at him and try to smile. I'm not sure how to talk to him. His proximity makes goosebumps rise on my arms. I try to think of something to say that will prolong our conversation, but the sound of weeping reaches us from the back seat.

"Hey... are you okay?" Rocket asks Luster, who sits in the row behind us, tears running down her perfect, shimmering cheeks. She looks up at him. Her irises are green at first, but then shift to aqua blue.

"Siren is dead," she tells him. "She was my friend. She was my same age. We grew up together."

Again, Luster descends into weeping. Rocket rises and moves to the back of the vehicle. He sits next to her and she leans into him, burying her face in his chest.

"Shh," he whispers into her hair. "I'm so sorry. She was far too young. I'm sorry."

I turn back to watching the trees and grass again. The sun is beginning its slow crawl back to earth. It will be dark in a few hours.

A brilliant bit of light and heat slips down my cheek.

XXII

The pavement runs out and we move onto broken asphalt. Little green plants have sprouted up along the cracks in the road, nature reasserting itself in the absence of human interference. I can no longer rest my head against the window. It's far too bumpy.

Broken asphalt turns to gravel. Gravel becomes packed dirt and tracked grasslands. We pass remnants of vehicles, abandoned and decaying buildings, skeletons of animals that have long since whitened in the sun. We enter an area that was once a sprawling neighborhood. The houses here have been flattened. Many evidence a massive fire that must have raged through a large section of the city, reducing homes and businesses to blackened, charred rubble. Only soot-coated bricks and the lonely spires of crumbling chimneys remain, interspersed with young trees—new life in the midst of death.

We find pavement again, but it is severely damaged. The further we push into the heart of the city, the darker it gets. The buildings here are massive skyscrapers. What few windows remain intact wink at us from impressive heights. None of them could match AI Tower, of course, and their style of construction speaks of a time in the distant past, but their sheer size is enough to create shadows on the ground, blocking out the evening sun long before its time.

We've had to decrease our pace even more. Broken down, abandoned vehicles and debris from crumbling buildings litter the road and the cracks in the pavement are so wide that the standard vehicles are forced to creep across them lest we bottom out. Decoy no longer disguises the tank, as we have reached a section of the state that few frequent. Instead, we have put the tank out in front. It clears a path for us, forcing cars out of the way as it goes.

As we near the shadows of the tallest building that remains standing, Miss Abilene stops the van and turns to Rocket.

"Rocket," she says. "Go get the tank to stop. We've arrived."

Rocket gently lets go of Luster, and crawls past me to the door. He exits and, with a burst of energy, he shoots into the air and lands on top of the tank. He bangs on the hatch. Badge opens it. A short exchange later and the tank grinds to a halt.

Miss Abilene turns the van into an alley off to our left and leads our small caravan of about thirty vehicles—mostly vans—into an old, concrete parking garage. She turns off the engine and gets out. I watch as she straightens her skirt and arranges her hair. Without success, she tries to buff out the soot stains on her blouse left over from the altercation at the compound.

"Okay... okay...." She leans back inside the driver's side door and says, "Just wait here. I'll be right back."

Where is she going?

She walks away from our company of parked cars but my vantage point is obscured from my spot inside the van. I crawl past Trinket and let myself out. Several other CCs join me as we stand near our cars wondering what we're supposed to do.

Rocket appears next to me. I swallow and take a deep breath.

"Now what?" he asks.

"I have no idea," I say. "She just said wait."

"Wait for what?"

"I don't know. Maybe she's going to meet somebody."

"Who? There's no one here."

I shrug. The image of Rocket cradling Luster returns to me.

"I need to check on Needle," I say and head off toward a blue van at the center of our cluster.

I peek inside and see Clarity sitting between Gauntlet and Needle. I haven't spoken to her since that day in the computer lab where she accused me of being untrustworthy and useless. She sees me now but quickly averts her eyes.

Clarity wasn't with us in our prison block, nor was she among those in the incineration chambers, but I know she witnessed what happened outside the prison and by the eastern gates.

"How is Needle?" I ask, afraid she'll tell me to mind my own business or something.

"He-He's doing much better," she says, fidgeting with a roll of bandages in her hands. "He's resting now."

"Good," I say, feeling awkward.

Needle appears to be asleep, stretching across three seats, his head on a folded military blanket. His shoulder has been skillfully re-bandaged. There is no trace of blood on this one.

"And how is Gauntlet?" I ask.

Gauntlet looks pale. His eyes are closed and he's leaning with one shoulder against the side of the van. He takes up two seats. But on hearing his name, he opens his eyes and looks at me.

"Oh, hey girl," he says, smiling, his voice weaker than I remember.

"Hi, Gauntlet. I came to check on you and Needle and the others."

"Oh, we're good… we're good." He closes his eyes again, takes a deep breath, and then refocuses on me. "A little thirsty, though."

"They need water," Clarity says, finally venturing to look at me. "And food. Food high in protein, if possible—meat, eggs, that sort of thing."

"Okay," I say, having no idea how I might procure a meal for them, but knowing somehow it must be done. None of us have eaten all day, but surely the wounded are the ones suffering the most right now. "Thanks, Clarity."

As I step away, I think I see her start to smile.

Hmm… Food….

"Where are you going?"

It's Rocket. He's seen me walking toward where I last saw Miss Abilene disappear.

"We've got to find her," I say. I keep walking as he moves beside me, hovering in the air at first and then landing to walk alongside me.

"What's the rush? She hasn't been gone that long."

"The wounded CCs need food and water. They can't wait. I have to find her."

"Okay," he says. "I think I saw her go this way."

We head toward some concrete stairs and enter the first floor of a decrepit office building. It's dark down here. So dark we can barely see where we're going. I consider lighting up the place. Maybe I can just illuminate my hand… but if I can't control it just right I could set the whole place on fire… Rocket, too. No… better leave well enough alone.

"Hey," he whispers. "I think I hear voices."

And then I hear something, too. It sounds like they're coming from below us. We head toward a flight of concrete stairs and lean over the side.

"…tell me who you are." It's a man's voice. He sounds nervous, threatened.

"It's Dara Abilene. I've come back."

"I don't believe it! Dara is dead! She was condemned as a Subversive and incinerated. I saw it on the news myself just this morning."

"You didn't see what happened after that? The CC rebellion wasn't televised? I thought that was a live feed."

"I heard about an attempted rebellion. But the last I saw all the Subversives were incinerated."

"They must've been able to stop the feed just in time," she mutters. "Or maybe the blaze itself knocked out the broadcasting equipment too early, giving them a chance to rewrite history."

"What are you talking about?"

We creep closer, moving down the steps as quietly as we can. Soon we're able to see into the lower garage. Miss Abilene stands outside what looks like an old elevator. Only a dim, flickering light illuminates the space. Whoever she's speaking with is inside the elevator, behind a closed metal gate, obscured from our line of sight.

"Look, I don't have time for this. Just tell Diamond that I'm here." A pause. "Well, do it!"

The elevator shifts into motion and rises. It returns a moment later.

"Diamond," Miss Abilene speaks to the person inside the elevator who remains outside our line of sight. "Don't you know me anymore? I know we left it badly last time we were together. I said some things.... I didn't mean them. I was just so hurt. So angry... and I didn't see things the way you did—not until that day... that horrible day. I've thought of you often over the years, you know. Everything I've done, I did for you... so you would think differently of me."

It's quiet for a moment but then we hear the sound of a chain being unlocked and watch the metal gate opening. A man wearing a white t-shirt steps out of the elevator. He's carrying a large gun, but he's holding it down at his side. He moves close to Miss Abilene and hesitates for a moment. She's looking in his eyes. Suddenly he grabs her and pulls her close. She melts into him.

"I'm so glad you're okay," he says.

They hold each other for a long time. I begin to feel awkward spying on them. I start to take a step back but startle at the sound of an energy rifle charging just behind my head. Rocket and I swing around to find three men standing behind us, each of them holding weapons aimed at our heads.

"Hands up!" they order and we obey.

"Diamond!" one of them says. He's a large bald man. He peers at us across the sights of his older model energy rifle. "Get up here! I'm about to waste a couple of spies!"

Rocket glances at me and then back at the bald man and laughs. "That is a very bad idea, my man. A very bad idea."

"Who's there? Come out!" Diamond yells at us from below.

We turn around and obey. The three Subversive militia members follow us down, still training their weapons on us. I still have my hands in the air. Rocket doesn't bother.

"Hey, get your hands up!" The bald man orders again gesturing at Rocket with his weapon as we step from the stairs onto the lower level.

"Go ahead," Rocket says, "but I promise you won't like the result."

"No!" Miss Abilene yells, hands out toward the armed men. "Don't shoot! Whatever you do! Not in here!"

"Wait, wait!" Diamond says, moving closer. "What's going on? Who are these kids?"

"They're with me," Miss Abilene answers, right on his heels. "And that little girl right there is the most powerful CC I've ever seen. Trust me. You don't want to discharge those weapons anywhere near her."

"So, she's valuable, then?"

"They're all valuable, Diamond. …You taught me that."

Diamond glances at Miss Abilene and then back at his men. He gestures for them to lower their weapons. They oblige.

"Well," he says. "I guess you'd better come inside and explain."

"Thanks," Miss Abilene says, "but before we do that you should know that these aren't the only CCs I brought with me."

"What? How many more?"

"I'm not sure, exactly… but I'd say there's nearly three hundred of them."

"Three hundred!" the bald man says. "What are we supposed to do with three hundred?"

"We'll need places to stay," Miss Abilene answered him, not letting his outburst intimidate her.

"And food and water," Rocket says with equal bravado. "In fact, we have wounded who need to eat as soon as possible."

"Dara," Diamond says. "I'd love to help you, but we just don't have enough supplies for that many. You know how we live."

"I know," she answers, "but these are AI CCs, Diamond. They'll earn their keep."

"I tell you what," Rocket says, stepping forward. "You get the wounded—just the wounded—some food and water right now, and Galaxy and I will bring you as much venison as you and anyone else you got here can eat."

"What did you get me into?" I ask Rocket as we leave the building. "I don't know how to hunt."

"But I do. At least, how hard can it be?" He lifts his robotic arm, and with a quick burst of motion loads his guns. He laughs. "Come on. I saw a forest on our way in. I think it was that way." Rocket slips his good arm around my waist and says, "Hold tight."

I have just time enough to grab onto him before he whisks me into the air. We soar above the buildings and angle away from the city.

I try to catch my breath as we burst through the air in flight. It's exhilarating. But I don't know what's more exciting—the feeling of flying or Rocket's arm around me.

I remind myself that only moments ago his arm was around Luster. I try to focus on the task at hand.

"There," he says, spotting a field where a flock of deer graze.

He drops us down behind the tree line near the field. He takes off again, fires a few shots, and returns.

"Well, we should have plenty of meat for tonight's dinner," he says with a smile, pleased with himself.

"That's great, but I still don't know why you brought me along." I'm still a little sore at him, but he doesn't seem to notice.

"I'm pretty sure your friends are going to want their venison cooked."

"Oh, right."

"But not burned to a crisp. Okay, Galaxy? No charcoal, please."

I snicker at that. "Okay. I'll do my best."

It takes a little time, but eventually Rocket is able to fly all the roasted pieces of venison back to the rebel hideout. By the time he takes me back, most of the CCs and Subversives have eaten their fill and sit around a large upper room in little groups lounging and talking. It's a rare thing for CCs to get a moment to enjoy themselves and the company of others. A few of them don't know how to handle it and keep getting up to ask Miss Abilene for her orders. She waves them away, assuring them there'll be plenty of work tomorrow. Now it's time for rest.

I sit in a small group next to the bed on the floor they prepared for Needle. There aren't enough beds or blankets for everyone—just the wounded, but the floor is carpeted. It's a big improvement from the cement floors of our prison cells. Rocket sprawls nearby, already dozing off.

Gauntlet rests a few feet away from me, looking a lot better. He chews loudly on a piece of fatty venison with a satisfied look on his face. Gash is next to him, his head back against the wall and eyes closed. His shoulder has also finally been bandaged.

"It looks like you're going to be okay," I say to Needle. "I was worried about you. They wouldn't let me ride in the van with you."

Needle smiles weakly. "Yeah. I'm feeling better already."

I know he's lying, but it's okay.

"This is all because of you, you know," I tell him. "If it hadn't been for you, we wouldn't have had a chance."

"No, Galaxy. It may have been my idea. But you made it happen."

I shrug.

"Actually, I think Absalom made it happen."

"Yeah."

"He planned this from the beginning, didn't he?"

"Evidently."

"He thought of everything—even of providing me with a special suit that doesn't burn or melt."

"Yep."

"Somehow he knew I would end up in that incineration chamber." I take a deep breath. "And so he made sure I would be okay. ...But why would he do it, Needle? Why go to such trouble and expense for me?"

"I know Absalom cared about you," Needle says, "maybe even loved you. ...But I don't think his plan was only about you."

"What do you mean?"

"Think about it, Galaxy. Absalom made you impervious to every weapon they have. You can do more than just save yourself. You can save us all."

I'm walking down a long corridor toward a door at the far end. A voice is whispering my name—a woman's voice. She calls to me from behind the door. I speed up to reach her, but the corridor gets longer, stretching before me so that I don't make any progress.

"Galaxy…. Galaxy…. GALAXY!"

I run, desperate to reach her. She needs me.

I reach for the door handle. Finally, I catch hold of it. I push through only to find myself surrounded by flames. The voice that had begun as a whisper is now a scream of agony.

"GALAXY!"

"I'm here! I'm here! Let me help you!"

"Stop, Galaxy, stop! You're hurting me!"

She's burning to death, screaming in terror and pain. I can't find her. The intense flames surround me, blind me. But she keeps screaming and I keep searching.

"Galaxy, stop! Please! You have to stop!"

The voice has changed.

"Galaxy, stop now!"

It's Needle's voice. I open my eyes. I'm on fire. The floor is on fire. The wall next to where I was sleeping is burning in orange and red flames. Someone cries out in pain.

Suddenly I remember where I am. I focus all my energy on pulling the blaze back inside myself. Soon the fires are gone and only a black, singed place remains where I had once been sleeping.

"I'm so sorry!" I cry. It's dark in the room. "Is anyone hurt?"

Everyone is awake now. Those closest to me cough in the smoke. Someone turns on the lights. A whimper to my right and I turn to see Needle holding his real arm next to his chest. It looks red and blistered.

"Oh, no! Needle! You're burned!'

"It's okay, Galaxy. It'll be okay. You stopped in time."

"What happened?" Miss Abilene comes over, hair disheveled from sleep.

"I'm sorry," I confess. "I... I must've been dreaming. I didn't mean to—"

"Galaxy, you're going to have to learn to control your ability," she chides. "Needle, are you okay? Let me see that arm."

"It was an accident," Needle says. "It wasn't her fault."

"I'm not concerned with who's at fault—merely with keeping everyone safe," Miss Abilene says, examining Needle's burn. "This is bad. I'll get a med kit." She rises to fetch it.

"I'm sorry, Needle," I say, bright, burning tears welling up in my eyes. I wipe them away quickly.

"Don't worry, Galaxy. We'll figure this out."

I back away from him—from everyone I nearly killed. I shouldn't be here. I'm not safe to be around. I can't control this thing inside me. I turn and walk toward the exit.

"Wait, Galaxy," Needle pleads.

"Don't go," Rocket says. "Needle's right. We can figure this out."

"I have to go," I say. "I'm sorry."

"No, wait!" Needle tries to get up to follow me, but his earlier gunshot wound prevents him. He's too weak and in pain to move.

I slip out of the room and find the stairwell. Moments later I step into the night air of the ruined city of Baltimore. The cloudless sky is dotted with stars. The moon is large overhead, reflecting light from the sun. I can feel it. Even that small amount of sunlight is enough to energize me.

The feeling scares me.

I pick a direction and start walking.

The End

About the Author

S. E. Thomas's work has been previously published by Focus on the Family, CBH Ministries, Judson Press, Mozark Press, and Feminists for Life of America. She won first place in a short-story contest with Mozark Press in 2010 and Grand Prize in the 2014 First Paragraph Contest with Women's Memoirs. She has her B.S.E. in English Education and a master's in philosophy. She enjoys writing historical fiction, YA dystopia, and Christian non-fiction. She works and lives in Lolo, Montana.

Follow S. E. Thomas

Amazon: http://amzn.to/2yLX8Qa

Facebook: Facebook.com/AuthorSEThomas

Twitter: @susanethomas1

More From:

The Dramatic Pen
TheDramaticPen.com
Facebook.com/TheDramaticPen
@TDPPress

The Holy Land Mysteries Series

Book I: The Sixth Hour
The rebel, Yeshua, drove the merchants and moneychangers from the Temple with a whip. Hours later, one of them was murdered. Now fifteen-year-old Darash must find a way to protect his family from poverty even as he struggles with the grief of losing his father. When another murder is committed, Darash finds himself searching for a dangerous killer and relying on an old, blind basket weaver for help. Despite the odds, Darash discovers he has strength of character, a deep compassion for others, and an uncanny knack for problem-solving. But will he be able to expose the killer before the killer finds him?

Book II: The Brazen Altar
A four-year-old boy disappears when bandits attack a family traveling from Samaria to Jerusalem. Magistrate Quintus Arrius enlists a clever but unlikely helper: a Jewish merchant boy named Darash. When Darash learns of a revival of the ancient cult of Molech, he fears the worst. This notorious cult frequently demands the lives of children as human sacrifices. As sole supporter of his family, Darash has troubles of his own—a demanding mother, a younger sister, and a new servant girl with a past as painful as her midnight cries. Still, the youth finds himself drawn into a race to find the missing child, terrified of what he might discover.

The Scrolls of the Nevi'im Series

Book I: Habakkuk's Plea: A Prophet of Elohim
A prophet of God should have answers.... But Habakkuk has only questions—questions wrought from sorrow, suffering, and night visions of evil. When Habakkuk is asked to take in a young refugee—accused of murder—Habakkuk immediately worries about what this will mean for his family of girls. How can he protect them if he brings the enemy under his own roof? But Habakkuk soon discovers an even greater evil residing in the hearts of his kinsmen. Can one man convince a nation to set aside their love of foreign idols and fear the One God alone?

Book II: Habakkuk's Plea: Evil Persists
Though he tries to convince the people to turn to Elohim, they will not listen. Will Habakkuk find a way to reach them before it's too late? Elohim is testing his heart, testing his compassion. Habakkuk must learn to love the people he is called to serve. But when someone close to him dies, he cries out in agony. "O LORD, how long shall I cry, and You will not hear?" Will Elohim give Habakkuk the answer he longs to hear? Or is this only the beginning of his test of faith?

Book III: Habakkuk's Plea: Elohim Answers
His land will be sacked and burned, his countrymen killed and exiled. How can he place his faith in a God who allows such suffering? Warned by a terrifying vision, the prophet Habakkuk knows only one end awaits—the destruction of Judah. It falls to him to warn the People of impending disaster, but can he overcome his own struggle to understand the God he serves? As the Babylonian hoards descend upon them, as death and exile threaten his wife and daughters, will Habakkuk's God remember mercy? Book III of the "Scrolls of the Nevi'im" series.

**Interactive Mystery Party Games
for Teens and Adults
S. E. Thomas
Who Invited the Stiff to Dinner?
Murder at Surly Gates
Accuracy
Let Them Eat Cake**

**A Reason To Celebrate
A Full-Length Christmas Production
S. E. Thomas**

For most, Christmas is a time filled with joy. But for many, Christmas can be a difficult season. But let us consider a moment what Scripture tells us of the first Christmas. What really happened? For the first time, God Himself—the Creator of the Universe, the King of Kings, the Everlasting Father—stepped into our world! He stepped in—not to enjoy the wealth or the beauty or the joys—but to experience our suffering, our longings, and our sorrows. From the moment of His birth, He experienced far from ideal circumstances. Yet, we remember His words, "In this world you will have trouble. But take heart! I have overcome the world."

Acting Out Loud
Christian Skits for All Occasions
S. E. Thomas

Whether you are a pastor looking for a skit to help drive home your message, a ministry leader desiring a dramatic reading to speak God's love at a retreat or conference, or a youth group leader hoping to spice up a youth meeting, we have the material you're looking for! Find over thirty skits, short plays, and dramatic readings that cover the following areas: Biblical Tales, Christian Living, Evangelism, Special Events, Holidays.

Lazy Dog
carol fields brown

"The quick brown fox jumps over the lazy dog." This sentence is called a pangram. A pangram contains every letter of the English alphabet at least one time. This storybook starts with this famous pangram. The Lazy Dog and the Fox start us on an animal adventure. You can write the sentences and color the pictures. At the end of the book is a chart to help you make up your own sentences. At first you may need help, but soon you will be able to make your own. Every sentence can become a story. Do you know why the Fox jumped over the lazy dog? I wonder…. What do you think? This coloring book provides an opportunity for young learners to explore the intricacies of the English language, practice their handwriting, and explore a variety of animal behaviors in a fun and creative way. Full-color illustrations, matching coloring pages, and lines for handwriting practice are also included.

Sourdough Secrets… Revealed!
From Making the Starter to Sourdough Success!
Ray Templeton

Step-by-step instructions that will allow you to make your own starter, make your first loaf, and even learn to make sourdough bread in your bread machine.

Is My Faith My Own?
A Resource for Christian Young People
Leaving Home for the First Time
S. E. Thomas

Everything was going along fine... then you got out on your own and realized it's your responsibility to get the rest of your life right. From here on out, if you're going to follow God, you're going to be doing it on your own. You can no longer coast by on your parents' faith, your pastor's understanding, or your youth leader's morals. Now it's up to you. And you have some questions: Is my faith real? Is it growing? Is it my own? (A *Finding Hope Resource Guide.*)

Complex Simplicity:
How Psychology Suggests Atheists are Wrong about
Christianity
Dr. Lucian Gideon Conway III

In *Complex Simplicity*, prominent psychology researcher Dr. Lucian Gideon Conway III addresses the modern atheist attack on the psychological effectiveness of the Christian religion. As an expert in the science of cognitive complexity, Dr. Conway uses scientific research and personal narratives to argue that Christianity is an effective guide for reconciling the many complexities built into the human psyche. Directly contradicting what many modern atheists believe, he shows that, in approaching human psychology from a complex perspective, Christianity meets our complex needs with complex solutions. To Christian believers, he offers psychological reasons to believe their faith yields positive benefits. To skeptics, he offers a challenge to the growing cultural belief that Christianity is both simple-minded and ineffective. *Complex Simplicity* is important reading for anyone curious about the intersection of Christian teaching and human psychology.

Daily Life in Bible Times
Small Group Study
S. E. Thomas

Workbook & Leader Guide Editions

Come face to face with the people you read about in Scripture by exploring what their daily lives would have looked like. Learn how a young man selected and courted his bride, what occupations they had and how they trained for them, how infants were cared for, and how the ancients mourned and buried their dead. We will also look at the economic and political climate, learn about crime and punishment, and even find out what they ate and how they dressed. And as you come to know the culture of Jesus Christ, you will see Him more clearly, as well. *This is a 10-week Bible study.*

Please Visit Us Again!

Find fiction and non-fiction books, study guides, plays, skits, mystery party games, fundraising resources, free downloadable templates, writers' resources, and much more at:

www.TheDramaticPen.com

Write To Bless The World

www.ingramcontent.com/pod-product-compliance
Lightning Source LLC
Chambersburg PA
CBHW060932180626
46817CB00004B/1497

* 9 7 8 1 6 4 1 5 7 0 0 6 0 *